Invitation to a Haunting

By Matthew Campling

Invitation to a Haunting

This book was first published in Great Britain in paperback during May 2021.

ISBN: 978-1916180376

About the Author:

Matthew's career has been shared between being a psychotherapist (MA Psychotherapy, BA Hons Counselling) and many writing jobs. He's been a magazine Features Editor and Assistant Editor and a columnist for film and theatre. For 10 years he wrote advice columns as an agony uncle, and he was a regular guest expert on TV and radio, especially on ITV's 'Trisha' show. He is a multi-award nominated playwright and has had 11 stage plays performed. He lives in North London.

Other Books by this Author

Fiction

The Secondary Victim
Who Is Killing All My Ex-Boyfriends?
Life Passing By

Non-Fiction

The 12-Type Enneagram
Eating Disorder Self-Cure
Therapeutic Weight Loss
Diary of a Male Anorexic

Dedication

For Harry, again

One. Prelude to Evil

Merlin lies sluggishly in his sleeping bag, sensing where his body connects uncomfortably with the hard wooden floor. The night was difficult. First his mind was racing, then every noise in the building nudged him back to consciousness. When he did finally sleep his dreams were intense, confused, nightmarish. At one point he woke up and there was definitely something in the room. Something that sniffed. Alarmed, he fumbled for his torch and flicked it on. The noise stopped. The room was empty. The door was closed.

Remembering this he now notes that the door has somehow opened, despite the two bricks he laid against it. The exposed corridor seems to mock him. Merlin runs a hand from his chest, down his body, feeling his stomach, cupping his genitals. It's as though he needs to check everything's still there.

His phone tells him its nearly 9am. He tries to call Maria, his girlfriend, but for some reason he can't get a proper signal here.

Merlin pulls himself up, his t-shirt the only barrier between himself and the morning chill. He drags on yesterday's boxers and a pair of jeans, plus a zip-up top with a hood. He looks for his glasses, but they elude him.

He shuffles down the corridor to the toilet and relieves himself, then returns to the room he has made his bedchamber. His glasses greet him as he stands on them.

Fortunately they are not broken so he puts them on, looks round, scratches his head. He wishes takeaway was as close in this place as it is at home. Instead, he heats water in the picnic jug and makes a cup of black coffee. He activates his phone's recording function.

'March 5 2021. Nine a.m. Merlin's morning broadcast. I'm standing ... ' here he stops, swings round. WTF? He punches the phone again. *'For God's sake. I know someone's standing behind me. They're watching me. Can I say to 'you', and all the rest of you, JUST PISS OFF AND LEAVE ME ALONE!'*

He pauses and there's nothing, not even a sigh of wind, creeping into the building through one of the broken windows.

'I don't know how much more of this I can take.' As he says this, a vision of his last physical challenge jumps unbidden into his raw awareness. The desert. Crossing the desert with a bunch of other Iron Men. At the thought his muscles tense. *'Yeah'* he says into the phone, *'I have survived deserts. I'm a decorated Iron Man. I've got medals. My body is a machine.'*

So empty, these boasts, now. He can do miracles in actual terrain. But he can't fight the invisible. However many sit-ups, he can't explain who moved the bricks and why this place is making him more frightened than he's ever felt, whatever the odds. Even when he bungy jumped for the first time, and that day a shark appeared next to his surfboard, he wasn't as disturbed as he feels now.

'Okay, so I'm ready to quit.' At these loser words his heart jumps and starts pounding. His father would despise him. Yeah, but dad's dead and doesn't have to put up with the shit I've had thrown at me the last 14 hours.

He glances round the derelict room, mentally assembling his few possessions into his canvas holdall. He can smell the mould in the air, see the wet floorboards. The damp wall patches offend him, even though he's slept in plenty of temporary beds just as crude. They weren't *this* place. Two minutes to get ready, put on shoes, find the front door key, get out. Get out. Get out.

A couple of minutes later Merlin tentatively begins to walk down the ornate, ruined staircase. Below he sees the magnificent, broken entrance hall. The graffitied walls, the missing floorboards. The air is heavy and he instinctively takes shallow breaths so the dirt doesn't clog his lungs. He is aware he is having to force himself to take each step forward.

He's never felt paranoia, never acted as though something was going to suddenly rush at him. He's aware of goosebumps on his legs, chills running up his back. If only he can get to the door and the safety outside. With fumbling, trembling fingers he reaches the safe haven of the iron-studded front door. He turns the key. He swears, kicks the ancient, worm-holed wood, and tries again. The key won't turn in the lock. WTF? Yesterday, when I came into this shit hole, it worked smoothly. They told me they'd oiled the lock. So, what's the problem now?

After a few more attempts Merlin accepts that he is going to have to find another way out. As his eyes rake the grotesque caricature of a once-splendid entrance hall he hears a click and sees an open door on the side of the stairs. He hadn't noticed it yesterday. He thought the panelling was solid but now this door has popped open of its own accord. Merlin activates his phone.

'Okay, I'm in the entrance hall. Marble and wooden panelling and shit. Broken crystal chandelier. And what seems to be some sort of secret entrance. I mean, it's not like a secret panel, it's under the stairs, so I guess it's a cupboard. Or maybe the entrance to the cellar.' Merlin thinks. *'Okay, so let me gather my thoughts. Everyone knows that if you're in a scary as shit house, the last thing you want to do is to investigate the cellar. But I can't get out the front door anyway. I'm going to need to find something to break a large enough window. And the most logical place to find that is down there.'*

Merlin nods as though there is someone watching who can approve this logic. He takes a few breaths, his usual method for calming and focusing before undertaking a strenuous activity. He walks towards the open, inviting, door, feeling the physical power in his leg muscles propelling him forward. At the door he tenses, watches dispassionately as his muscular arm reaches out to push the door even wider. He is a physical machine, just remember that. He looks down into a void of blackness. Although not quite. It appears there are windows on the far side of the cellar. There is just enough murky light to illuminate a staircase of dubious wooden steps.

'I'm going down the stairs into the cellar now. There are windows. I'm okay.'

He knows that the wood may be rotten, that a fall would be disastrous. So he moves slowly down the stairs, feeling each step out before placing his weight on it. He counts 12 steps before reaching the cold concrete floor. The windows aren't barred, they might be the quickest exit. But this place gives him the total creeps, he wants to grab and get out. He looks around for something suitable for breaking a window. There are benches on either side, and a clutter of domestic detritus, presumably left by the former occupants. From a pile of rusted hardware Merlin selects a length of piping. There's also a pile of dusty and dirty plastic sacks, useful for wrapping round his hand and protecting his eyes. He gathers a couple and turns to ascend the stairs.

'Who's there!?' he cries out. All he can see is a shadow, standing on an upper stair. 'For God's sake, don't piss me about. Has it been you all the time?'

There is a moment, then he hears a whisper, almost a clear chuckle, from the shadowy figure. Merlin relaxes.

'Okay, so very funny. Are you working for Carl Raeburn? Is this part of my experience? You tell Raeburn he doesn't play fair. And I still want my money. Or I'll kick the shit out of him and enjoy it.'

The shadowy figure says nothing and Merlin's nerve suddenly gives in a way it never had when he was in the sunshine, surrounded by well-wishers and fellow team members.

'You're not funny, bro …' he whispers, and tension rises in him as he feels a strange paralysis entering his body. Even his voice is fading, it grinds to a croak. Around him, the very air seems heavier, as though he's now attempting to wade through water. Thick water? Now he can't breathe, there's a great weight pushing him from all sides. Merlin tries to make his breaths light, to compensate, so he can ascend the stairs again. But his legs, it's as though someone's tied lead weights to them. He can just about access his phone.

'I ... don't know what's happening. There's something in here with me. The ... the air is against me. I can't move. I can't breathe ... Now ... now I feel ... the ceiling's pushing down ... on me ... I can't ... I can't walk ... It's watching me ... Please ... stop doing this ... for God's sake have pity ... I can't ... please... I have people who... love me ... don't let this happen ... please ... stop it ...'

Merlin is pushed to his knees, and then onto the floor. The great invisible weight bears down on him, like a giant kneeling on his back.

'Can't move ... can't ... breathe ... tell Maria I've always ... loved her... this was so we could ...start again ... Can't ... breathe ...'

The shadow on the stairs melts away. Perhaps it was only an effect of the sunlight, advancing tentatively through the gloom. Merlin's hand drops his phone. His body appears to be attempting to push itself through the concrete floor. There is a moan as his last breath is expelled from his lungs, before the terrible pressure squeezes out his life.

After a time, there is a movement. Something lifts up the phone and hurtles it against the wall. The frail plastic flies apart. Then there is one last movement, one last ordinary domestic noise, as the wooden door to the cellar squeaks shut.

Two. Martie

I lie in bed, listening to the high-heeled shoes of the woman upstairs clack-clack their way across the floor. These flats are supposed to be carpeted but I don't complain, her footsteps are cheaper than an alarm clock and more reliable. I would like to jump out of bed and embrace the day but I have to go to work and I hate my work as much as work hates me. Both sides are waiting for me to crack, or for my work to get so poor they can fire me. Meanwhile I need the job to pay the mortgage on my lovely ex-council flat, so I go to work, put on a brave face, do a job I hate that I'm crap at.

I was extremely lucky to get this flat. I didn't have any money saved: it was only because I work for the local council that I could get a 100% mortgage. I'm a great believer in making allies even if I can't see up front how I'll need them. In this case, the council's Director of Finance is someone I've always made a habit of greeting warmly, and it was the DoF the mortgage company approached for the official tick. Pays to think ahead. I'll have to find a way to thank him that doesn't involve having dinner and being chased around the table. Would a cheerful card do it?

I'm on the bus now. The 137 that starts down south, picks me up at Battersea Park, takes me and a bunch of other commuters over Chelsea Bridge, and deposits us near my most favourite tube station in London: Sloane Square. Location of The King's Road. The birth of the cool. Then it's a few stops on the Circle Line up to Kensington High Street tube. And a short walk to the dreaded Kensington and Chelsea Council, for whom I am a barely tolerated and lousy Personal Assistant to the Head of Private Care. I got the job because I can touch type 65 words a minute. I can also lose filing, forget to put appointments in the diary, overlook to post urgent letters and generally add life and spark to the department.

I'm enlivening the walk up the street to the council's offices by catching up on Twitter. There's an intriguing tweet from a name I seem to recognise. I could explain why it's intriguing but it's easier to just quote it:

'Do you believe in ghosts? I'm putting together an art project involving a group of people who have had an actual encounter with the supernatural. Check out my website: www.carlraeburn.com. Serious replies only.'

'Yes, I have' I mutter, stopping in my tracks and causing the person behind me to swerve into someone going the other way. There's a whole stream of people behind me, I'll have to wait till I'm at my desk to reply. However, my brain is now full of half-sentences, images, anecdotes. What sort of art project? I'm thinking it could be a play, there's been a few plays about ghosts and the public seems to like them. *The Woman in Black,* for example, has been running over 25 years. I mentally compose a response tweet I hope will find favour:

'Yes! When I was younger, I had an unbelievable experience. Except you can believe it. I swear. I'd be perfect, I don't scare, I don't have allergies and I make friends easily. I'm available any time.'

Since I'm on the rim in terms of sick leave, and I've used up my holiday allowance, this last isn't technically true. But it's *ghosts!* I mean, one of the few areas in which I have some claim to expertise.

It's later in the day. I'm checking Twitter every ten minutes and Carl Raeburn has not replied to me. I'm supposed to be ringing round for Jenny, my boss, arranging a high priority, service managers meeting. I know, you're not the only one who could die with boredom. I only hope the tweeter is serious and has some project in mind so glorious that I can helicopter out of my crap life.

It's now after lunch. I'm at my lowest after lunch. If I could, I'd throw myself out the window I'm so exhausted from the morning's grind.

But I can't be bothered to get a key from security to open one of the windows. So I'm on Twitter and still nothing. I'm thinking perhaps I should send another tweet when I see my DMs have a message:

'Thanks for your reply. I'm having a get together with a small number of respondees. Can you make 6pm tonight? Sorry for the short notice, explain later.'

There's also an address in Knightsbridge. Perfect. I can walk to Knightsbridge through Kensington Gardens, which is a few blocks north of where I work. During the afternoon I surprise Jenny by accurately relaying to her a phone call that came in while she was out. I surprise her further by finishing all her mail and leaving it for last post. I suppose all I need is a bit of external stimulation. I hope they're taking note. Of course, since I haven't told them about the tweet, they must think I've just decided to put more effort into the job which pays me. Sweet innocents!

I leave, as I always do, at five on the dot. The two middle aged female viragos I work with make a point of always working a few minutes overtime, to illustrate their devotion to the job. I'm young, I'm easily distracted, I'm out of there as soon as.

The walk from Kensington High Street, through Kensington Gardens, with Kensington Palace and the boating pond on the left, up to the Royal Albert Hall and Knightsbridge, is always delightful and one of the benefits of my crap job. I'm so happy to be walking, not working, I get to the address ten minutes ahead of schedule. So I hang around. This also gives me the opportunity of seeing who else might have responded to the tweet. As far as I can tell, taking into account some people might be going through that front door on other business, the respondees appear to be:

1. A well-built woman, well but unsuitably dressed, giving her the curious look of a truck driver in drag. She has long blonde hair with dark roots a couple of inches long. She seems to be South African, judging from the sentences she shouts into the intercom by the front door.
2. An incredibly hot guy. Short hair. Muscular build.
3. A woman who looks like she's on her way to a cemetery. Shame. I'd definitely say she's someone who sees ghosts.
4. A big black dude. He has face scarring like Seal. I don't know why it's so attractive but it is.
5. Very pretty young woman. Looks a bit of a princess. Something smouldering about her though, she could probably take on the hot guy and the black dude and still have room for other interested parties.
6. Some guy about 35 who just looks angry. I wonder what he's angry about?

There was also an older woman who got out of a taxi, went to the front door, rang the bell, *literally clutched her pearls,* evidently changed her mind, got back in the taxi and left.

By the time I've processed these phenomena it's about twenty minutes after, so just about time for me to arrive. I buzz the intercom. A cool, male, voice responds, tells me to push the door open. They're apparently gathering in the study, turn second right in the hallway.

I give myself a moment in the hallway. Because Knightsbridge, like Kensington, is one of the most expensive areas in London, I'm expecting a decent decorative show. This is spectacular. Wide, long, high – my dream entrance hall. Marble floor, white walls, a number of vibrant contemporary paintings in gilt frames plus some 3-dimensional floor works by people like Jeff Koons and Elizabeth Frink. I follow the sound of voices. Someone's having an argument already. Magic. My kind of people.

I enter, pause, sadly no one's looking at me. The angry man is now apoplectic and pointing a shaking finger at a man about 40, casually and expensively dressed, who must be our host.

'No, don't give me that bullshit!' the angry man thunders. 'You're trying to interfere with natural laws. You're unnatural. These people don't know. They're your victims. I know. You're evil!'

The woman with the two-tone hair speaks. A sort-of pleasant South African drawl. 'Doll, if you've got a problem, just go. Let us who know what we want listen to this nice man. I'm being polite now. Next time I speak I won't be so polite.'

I like her immensely.

'Idiots!' the man shouts. 'Cannon fodder! He'll eat you up and shit you out!'

'Okay' says the man in charge, 'that's enough. Leave.'

The angry man looks round. The hot guy and the black guy look annoyed enough to take contact up the physical level. The angry man steps back and when he speaks again it's more a weak whine.

'I'm just trying to save you. He's a monster.'

This is impressive stuff and the group does think for a moment. The hot guy speaks.

'Okay, you've warned us. Now let me tell you. I wouldn't be here, and I suppose the others wouldn't either, if we didn't have a powerful interest in this area. The supernatural. We've all experienced something. I'm guessing we all want answers. So why don't you either shut up and let Carl speak, or go?'

Hot *and* articulate. I'm in love.

The angry man throws himself into an armchair, which squeaks comfortably, folding him in its expensively padded interior.

'Right on, Glen' says the two-tone hair. I'll have to learn all their names.

The one identified as Carl, who is presumably Carl Raeburn, since I recognise the signature on some of the art in the hallway, looks to me and smiles. Everyone looks in my direction. At one time in my life I would have dissolved like a snail at so much outsider attention. Gay teenagers eat to feel invisible. Yet I now feel confident in my outward appearance. So I merely brush some invisible hair out of my eyes, a gesture that's been called sexily vulnerable.

'I'm Martie Collins. Sorry I'm late.'

'No you're not' says the two-tone. 'I saw you outside watching us arrive. I'm Becca Rose.' I'm embarrassed but the group seems easy going.

'Why don't we all go round again?' asks Carl. 'I'll start. I'm Carl Raeburn.'

'The artist' I say, and smile. He smiles back.

'I'm Don Shaw' says the hot guy.

'I'm Alix with-an-I' says the scarred guy. 'Alix Bains.'

'I'm … I'm Sylvie' says the sad woman. 'But you don't need my surname. I don't think I'm going to stay.'

This immediately makes everyone turn to her, mumble empathetically. After a minute of heavy emotional strokes she manages a weak smile. 'I'm Sylvie Hughes.'

A voice like honey being poured slowly over hot chocolate calls our attention. 'My name is Attracta Allen' says the very pretty woman, seated on the side where she can watch the rest of us.

'A tractor?' asks Becca.

'It's Irish. Attracta.'

'Attract with an A on the end' I suggest and she nods.

We all spontaneously turn to the angry man in the chair. He twists his mouth.

'I'm Glen. Why do you need my surname?'

'Thanks for giving me my cue' says Carl. 'Because you're all going to get to know each other a lot better. If you decide to stay with the project.'

'What is the project?' asks Alix.

'It's an art project. You've seen outside and in here some examples of different sorts of art. I've made a name for myself as a framework artist. Now I'm wanting to branch out, be more experimental. Do you know the work of Bill Viola? Videos? Or Dan Flavin? Neon tubes? Or Christo and Jean-Claude who wrap everything from a building to an island?'

'I don't know those people' says Becca in a way that makes it the artists' fault.

'I don't know what I expect from this' says Carl, in a sober, reflective way that makes the group suddenly eager to please him. 'I know I want to do something different. Collaborative. And I've got shedloads of money to help.'

'I like that' I blurt out and they all look at me. 'Why are you all looking at me?'

Carl laughs. 'I mean I have the money to make life work for me, rather than the other way round. Consider yourself … social experiments. You know those ads you see that say, for example, that if you're asthmatic or a migraine sufferer you can make a couple of grand testing new medical cures.'

'I'm not with you' says Becca, again in a way that lays the blame with Carl.

'I am' says Alix. 'You're gonna use our bodies to make art. Like we're gonna be rolling around in paint, like the butterflies Damien Hirst used to make art.'

'That's disgusting' says Sylvie. 'I condemn anything that abuses animals. And I certainly won't be up for it.'

'Now hold on' says Carl gracefully, his face a study in relaxed ease in the face of the criticism. 'I'm not saying anything like that. I just want you to record stuff.'

'What stuff?' asks Don.

Carl opens a leather, embossed folder that's been lying closed on his impressive glass and chrome desk. It's a picture of a magnificent country house.

'Does anyone know where this is?' he asks.

'I've seen that recently' says Don, although a little doubtfully, as though he's saying if I've got it wrong, don't blame me.

'I bought this house last year. Apparently it's haunted.'

There's a mumble of shared comments.

'That's no surprise' says Becca. 'I mean you know we're all interested. So what? You want us to visit your haunted house and see if we can sniff out the supernatural?'

Carl stares intently at Becca. She deliberately stares back 'So what?'

'Yes, sort of' says Carl. 'I was going to put it more elegantly. What I'm suggesting is you stay, obviously at my expense, in this beautiful country home. Get to know each other. You'll each have a recording device. You'll each spend the night alone. And record if anything happens. You will also find a couple of ruined buildings in the grounds. I'd like your opinion on those as well.'

'This is bullshit' says Glen from the chair.

'He's not finished' says Sylvie. 'Why would we do this, Carl?'

'Yeah, what's in it for us?' say both Alix and me. We look at each other and mutually frown in agreement.

'I have a bucket load of money' says Carl simply.

'Carl, darling, believe me we heard that the first time' says Becca. 'So how much are you thinking of sending our way?'

'I'll pay you each three hundred pounds per night you stay in the house. And a bonus of three thousand pounds for all of you who manage a week.'

There's a brief moment. I whip out my phone and activate the calculator.

'Five thousand one hundred pounds' I conclude.

Becca grunts. 'You're worth nearly a billion pounds' she says to Carl. 'According to my phone.'

'And I earned it. And you can earn over five grand in a week.'

There's another silence.

Sylvie speaks. 'If I did this, it wouldn't be for the money.'

'I'll have yours' say both Alix and me. This time we grin at each other.

'I want you to have the money' says Carl, seriously.

'I've got stuff going on' says Becca. 'I can make five grand in a week. Will you compensate me for lost earnings?'

'If you can prove lost earnings, yes' says Carl. Becca looks embarrassed. Judging by her clothes she's not exactly living the London dream. I wonder how long she's been here from South Africa. I know new arrivals struggle.

'I could do with five grand' I say, surprising no one.

'Yeah me too' says Alix and we again smile.

'Five grand's an insult' opines Don, but he doesn't storm out. Which at this juncture, Glen does. Sylvie goes after him and we hear her gentle voice, and his loud one, echoing from the entrance hall.

'Make it four hundred' says Don. 'And eight grand if we do the week.'

Everyone turns to Carl. Suddenly we're hardened union workers, presenting a united front to management.

'Sorry. That's way too much' says Carl. 'You're only the first tranche of respondees. I've got more people coming later tonight and more tomorrow.'

This takes the wind out of our sails. We're not in as strong a position as we imagined. From the entrance hall there's a loud slam and a few seconds later, Sylvie sadly returns to the party.

'He wouldn't listen' she reports.

'So what?' says Becca. 'He looked like a real prick.'

Sylvie shrugs gentle shoulders and I want to hug and comfort her.

'We shouldn't fight' says Sylvie, simply. 'We should look after each other.'

'Yeah, that's not happening' says Attracta. 'I'm used to fighting my own way. I'll do it but not if we're all supposed to hug and be there for each other and shit. I'm a loner.' This is interesting from Attracta. Up till this moment I had her pinned as a Page 3 type. Who presumably need to make lots of contacts if they're going to leverage a good body into a stellar career, like Katie Price.

'I think the point is… the point is…' says Don, waiting for everyone to look in his direction. 'The point is we're all different sorts of people. That's good. Carl's not asking us to be different.'

'He's short-changing us' mutters Becca.

'Oh come on Becca' snaps Alix. 'Anyone else giving us five grand to hang out in a cool country house for a week? And scream the place down if we see The Grey Lady?'

There's a general laugh and easing of tension. Which I'm happy to join in.

'Do you want to know about our past supernatural experiences?' I think to ask.

'Not really' says Carl. 'And whatever you do, don't go for coffee after this and start trading stories. You're going to be alone together for a week. All the stories will be told, at the right time.'

'But what are you going to do with the recordings?' asks Becca.

'I'm not sure. Because I want it to be spontaneous. I mean, who gave Christo the idea of wrapping the Reichstad? Art can't be predicted.'

'So basically we're being paid for a modelling job?' asks Don.

'Have you modelled?' asks Becca.

Don just nods. So cool. Our babies would be beautiful.

'And you'll want us to sign release forms?' pursues Don.

'Yes' says Carl. 'The usual kind of release. I can use your commentary and your faces however I like. With one extra clause. I can't take responsibility for anything you encounter. It's a haunted house. You can't sue me because you have a bad experience.'

Becca says this is bullshit. Alix agrees and looks like he wants to throw something. Don laughs. Sylvie sits in a chair and starts crying quietly. Attracta moves towards the door.

'No way. I'm out' she says. 'I've been in a haunted house. I was terrified. I'm not going back there again.'

There's an impressed silence as we all take a moment to remind ourselves of our encounters with the supernatural.

'Okay. Six hundred a night. Plus six grand bonus.'

There is a silence while my calculator does its work. 'Ten thousand two hundred' I report.

At the door, Attracta looks torn. 'I need that sort of money' she says.

'Babe we all do' responds Becca. 'I told you crap about making money. I'm sleeping on a friend's couch and she wants me out. Frankly The Grey Lady can do pilates in my room all night as long as I can sleep in a comfortable bed.'

Everyone laughs again and there's a general sense that we're coming on board.

'But what about you?' says Alix to Don. 'I mean, you're the kind of dude who can make plenty flash doing modelling.'

Don frowns. 'Maybe I think this is an interesting project. Maybe I've got unresolved issues.'

'I'll have to ask work. Work hates me' I share with the group.

Becca coos at me. 'But you're so pretty. You're the prettiest man I've ever seen.'

I can't help glancing at Don, but the look on his face doesn't indicate he shares her sentiments.

'I'll have to tell them I'm sick again' I finish, lamely. 'Or maybe I could go off with work stress?'

Sylvie speaks. 'I could do with the money. And the supernatural is an issue very close to my heart. I'm in.'

Carl casts a look round the group, asking with a raised eyebrow if we are in or out. We go round and everyone signals assent.

'I'm in' says Becca. 'Can I get an advance on my first night?'

Carl laughs but doesn't agree. The group drifts over to the drinks tray. The hungrier among us dive into the excellent snacks.

'No deep intimate talking' warns Carl. 'You'll have enough of that on the week.'

'When is the week?'

'As soon as you can start.'

'I can start tomorrow' says Becca, frowning as she does so, realising she's emphasising the weakness of her position. 'I've got plenty of irons in the fire' she reports although no one's listening.

A couple of minutes later we've all exposed the weakness of our positions. A warning voice in my head is telling me something. I'm wondering how many other people replied to Carl's tweet. On what criteria were we selected? I hope it's not vulnerability. Then I look at Don and Alix. And Becca and Attracta for that matter. They appear financially weak but physically strong. Sylvie and I are clearly the sensitive ones. We actually make up a good team. Maybe Carl's put more thought into this than he seems to want to show?

After some more debate we settle on the project beginning the week of Monday next. That helps me, I'll need a couple of days of bursting into tears at my desk before they'll give me any more time off.

Becca won't leave until Carl gives her something in advance. Looks like about five hundred, cash. He makes her sign for it. Alix also wants an advance. I get the feeling Don would like one too, but he's too proud, yet he doesn't fight when Carl puts the same amount in front of him. I'm basically okay and I keep quiet. After a moment Sylvie, shyly, also asks for an advance. So it's only me and Attracta who aren't boracic.

We leave together but bearing in mind Carl's dictum that we not exchange personal information we nod or smile tightly to each other and then each goes their own way. I walk all the way back to Kensington High St. tube so I'm not walking with any of the others. I use the way to think. This isn't what I was expecting. Still, an extra week's leave. Some interesting people. Everything paid for plus a big bonus at the end. And I know ghosts. People are frightened of them because they think they'll attack them or something. But they don't. You just think 'Oh, there's a ghost. No problem.' Ghosts are harmless.

Three. Alix

Jumped the barrier at Knightsbridge. Didn't need to, got skrilla in my pocket, just like to see the shocked white faces. Changed for the Victoria Line up to Tottenham. Up goes the hoodie. My scars are a warning sign but they don't always work. Excited. That meeting was insane. Looking forward to more of the lovely Attracta. From where I was standing I could smell her across the room.

Greet my bros on the street. Don't stop. Don't want them to ask me about the suspicious bulge in my jeans. Gotta get home.

'Yo Mum'. She's in the kitchen, doing somethin'. Always doing somethin'. Woman never stops working. I pull skrilla out my pocket and slap it on the table.

'Where did that come from?' she asks, suspicious.

'Cool it, Mum. Told you I could get skrilla. It's all for you.'

I see her eyes light up with happiness. But she's also wary. My big bro used to give her skrilla 'til the cops came one night and hauled his criminal arse off to jail. Now it's just me and her. And all the people she does stuff for. Fair dues, they pay. But I'd pay to see this woman put her feet up for once.

'I told you. This rich dude wants me to spend a week checking out spooks and stuff. Five hundred in advance. It's all for you, Mum, minus a hundred for expenses,' I say, picking up some of the notes and stuffing them back in my pocket.

Mum looks wary. Don't blame her, all the Mums on this street doubt life can give them one good thing for free.

'What do you have to do for it?'

'Nothing crim, nothing bad. Just a week, all expenses paid, in a castle in the country.'

Mum looks even more suspicious. I laugh. 'He don't have plans on my body, Mum. There's a whole group of us. We've all seen ghosts and stuff. He's an artist' I say, remembering an important point. 'He wants us to help him with his art project.'

Mum looks happier. She takes the skrilla, counts it, puts it in the drawer next to the cooker.

'So I'm gonna be out your hair for a week. Starting next week.'

'What sort of artist? Would I have heard of him?'

I show her some pix on my phone. She grunts. 'People pay for that? I can't even see what it's supposed to be.'

'Yeah. That's what they want. They want people to know they've got so much, they can buy stuff that looks like shit. 'Cause when they're tired of it, guess they just throw it out the window with the other trash.'

'And he's not going to want his money back? If you don't see any ghosts?'

I think for a moment.

'That's a good point, Mum. No, from what I remember, he just wants us to be in this house for a week. 'Cause we've already seen ghosts and stuff. Oh, and he's gonna give us new phones so we can record it all.'

'What all?'

'All the stuff. The groans and the eerie cold places and the people walking through walls and shit like that.'

'What if there isn't any? What if having a herd of cattle like you and your friends scares off the ghosts?'

'We're there for seven days. Not our fault if they don't play ball.'

'So. Five hundred for seven days. That's okay.'

I laugh, grab Mum and kind of dance her round the kitchen. Small room. Bit complicated.

'Mum, this is only an advance! I'm getting … wait for it … six hundred *a day*. And if I make it through the whole week, at the end, a bonus of six grand. This little gay guy worked it out. It comes to over ten grand.'

Mum pulls away from me. Rather than the happy look I thought I'd see, now she looks even more stern. She's got that look she had with my big bro.

'Alix, no one gives you that sort of money for free. There's something more going on here. You'll find you have to run guns or be a dealer or worse. They'll want you to kill someone or something like that.'

'Mum. And I'm speaking to you serious. It's nothing like that. You should see where this dude lives. I looked up the cost of houses in that area. They're like ten, twelve, fifteen million. This is chicken feed for him. He's a famous artist. He can make some shit in a morning and sell it in the afternoon for more than this whole effort is costing him. Chill. It's legit.'

I can see she's not convinced.

'When I come home when the week's up. Then you'll believe me. And then I'm taking you on a fucking cruise.'

She doesn't like me to swear but she likes the sound of a cruise. Her eyes sparkle.

'Alix, you've been promising me a cruise your whole life. You really think this time it's for real?'

'I know it's for real. You should see this man. If you've been around poor folk all your life like I have, you can see genuine money. Not pimp money, not crack money. Mum, he breathes money.'

Then she makes me dinner so we eat it at the table. She's not saying anything, which is cool. I've got thinking to do. I know I look cool, but those others, they know all about spooks. I wish I had their confidence. I don't know what's gonna happen to me, I hope I don't wet myself. But I gotta stay the whole week, so I can take Mum on a cruise.

'Listen' I say, 'you gotta put that skrilla somewhere safe, huh? Don't go leaving it in the drawer. 'Coz when you tell your friends about my big deal, and they'll tell their friends. Soon there'll be the whole street in your little kitchen, looking for it. You keep your mouth shut, okay, and you put it in the bank.'

'I know' says Mum, and she looks at me all kind like. She knows I love her.

'You're a good son' she says, and she reaches out and touches my scars. She's the only one I'll let do that. I'd do anything for my Mum.

'Promise me you'll be careful. And if anything, you know, weird or scary happens, promise me you'll get out of there and come home. I won't think badly of you. I'm gonna be worried all the time you're away. You just come home and we'll be together just the two of us as always.'

'Of course, Mum' I say. Inside I'm saying no way am I leaving. I'm kinda looking forward to them throwing shit at me. I'm gonna kick their dead arses.

Then Mum wants to clean up so I go to my room. I sit down carefully on the bed. We found it in the street and if you sit down too quick the legs fold and you land on the floor. It's an art. Yeah, not an art like Carl's, no one's gonna pay me to sit on my bed, but I've seen my friends try it and they always end up on the floor with bruised bums. Yeah, that's an idea. First I'm gonna take Mum on a cruise. Then I'm gonna go into Tottenham Court Road, to one of those fancy furniture places, and buy the biggest bed they sell. I'll need a double, of course, maybe a king size. Nothing less will do for my princess. My princess Attracta.

Just thinking about her gets me hot. I wedge a chair under the handle to stop Mum coming in. I get to work pleasuring myself thinking of Attracta's mega titties. I think of that other ho, Becca. She's got a big bootie but she's also got a big mouth. She looks like trouble. Maybe I'll have to get her to leave early. Won't be difficult. When we're there, no rules, right? Survival of the fit and everyone else down the shitter. That Don, he's my man. That little poofter, he must try something, I'll stop him cold.

Stop it Alix. You're supposed to be thinking about Attracta. Yeah, that's better. Oh, that's much better. The next time I see Attracta I'll look at her. She'll look at me. She'll see I know all about her. She'll come to me. Then I'll take her for real.

Four. Becca

I would have preferred spending the week with a different group of strangers. This bunch gave me a weird vibe. I wonder if I should call Carl, tell him I'd like to meet whoever he's got coming to see him tomorrow? But Becca, my girl, what makes you think he wasn't lying to us, when he said he had other people? I mean, how many people have had the sort of experiences our group has apparently had? I know when I speak about my experience, I get lots of sympathetic stares, some doubters. A couple of times someone has talked about their own experience, but it's never as impressive as mine.

Also, he gave those who wanted it five hundred pounds advance. I guess it means nothing to him, but doesn't that sound like we're the only ones? He's pulling us in with his vulgar cash. I have no strong objection to be lured by money, I'm just saying it's more logical he would only give us money if we are his only group. His control group. Or whatever he wants to call us.

I have to say when I arrived in London I thought my life here would be *so* different. I mean, I knew London's hard and all that, when you arrive from SA with just your white skin and a big smile you must expect a rough ride at the beginning. I've been here fourteen months, though, and it's been nothing but rough. People who were my best mates back there open the door take one look and slam it in my face. Guess I'm not the first looking for somewhere to crash. I'm meeting a lot of South Africans in London who're going home in a couple of weeks. They can't adjust to the sudden drop in their lifestyle.

Although it's been tough, I've never for one moment considered going back to Johannesburg. Going *back*. I won't do it. Every day I'm here in London is one more day I've survived. It's not so bad. The first couple of months were worse. I've done a bit of this and a bit of that.

Temp jobs. Cash-in-hand jobs. Once a guy gave me a hundred quid for a blow job. I was so nervous, so crap at it, I thought he'd want his money back. He was also nervous, couldn't wait to come so he could pay me and I'd leave.

I've thought about maybe going on the game professionally. I even talked to a couple of girls who were living in lovely flats, warm, thick carpets, dishwashers. I couldn't. I don't mind cleaning rooms and making beds but I'm not going to stare up at the ceiling while some sweaty guy grinds himself into me thinking he's banging Scarlett Johansson. I'd make a terrible courtesan. When I'm having sex I'm always looking for their weak spots and pointing them out.

My five hundred we screwed out of Carl's nearly gone. Just a couple of celebratory dinners and a few drinks in a decent hotel. London is *expensive*. Good job we've got our week starting tomorrow. Back in Johannesburg when I was in Marketing I always liked to prepare for an assignment. It's easy now you can look up people and companies online. So I've trawled extensively using search word 'ghost'. As you'd imagine, there's a lot of crap. Lots of people making hysterical and unsubstantiated claims. I wonder if it's important that Carl *didn't* ask us what we'd experienced? Although I did go into details in my response email, probably everyone else did the same. I wonder if he's got his own story? Is that what got him interested? He's not married, I don't think he's gay. Pity he isn't coming on the week. Seven days in the country, and we're expecting decent weather. Lots of opportunities for us to go strolling round the spacious grounds. I can imagine finding my way into his bed 'help me, I'm so frightened.'

Yeah, Becca, he's not coming with us. Still, if you discount little Martie, there's still the lovely Don and the lovely Alix. I wouldn't even mind taking aim at Attracta, she looks like she knows what to do with her tongue. That Sylvie, she's going to be a pain. I've said five words to her and already I know I hate her. She's whiny. She's 'sensitive'. I know when she starts opening up about whatever's in her past I'm gonna get up, bang my head on the wall, and walk out the room.

Cool it, Becca. Remember what happened when you finally got a decent house share? I mean, they fucking hated you by the end of the first month. People just get so sensitive around politics. Better you take it easy, my girl. Tell them whatever will get you through the seven days. You don't have to make besties of them. But you know how easily people take against you. Don't give them a reason. Be nice. Even to fucking stupid Sylvie. You might even find you like her. Hah! Just kidding!

Ten grand would be wonderful, though. Ten grand and I'll have the deposit for a flat. I'm thinking a two bedroom so I can get someone in to pay most of the rent. I look around me, when I'm in the street, I say what have these people got that's so special, they can go home and open their doors and step into their comfortable homes, and I'm struggling?

You know the worst thing about England? Some people's privilege. Remember when I did that temp job and dear little Felicity told me how her parents had given her a flat in Earl's Court? *Given her a flat.* I got so angry I choked on my food. I had to tell her I was allergic to mayonnaise. This spooky deal is the first decent thing that's happened to me since I arrived. I deserve this break. And it's come at just the right time. Felicity's let me crash on her couch but her boyfriend and the other roomie have somehow taken a dislike to me. I was about to be out on my arse. Except instead I'm going to be living it up in a castle in the countryside. I've told everyone I know, I'm getting dozens of likes and excited responses. I haven't told them why I'm going to be there, of course, let them think it's because I've finally arrived. When I got here someone told me South Africans do well in London. Partly because we work hard, but also because we're used to a better standard of living, and we keep fighting till we get it.

I have to say I'm getting so tired of fighting. I can't go home, but I sometimes think longingly of taking a trip down to the Thames and throwing myself in the river. Why not? Who would miss me? A few people would post sad faces on Facebook, then the world would go rolling on without me.

Maybe I'll have an experience so horrific it will turn my hair white and people will think I'm old and feel sorry for me? Or maybe I'll have a heart attack. That's a point. We should make Carl insure our lives for millions of pounds in case one of the spooks goes too far. Probably too late now, and I've already taken his advance, wish I'd thought more laterally sooner.

The whole caboodle's whacky, of course. Documenting our experiences. Cue us babbling shit into our phones, very *Blair Witch Project*. Watched that again. Not scary once you know what's coming up. Steve McQueen was an artist before he became a film director. Is that what Carl's got in mind? In which case shouldn't we be making a whole lot more money? The girls who were in *Blair Witch* got proper Hollywood careers out of it. Would I be any worse as an actress?

I didn't come to London to make it as an actress, of course. I didn't know what I was going to do here. Just had to get out of good old SA. I'm not bad looking, I mean I'm not *pretty*, I'm not slutty like Attracta, I suppose I could be the heroine's best friend or something. Anyway, I don't want to be an actress. I don't give a shit what Carl's planning to do with our tapes. Tell me when it opens and I'll attend the premiere, that sort of thing's okay. Till then, just give me the money. And if you want me to scream, I'll scream. Tell me how loud you need me to scream.

Five. Sylvie

I can't believe I'm going to do this. A hundred times I've looked at Carl's number. I should have just called him and said I've changed my mind. People do that. I could have called him last week. He'd have had lots of time to find someone else. One of those other people he mentioned to us.

Here it is, Monday morning. I'm standing outside my block of flats. I have a big suitcase and a small one. Plus my coat which I'm carrying and my hat that I'm wearing. I'm standing here waiting for the minibus to pick me up to take me, and a group of complete strangers, to a castle in the country called Strawberry Manor. I've looked it up and it looks wonderful. It also has a reputation for ghosts. So, again, I can't believe I'm going to do this.

And they're such a strange group. Attracta's clearly giving up a week's prostitution to join us. Alix looks like he's on the run. Becca, the South African loudmouth, I know I'm going to keep out of her way. Don is very attractive, when I first saw him my silly heart fluttered. I know exactly what he is, and that's one good reason for having Attracta with us. I shouldn't think we'll see much of either of them. All the groans and creaks will be from their bedroom!

Martie seems a sweet boy. I can see the two of us teaming up. If things get really hairy, I wouldn't mind him shyly creeping into my bed. I've always got on better with gay boys than straight men. I'm not one of those stupid women who thinks she can convert gays, or who doesn't understand that gay men simply don't respond sexually to women. I know, just as I know I am entirely uninterested in women, that gay men are entirely uninterested in women. So we can make wonderful friends for each other.

The minibus is a little late. I wonder who wasn't ready on time? Attracta, of course, probably hadn't got rid of last night's gentleman. And Becca probably couldn't locate her diaphragm. Although I also think Attracta's … not just your straightforward slut. In fact she could be interesting to unpeel, like an onion.

I shouldn't make fun. I don't like people making fun of me. I'm so sorry I wasn't able to stop Glen leaving. Obviously if he wanted to join our party, he has some sort of supernatural connection. He was so angry, though, nothing I said helped and if I pride myself on anything, it's my ability to pour oil on troubled waters. Nothing I said helped, he stormed off into the night. No one else was much bothered. That's a bad sign, of course, shows they're all essentially selfish.

I'm trying to retain an open mind on what this week's going to be like. One thing I do know for certain, we're going to be very close to each other, and we really must all make an effort to get on together. I can see Becca is the one most likely to throw all her toys out the pram. I mustn't let my natural antipathy for her give her the opportunity. If the castle *is* haunted, if we are besieged by supernatural entities, there'll be no room for all-too-human temper tantrums. We must stick together.

At last. The minivan. Martie immediately endears himself to me by throwing open the door, jumping out and putting my bags in the boot with the other luggage. Looking around I see I'm almost the last.

'Where's Don?' I ask.

'He wasn't where he should have been' explains Martie, with a twist of his mouth that indicates he feels this deficit personally.

'I'm sure he'll turn up' I say with a smile. I keep the smile firmly plastered on my face as I greet Becca, who is wearing totally unnecessary sunglasses, and Attracta, who is reading *Hello*. Alix is driving. 'Are you getting more for doing the driving?' I ask Alix. He frowns, he looks like he wishes he'd ask Carl for a bit more.

'No fucking Don' is Becca's aside to me. 'Weekend's shit before we start.'

'Never mind' I say in a whisper, 'there's still Alix.'

Becca grunts in what I can only call disgust. She turns away from me, looks out the window. I'm left with the ugly thought that Becca doesn't fancy Alix because he's black. Oh, that's a poor start right there.

'Anything interesting in there?' I say brightly to Attracta, who looks at me as though I'm completely mad. 'I mean, what's Meghan up to this week?'

'I'm reading a very serious article about Lord Spencer's plans for Althorp.'

'How interesting' I reply. 'I've been to Althorp.'

'Yeah' says Becca, 'was it for a week like we're doing now?'

'Of course not' I can't help slightly snapping back. 'I was a tourist like anyone else. It's still a marvellous and beautiful home.'

'I'll have to drop in on my way back from Strawberry Manor' says Becca sniffily. I don't know what her problem is. I suppose like most South African whites she comes from a great deal of money. Still, I remember she jumped at Carl's cash advance, so I wonder if she isn't all front and behind that she's really only a frightened girl in a strange country? This thought does the trick, and I smile at Becca with genuine warmth. She lowers her glasses and looks at me directly. She has that sort of distrust I've seen before in white South African eyes. When she sees I'm being genuine she smiles back. It totally transforms her face. Then the smile snaps off again and she replaces the glasses.

'I wish Don was here' says Alix. 'I told Carl I could drive. I didn't tell him I never got my license.'

There follows a long argument that ends when Becca, who apparently can drive on an international driver's license, takes over. I must say we proceed more smoothly. I smile at Alix and he gives me the sort of look men always give a woman, however unsuitable she may be, if they think they may have a chance. I turn away from him a little too abruptly.

Then there's a debate about which radio programme we should listen to. I vote for Classic FM. Surprisingly, so does Attracta. Must be her romantic Irish background. So does Martie, although I think that might be out of a growing loyalty to me, which also makes me happy. I've never heard of the one Alix wants, but since Becca's driving he has to keep quiet. So we are wafted out of London to the glorious sounds of one of my favourite tunes, Ralph Vaughan Williams' *The Lark Ascending*. A country tune. So apt.

I drift off for a while and when I wake I've been sleeping with my head on Alix's shoulder.

'I'm so sorry' I say politely. He laughs. Perhaps he will be fine.

'How far to go?' I ask Becca.

'About twenty minutes' she says. 'Although I find these tiny English roads a total pain. In SA we've got proper freeways.'

'Yes' I say, 'that's the problem with most of these single roads having once been cart tracks.'

'Yeah?' she says with what sounds like genuine awe. 'Yeah, you're probably right.'

I could tell her I'm absolutely right. Instead I try to forge something out of this moment of connection.

'The wonderful thing about the English landscape is it didn't all come at the same time. I love looking at photos of London in the mid-19th

Century, or 18th Century engravings, where there's a single structure and around it open countryside. Our history is the gradual eroding of all the open spaces. It's a shame.'

'People have to live somewhere' responds Becca tartly.

'Of course, you're right' I respond. People like hearing that they're right.

'But I know what you mean' she says, more kindly, 'I'd love to have the money to live out here. Wherever I go in England, I want to live there.'

Alix laughs. 'Guess you haven't come to my street, hey?'

'What's the protocol when we get to the castle?' Attracta asks.

'Didn't you read the long email Carl sent us?' I reply, carefully not making it clear that she should have.

'Tell me the important bits' replies Attracta, still spelling her way through *Hello!*

'The front door will be open. Well, unlocked. People from the local village will have set everything up for us. They probably won't be there, they don't like the castle. We have to give up our usual phones, post them through a locked box in the study. There will be other phones that we can't use to call the outside world. They are only recording devices.'

'So we can make home movies' says Becca. 'I'm not giving up my phone.'

'You really should have read the email' I say. 'We have to film ourselves posting our phones into the locked box. Or we get fined half a day.'

Attracta sits up so violently she tears her magazine. 'Shit!'

'What's the problem?' asks Becca, seizing on her discomfort. 'You have to take this seriously, you know. This junket is costing Carl serious bucks. We have to be responsible.'

Attracta calls Becca a stupid bitch. Oh dear, I was afraid relations would swiftly deteriorate.

'Stop it' says Martie, unexpectedly taking control. 'We're here for a week. I'm already shitting myself. Please let's not fight.'

That was exactly the right sentiment. We all withdraw into our internal world. I don't know what anyone else is thinking, but I'm remembering that night the world stopped being logical. Stopped being certain and safe. Instead became a realm of sheer horror. Again, I ask myself why, why I would willingly put myself back in that frame? Of course, this castle if it is haunted will have its own resident spectres. I very much doubt what happened to me will happen this week. Yet I've never been able to speak about the events of that night. I've never wanted to, always I've pushed away any thought connected with it. If I'm in that sort of conversation I may say 'I know that there is true evil in this world. That it can come into the room at a moment's notice and tear your sense of sanity apart.' That's always been more than enough to change the conversation. Yet here, in this week to come, we will be here entirely for the purpose of unleashing the phantoms and demons of this world and whatever is beyond the veil of life.

So again, why am I here? Because I might also experience the echo of what I lost over 10 years ago. Because before that night when hell took over, I again had a glimpse of Hailey. Afterwards I regretted not saying anything of what was in my head and my heart. Yes, I was terrified, but I also threw away my only opportunity to tell my dearest, darling daughter how much I loved her and how much I miss her. Perhaps by a miracle I will get another chance this week. So I must take it. Whatever the consequences to me.

Six. Attracta

We've just seen the first local signpost to Strawberry Manor. Cheers, high-5s, clapping. FFS. You'd think they'd never been out of London before. So it's a castle, big deal. I'll be excited when it's *your* castle. My great aunt got married in a castle. She was a beauty queen – Miss Eire – I have to explain down south 'that means Miss Ireland.' She was blonde and green eyed like me. She was smart. She grew up in the same messed up family as my grandmother, but she knew what she wanted. She used her looks, and then her beauty title, to marry up. My grandmother, sadly, messed up and married down. If she even actually married the waste-of-space that was my grandad.

He was dead before I was born, drink, women, too many falls into the canal or down stairs. She loved him for his wild looks, then she hated him for his wild behaviour. Now I've got Alix shrieking in my ear. Give it a rest, mate, you sound like you're seven. I did have to laugh when he was made to stop driving the minivan because he didn't have a license. I think he thought driving would impress me. I think he thought he lost face when he got demoted. Dream on. He never had a chance with me. Not that I've got anything against facial scars. In the 18th century sabre scars were deemed highly attractive. As long as the possessor also had a family house and a title.

Carl doesn't have a title, of course, unless it's mega-rich-artist. So what, the world's a meritocracy now unless you were born into privilege. I like the women who made it up from the shitheap. Evita, Madonna, even Carrie bleeding Symonds. They saw the main chance, they took risks, they got everything they ever wanted. And I want Carl. My great aunt didn't have much to do with our branch of the family. We were the poor white trash. I met her only once, at my grandma's funeral. I begged her to take an interest in me. To rescue me, as she had been rescued. She gave me a cold beauty queen smile and wished me 'best of luck.'

Strange. For three years we lived in a shack where doors would open or close of their own accord. Where you couldn't put anything down in the kitchen because it ended on the floor. And knives. I remember my mother sharpening a knife on the whetstone outside the back door. She put it down to wipe her face and next thing it was flying through the air. She screamed and I ran in. The knife was embedded so deeply in the wall we had to leave it there. It was still there when we moved out.

Yet that was my experience, that is what has qualified me for this hilarious week-long wank with this busload of losers. And Carl. He's made it clear that we're on our own. However we have to return our modified phones to him personally, to get the tick before we get the cash. In between dodging flying knives and whatever else shit the castle can throw at us I plan to be sunbathing in my bikini. I'm going to look fantastic for my exit interview. And this time, I'm not going to be put off with a 'good luck and goodbye.' This time I'm going to find a way to move my flimsies into his bedroom.

So now we've drawn to a stop. There's been a high, green hedge along the road, but now it suddenly disappears. The reason is obvious: on the other side of a valley is Strawberry Manor. I'd recognise it anywhere, thanks to the reading up I've been doing. I know something of its history but the books are pretty vague about what actually goes on here. A couple of blurry shots of bricks flying through the air, what looks like a puff of smoke walking down the staircase. I'm hoping I'm going to be the one who gets the killer pix. The money shots.

Which means I'm going to have to put myself out there. Fine to lie around during daylight hours but come the night I'm not going to be hanging round with this lot. I'm going to be traversing the castle, starting with the unoccupied rooms, then the supposedly haunted rooms, then the real spooky stuff like the attics, the cellars, the burned down outbuildings. If I get only one great shot a day I'll still have seven. Seven pictures to be the key to my new future.

I remember when I was a Page 3 girl. I was only just 18. They made a big thing of my still being a virgin. Eventually I sold my virginity for enough money to travel for a year. Stupid cow. I should have saved it. I should never have left Mayfair. How was I to know that at 22 I'd be on the heap? From 19 to 22 I lived in pure luxury. I met him at Annabel's and what do I care he's never got divorced? I had a personal maid. My own chauffeur driven car. An unlimited credit card I punished as hard as I possibly could. Then I turned 22 and he turned to me one night and said 'When did you get so old?'

I promised I'd get botox, I'd have my tits done. There's stuff, face peels, you can do that takes at least five years off.

He wasn't interested. I was out by lunchtime and I'm pretty sure my replacement was waiting in a taxi around the corner. I still had some stuff I could sell. He was always generous on my birthday and at Christmas. Imagine my shock when it turned out all the bling he'd given me was fake. Fake! I should have checked it at the time, but I was in love. As if.

So now I've been living in a one-bed. Okay, it's not as bad as couch hopping. I swear if I had to do that I would sooner shoot myself. I've just got to make a fantastic success of this week. I'm only 25 after all. I've still got it in me. Carl, he's not like other men, you can see that. I have to find out what really drives him and be exactly that woman. I've got to make myself indispensable to him.

We're here. You should hear the gasps. More clapping. I have to admit it's mega fantastic. And this is only one of his country houses! Who knew shit art paid so much? There are a lot of stupid people in the world, that's a fact. Of course, I seem to be travelling in company with some prime examples of that.

Sylvie gives me a big sympathetic smile, like she's been elected the soul of the group. I push past her, enjoying her momentary shock. I lock eyes with Becca. She gives me a look that says 'either, bitch, I'm gonna be your best friend, or I'm gonna hate you so much you'll want to die.' I decide that we've got enough unknown junk going on this week. So I give her a big smile and a wink and I see her visibly relax. So, she's not so brave under the attitude. Poor little South African provincial nobody.

What the hell happened to Don? I mean, he's no Carl, but I wouldn't have minded a no-strings week-long affair. Now he seems to have disappeared. Maybe the house got to him early. Haha joke. Just as well he's gone, don't want this lot gossiping about me to Carl. Carl's gotta see me as a jewel, not damaged goods.

'I suppose we should go inside' says Martie. Clearly the brain of the group.

Alix athletically jumps into the back and retrieves our luggage. You can always tell someone's wealth by his luggage. This lot are pretty desperate. Fortunately mine's the only luggage that matters: Louis Vuitton. Sadly no one in this group seems to recognise the famous initials. What a bunch.

'Whose is the Louis?' asks Martie, with a whistle. I smile at him. At least one person this week isn't entirely a savage. Maybe when Carl and I are living together we'll have Martie over for a weekend. Reminisce on the old days. The days, I remember with a shock, we haven't yet experienced.

I wonder what these others have been through? Sylvie looks like she's permanently on the edge of a mental breakdown. Alix's cheeks look like some ghostie took a scalpel to them. Ouch. Becca's a fat liar. I bet she's never experienced anything even slightly eerie. She's too dim to be sensitive. Pity we never found out what Don's hang up was. I can imagine keeping his mind off strange noises. Maybe I'd even go so far as anal. Sadly my body's going to be a temple this week. There's no one here I care to even French.

So now we're inside. It's warm outside but cold here. There's a fire in the enormous fireplace. Got a feeling we'll need all our woollies, even during the day. The entrance hall is properly castle-like. I'm not joking, I've been to some castles which are okay on the outside but pathetic inside. This one's the real thing. A double staircase. Two separate, wooden staircases sweeping up, meeting on the first floor, then running round a gallery to four or five corridors. Bedrooms presumably off the corridors. Is it best, in a haunted house, to be in the bedroom at the end of the corridor, so the spirit gets to you last? Or is it best to be in the middle? Is it best to sleep with the door closed, or open? Seeing it's a ghost, if it wants to, it can always open the door. But if it's closed, will anyone hear me when I scream? Would we be safer sleeping in like a dormitory?

No, I can't think like that. Safety last is the theme of this week. I'll have to volunteer for the worst room, the one with the bad reputation. I'll have to be the last to go to bed, in case I meet something on the stairs. I'll have to be the one who volunteers to find out what that funny noise in the darkest part of the castle is. That's why I'm here. If I'm going to be good enough for Carl, I've got to give this all I can. Otherwise, I really will be 25 and on the scrapheap. I call on the saints to bring me good luck. To keep me in their prayers. Saint Evita, Saint Madonna, Saint Carrie. You did it and I just know I can too.

Seven. Don

Like I would have travelled with the group. Never going to happen. First, I want my car handy in case I need to leave in a hurry. Second, Carl's not giving us the whole story. He mustn't treat me as though I'm stupid. So I call him last thing last night and tell him I'm pulling out unless he gives me the whole story. He laughs and an hour later we're drinking excellent vintage Scotch and he's being honest.

Seems our Carl is at a crossroads. Like Damien Hirst, he's a well-known BritArt face. He's made an obscene amount of money, somewhere up there with Hirst, Tracy Emin, the Chapman brothers, Marc Quinn. There's a lot of people willing to part with a great deal of money for something unusual to hang on the wall. Only he's running out of ingenuity. He's repeating himself. That's fine as far as it goes, a lot of collectors want what their friends have got.

He's not happy. Shame, so rich and so unhappy. Then he referenced The Beatles and I knew exactly what he meant. When The Beatles had had their first spectacular success in the mid 60s there was a period of 18 months when they went quiet. The buzz, the music columns, all were talking about how The Beatles were burned out. Turned out they were only taking time out to create the world's first concept album: Sergeant Pepper's Lonely Hearts Club.

When it came out they eclipsed every other artist. Even The Rolling Stones were still churning out singles. The record covered everything from the newly emerging mystic east to Ringo's flat tones asking for a little help from his friends. The point is they took sufficient time out to create something extraordinarily new, and then swept the competition away in a tsunami of creativity.

Which is kind of where we come in. Up till now Carl's been an actual artist, more like the German Gehard Richter, less like Koons or Jake and Dinos Chapman. Now he wants to take all the conceptual artists on at once. Wrapping the Reichstag, like Cristo and Jean-Claude, blew people's minds with its combination of technical brilliance and insane ambition. Carl wants to do something of that level. I remember reading an article about the man behind the idea for people to wear red ribbons on their labels to signify AIDS. Did you know he was actually an artist? He saw people wearing the ribbon as an art project, like a 60s 'Happening'. From what Carl said – it was excellent Scotch and he's a generous host – I think that's what he has in mind. Something to blow people's minds artistically.

I guess he's going to put all our recordings into one and then perhaps project images onto one of the concrete walls at Tate Modern. Or perhaps he'll take over a contemporary art gallery, like Whitechapel's White Cube, and recreate our week as an interactive installation. It's kind of amazing to think we're all going to be part of his creativity.

I told him that now I understood, I wouldn't share it with the others, and I was 100% happy to be part of the week. He seemed pleased. On the way home in the taxi I called a couple of contacts I have in the art world. See, I think modern art's made for dummies. I can see the point of a Constable, even a Monet, but for me art died in the 1950s. Once Abstract Expressionism comes into the picture, I bow out. As far as I'm concerned, now it's vultures circling round whichever rich sucker with no brains thinks they can impress their equally brainless friends with their latest heap of shit.

So whereas, as I told Carl, I'm totally on board for the week, I must be honest and acknowledge that I have very, very little interest in helping Carl with his latest venture. I have to be there, of course, but what really interests me is how I can create my very own little art enterprise. Something truly anarchic, like those two art students who bounced up and down on Tracy Emin's bed when it was installed at Tate Britain. Except I'm not going to so much as bounce up and down on Carl's project as cut his legs out from under him. Let's just say that from my time modelling I know some people in the media. And they're very interested to hear that Carl's up to something on the scale of Sargent Pepper's. Like those supermodels who won't get out of bed for less than £10,000 a day, I'm not going to be happy with making only slightly over that for a week's work. I'm looking for a big, big payday.

I park my car on a dirt road that runs by the side of the high brick wall surrounding Strawberry Manor. If I had all the bricks that have been put into the wall, I could build my own sodding castle. Walking towards the iron entrance gates, the sun on my back, it really does feel like I'm in the typical English countryside. What we've got left after the shit of Brexit, I suppose. I lift my head and feel the sun's benevolent warmth. Perhaps we should be starting off with high winds, a dark day and stinging rain, but the night will come soon enough. Take time to appreciate this perfect day before we settle down to whatever's waiting for us within these walls.

I walk up the long, long drive. My eyes intuitively search for the best escape route in case of emergency. The drive, the bushes and trees on either side, all meticulously maintained. Yet I know no one lives here full time. Perhaps this is another of Carl's art conceptions: blowing a million bucks a year on a castle in which no one lives. Like those two so-called artists who burned a million pounds. Of course, I remind myself, there must have been someone living here, at some time. How else could it have got a reputation for being one of the most haunted locations in the UK?

I saw the whole of the castle from the other side of the valley, but now, as I turn the last carefully placed obstruction, the genius of the architect stands fully revealed. There are some castles that aren't much more than unusually large houses. Three floors and a battlement doesn't necessarily add up to castle status. This one, however, does. From where I'm standing at the beginning of the drive all I can see is grey stone, soaring high over the surrounding landscape, commanding and somehow, demanding our complete attention. I don't know a lot of architectural terms but reading from left to right we've got a tower, battlements, several blocks of flats worth of walls with windows, a central entrance with huge wooden door, a stone portico and balcony above, and then another couple of blocks of flats worth to the right. In fact, I'm not even seeing the end of the castle, it stretches round and out of sight. A single ghost patrolling all of this real estate would be very lonely. Perhaps there's more than one?

There's a minibus parked in a sprawl on the wide expanse of gravel that leads up to the entrance. The doors and the boot are open so it's as though an unearthly insect, perhaps from the age of dinosaurs, has landed. I see that although a lot of the windows are small, diamond panes someone, probably in the 19th Century when there was the Gothic Revival, has fitted a two-story high stained-glass window over the portico. The front door is open so I'm guessing the rest of the group is oohing and aahing over the interiors. I'm in no hurry to join them: when I was a model I was often on display at some of the country's more trendy country estates. It has left me with a deep distain for the so-called upper classes. Rich scum sticks as a term because it's very true.

'You're here!' I hear an excited, lightly pitched male voice and turning round I see the gay boy, Martie. In his arms he holds branches of flowering shrubs. He looks like a travesty of *Primavera,* from Botticelli's painting. 'We're so glad' he continues, apparently the spokesperson for the group. 'We thought you'd bottled it.'

'Crap' I say by way of explanation. I pick up my bag, sling it over my shoulder and walk towards the front door.

'Wait till you see inside!' shouts Martie from behind me. I don't acknowledge this. I don't want to encourage him.

Inside the space is cold. There's a roaring fire in the Tudoresque stone fireplace, but I doubt the heat extends out for more than a foot or two. I put down my bag and take in the space. The floor is shining wooden parquet, more French than English, and beautiful. The floor area must be at least fifty square yards. There are two immense wooden staircases, rising from either side and meeting in the middle before sweeping up to various shadowy corridors. I instinctively look for the quickest way out and select the stained glass window. One quick heave and that will crack open like a walnut. The window itself is glorious. Principally golden, it depicts what looks like Adam and Eve in the Garden of Eden. Interesting that rather than an overtly religious theme, the builder has gone for a mythical, idyllic time at the start of humankind. Is that how he or she saw this house? Then what's happened to give it such a sinister reputation that no one wants to live here permanently?

'Oh so you came' says a voice in deliberately unimpressed South African tone. I don't need to turn to acknowledge Becca. 'Becca' I say, equally unimpressed. 'We thought you'd chickened out.' This I ignore. From my extensive past visits to country mega homes I know where I'll find the kitchen, so I drop my bag on a carved hall chair and make my way behind the stairs. I can hear voices, so I suppose I'm right in my assumption.

'Don!' says Sylvie in an honest, pleased tone. She's the only one I thought might have some substance to her, although I'll have to make clear I'm interested only in friendship. Nevertheless I don't stop her as she comes over and kisses my cheek. 'We thought you'd got scared' says another voice and I nod to Attracta. The day is warm but the castle kitchen is cold. There's no excuse for Attracta's barely there top and tiny shorts. I can see her legs are smooth, muscled and beginning to brown. Big deal. I've slept with supermodels and Attracta's like every slightly over-age narcissist I ever worked with. There's a series of bangs, like someone with an arm of wooden logs dropping them on a stone floor, and I see Alix, grinning, with that insane scarred face, with the expected logs piled up around his feet.

‘My man!’ he says. I like the simplicity. ‘Have you looked round?’

‘Not yet’ I say. ‘I bring you greetings from Carl.’

By now the group has gathered in the kitchen. When I say this Attracta demands ‘What? Is he with you? When did you see him?’

‘Last night.’

‘Why?’

I let a beat go before answering. Giving them time to acknowledge that I’m going to be the Alpha Male here.

‘I wanted to understand more about what we’re doing here. The money is nice, but I’ve made good money before. I wanted to understand what he expects to get out of us.’

‘Simple, stupid’ says Becca, in her charmless way. Attracta sidles up next to her, leans an arm on Becca’s shoulder. So they’ve teamed up, no surprise there.

‘We’re going to make recordings of ourselves. Our reactions, whatever. And he’s going to use them in an art project. So fucking what, we already knew that’ says Attracta.

I shrug. ‘Sure’ I say and make for the hotel-sized fridge. As I open one of the white enamel doors I say over my shoulder ‘If that makes you happy, keep thinking that.’

‘What do you mean?’ says Sylvie, her voice instantly resonating with fear. ‘What else might he be using us for?’

I turn to Sylvie and smile. My smile can soothe a herd of stampeding bison. ‘Nothing more. Just that. He wants us to record our most intimate thoughts and feelings. So if you wake up and a cold, dead, white hand is reaching out towards you, its flesh crawling with luminescent slugs, don't forget to hit 'record' before you scream and faint.'

'It's not going to be like that!' Sylvie cries. 'I don't want to be scared!'

'Then' says a drawl from Alix, 'you picked the wrong week, the wrong house, the wrong group, sister.'

'No' I say, and again I'm pleased to see they're waiting for my opinion. 'No, she's in the right place. I don't know what any of you have experienced, in fact I'm looking forward to finding out more. Sylvie, we don't know each other right now, and I can see we're maybe not the people we would usually associate with, but I know how these things go and I believe that by the end of the week we're all going to be looking out for each other. And you have my personal guarantee that if you feel scared, you come looking for me. Scream for me if you have to. In fact, consider me your guardian angel. I'm going to make sure you're safe this whole week.'

I don't know where this shit came from. I suppose it's that there was a space at the top of the pecking order literally crying out for someone to take charge. This is how you do it: you find the most helpless individual, you adopt them, the others feel crap for not thinking of it first, or for only thinking about themselves. I doubt that if I'm warm and sleepy in my bed I will give a shit if Sylvie starts screaming in the night, but just knowing I'm around probably *will* make her feel better. I don't mind doing someone else a good turn if it in no way affects my own personal comfort.

'Thank you, Don' says Sylvie, and she attempts to get so close to me I could put her in my pocket. 'I think my room's next to yours, so I won't have to call that loudly.'

'We have assigned rooms?' I say. This annoys me, I should have asked Carl about this. 'Yeah' says Becca, and her tone is superior, 'if you'd arrived with the rest of us you'd have known that. You'd also have got one of these welcoming sheets.'

She shows me a folded piece of paper.

'We didn't know you were coming' says Martie. He fishes in the rubbish bin. 'We, uh, we threw yours away.'

He retrieves an envelope with my name on it. I indicate he should put it on the huge, antique, scrubbed wooden centre table. 'I'll look at it later' I mumble.

'We're all unpacked' says Attracta.

'We've got the best rooms' says Becca.

'Not so' says Sylvie. 'We've all got the rooms Carl selected for us. Only you're in the smallest because Martie took your room.'

'I can switch' says Martie immediately.

'Wouldn't you prefer it if Don bunked with you?' asks Becca and she and Attracta laugh.

'Thanks Martie, I'd appreciate that' I say. I don't go so far as to smile at him, but I do nod.

'We were just making lunch. There's a magnificent formal dining room, plus what I suppose we should call the winter sitting room. It's a giant glass house. Lovely wicker furniture' says Sylvie.

'Lovely' echoes Becca.

'Lovely' repeats Attracta.

'How much do you know about group theory?' I ask generally.

'Oh crap' says Martie. 'Is this going to be like one of those work away days?'

Becca and Attracta laugh at this and move closer to Martie. Careful. I once read on Reddit about a conspiracy at a high school to destroy their good-looking PT teacher. The girls were angry because he rejected their advances. So they efficiently scapegoated him, made him a pariah, got him fired. The most appalling part was that even when the man lost his home and his fiancé they could see nothing wrong in their actions. They blamed him, they said, because he was too good-looking. I don't want that to happen to me.

'Nothing has to happen you don't want' I say smoothly.

'Unless it's being smothered by The Grey Lady' adds Alix and I realise I need to make one good ally here. Sylvie doesn't count. I punch Alix lightly on the shoulder, mano-a-mano and he grins. So simple.

'Why don't we eat, then we can meet somewhere and get some organisation into this week?' I ask.

'Excuse me' says Becca. 'Who died and made you our leader?'

Tough talk, but I see Martie moving away from the two of them, toward me, so I can now count on Martie, Sylvie and Alix to follow me. The other two will soon join them, once whatever has infested these ancient walls starts kicking.

'Okay, so whoever wants to can meet with me after lunch and we'll see what order we can put into place. This is a wild week, a wild adventure. We'll do better if we put in some ground rules.'

'The only ground rule I need' says Attracta in a loud aside, 'is for certain people to stop thinking they're channelling Indiana Jones.'

Sylvie, who has slipped automatically into the motherly role, puts out a pile of white china plates and we each help ourselves to the buffet.

'This is great' I say, meaning the cold chicken, the salads, the various cheeses. 'I really appreciate a good spread.'

'Oh,' Sylvie says, honestly, self-deprecatingly, 'I didn't do this. The women who got the castle ready left us this. A welcome. Very kind of them.'

'Really?' I say, finishing and handing the big spoon on to Martie. Our fingers meet and I'm sure he's blushing. 'Did you meet them?'

'No' she reports, 'Sadly they were gone by the time we got here.'

'I drove' says Becca. 'Alix drove at first but he's illegal.'

'Drop it' mutters Alix.

I'm not interested in whatever shit went down on the way here. I'm only interested in making this week work for me. I make my way out the huge kitchen, back to the vast entrance hall. Clearly this week is going to require a lot of walking just to get around. I can't wait to see the yardage in my bedroom.

After we've eaten, and I mean all eaten, Becca and Attracta join us although they contrive to somehow remain separate from the rest of the group. I signal Sylvie to collect the plates. Becca makes a big deal of insisting that women not be used as unpaid servants, so eventually Alix and Martie take the plates and whatever back to the kitchen.

'So now what happens?' says Becca in a loud aside to Attracta.

'We all drop our pants and see who has the largest dick' says Attracta, and they both laugh. I ignore this. My silence begins to get to them, and by the time Alix and Martie return they are no longer speaking, just flashing irritated, girl power looks at each other.

'So what do we need to survive this week?' I ask into the air.

‘No men’ responds Becca.

‘Really?’ I reply. ‘Since Carl picked three women and three men I would think Carl knows men are essential to the success of the week. Perhaps you’d like to talk to Carl about this?’

I stare at Becca and she looks at Attracta for support. Hilariously, Attracta turns out to be treacherous. ‘Actually, Becca, I think Don’s got the right idea. We’re not children. We need some sort of organisation.’

I risk a quick glance at Becca and she’s fuming. Also, her face can’t help registering panic. Sure. She’s the colonial, she’s the newcomer. She’s all front when she’s got a pal, but discovering there’s more sides to Attracta than she’d reckoned is thrusting Becca way out into the cold.

‘What’s happening here is exactly what I was talking about earlier’ I say, my voice richly shot through with gravitas. ‘This is why we need to understand group dynamics.’

‘That sounds interesting’ murmurs Sylvie.

I pause for a moment and the respectful silence holds.

‘Okay. Group dynamics. There are four stages in groups coming together to work as a team:

‘Forming, Storming, Norming, Performing.

‘In other words, Forming is the first stage, when the group comes together physically, then we Storm, we test each other out, we voice our opinions or prejudices. This can be scary, people feel scapegoated or put on trial or rejected. Then, because we’re here for a bigger purpose, we move towards Norming. In Norming we agree to put aside our differences and concentrate on functioning properly and normally.

And then we get Performing, where we work as a basically single unit, to accomplish the bigger task at hand.'

'Huh' says Becca. 'I wish you hadn't told me that. Now I'm going to feel really self-conscious.'

'Sorry' I say, although I don't mean it. 'We only have a week, and in fact we've only got a couple of hours before night begins to fall. Basically we're in the same situation as a bunch of troops being gathered together for a top priority mission. Yeah we could all piss about and do in here what we do out there, but we're in one of the most notorious houses in England and I for one would feel better if I thought you all had my back. Just as I'll have yours.'

There's a silence and I know I've got them. I smile inwardly. My knowledge of group dynamics comes from an introductory weekend to business tools. I didn't have the money to do the whole course. I need this gig as much as any of the group. My last girlfriend – well, I thought of her more as friend-with-benefits – kicked me out and I've been sleeping in my car or in a friend's caravan. It's pathetic how quickly the good money evaporates and then you have to hustle. But here I'm king.

'That's crap' states Alix. 'I mean, what a buncha shit. I'm not doing any of that stuff. I'm not watching anyone's back. You can all get scared shitless for all I care.'

Oops. I forgot the prime rule, you have to work at the pace of the slowest participant. This is not the time, though, to force anything.

Instead I stand and stretch. I'm aware my t-shirt is riding up, exposing my gut. I have a great gut. I have those curves between thigh and abdomen that all models need. So I reckon, just from this innocent stretch, I have all the others except Alix. And Alix doesn't bother me, he's not bright enough to be an Alpha.

'I'm tired' I say. 'Can someone show me my bedroom?'

'Find it yourself' growls Alix, but he's outvoted, so to speak, by Sylvie, Martie and Attracta immediately escorting me out of the room, towards the extraordinary staircases. I can hear Becca and Alix talking behind me but that also doesn't bother me. Those two are too different to form a significant cabal.

Martie's good as his word and does indeed swap his room, the largest, with a proper en-suite, for mine which is smaller and situated at the furthest distance from the group bathroom. I can see Carl has put us all in the same corridor. I suppose that's a gesture of concern, he doesn't want anyone too far away for the others to reach them in time. In time for what I have no idea. I let Sylvie help me put away my clothes. The cupboard is capacious, polished antique wood. Probably made up of 17th Century or earlier panelling. I can't imagine why Carl keeps this place, he could make a fortune breaking it up and selling it off.

Of course, none of this would be happening if Carl wasn't as rich as King Croesus. I hope Carl's enjoyed his years at the top. When I'm finished with him, maybe he'll be grateful he can still sell off all the shit in this castle. Providing whatever happens this week doesn't level this place to the ground.

Eight. First Evening

Once Martie has obligingly swapped his huge room with en-suite for a smaller room with a trip to the bathroom, the divisions of rooms appears thus:

	Corridor with unoccupied rooms	
Sylvie	Corridor	Martie
Becca (en-suite)		Attracta (en-suite)
Don (en-suite)		Alix (en-suite)
	Staircase	

Purists, or those experienced with accommodating large parties of visitors, might cavil that the two most vulnerable visitors were the furthest from the staircase, that the two most aggressive were cosily ensconced between occupied rooms, and that the other men were closest to the staircase. Yet no one, at least so far, is willing to argue with the rest of the placements as decided by Carl Raeburn, celebrated BritArt artist and their physically absent yet generous host. Perhaps the key, as practised by all the more distinguished hosts and hostesses, is to put the people more likely to kick up in the best rooms and leave those who won't speak up for themselves to pig it.

For some reason even the distinctly physical types like Don and Becca find themselves taking lengthy late-afternoon sleeps. If they thought about it, perhaps they would put it down to the soporific country air. Perhaps they should keep thinking that. By the time everyone has dragged themselves up from an unusually sound slumber, had a bath or shower, and put on their best clothes for the evening, the sun is almost down. It is that moment the French call *l'heur bleue*: 'the blue hour', a charming concept from a refined and cultured country.

'I've got such a fucking headache' comments the less refined and cultured Becca, newly arrived from the former British colony of South Africa and no better than she ought to be. 'I really shouldn't sleep in the afternoon' she concludes. After this she leaves a slight pause, expecting one of the others present to make some polite comment, yet no one does, so she wanders out to the kitchen in search of a cold beer. By unspoken agreement the group has gathered in the drawing room, a huge and impressive space, the walls bearing crimson red flocked wallpaper and a scattering of antique, gilt framed paintings. Sylvie continues to stare out the window, watching the last of the light being squeezed out by the approaching country night.

'It's going to be so dark' Sylvie comments, and immediately Martie and Don respond.

'Yes, you can see so many stars in the country' says Martie.

'I think we should make sure all the windows and doors are locked securely' says Don.

'Do you think there are burglars?' asks Sylvie, her nervousness never far from the surface.

'I was wondering if Carl is planning any surprises for us this week. You know, he's hired us to be ghost watchers. What's to stop him hiring a bunch of students dressed as ghosts?' asks Don.

'Oh! Do you think that's his game?' asks Sylvie.

'I have no idea. I'm still going to check all points of entry and exit are secure' says Don.

'I don't think he's going to do that' says Martie, carefully. 'Isn't the point about us as a group the fact that we've all experienced the supernatural? Wouldn't it defeat the experiment to mess around with playing ghosts?'

'Possibly' grunts Don. 'Don't forget we're already disposed to believe in the supernatural. That makes us soft targets.'

'You don't look like a soft target' says Martie, running an unguarded eye over what he can see of Don's physique.

'There's one problem with all human beings.'

'What's that?'

'We all have to sleep. And who knows what can happen in our sleep?'

'Perhaps we should ignore what Carl said, and everyone should share a bed?' asks Martie with a joking note of hope.

'Piss off' says Don, and he walks out of the room for emphasis. At the doorway he brushes against Alix, carrying a beer. The beer jumps out of Alix's hand and smashes against the wall.

'Shit!' shouts Alix.

'Sorry, mate. My bad.'

'No, no it's not that. I mean you banged into me. But… but it felt like something literally pulled the bottle out of my hand and threw it at the wall.'

Everyone reacts to this.

'So it begins' says Don. 'Is someone making a recording of this?'

'Yeah' says Attracta, who up till now has been in the depths of another part of the vast room. 'And I'm using an official recording device.'

Becca enters with her own beer, sipping from the bottle. A few words get her up to speed, then while Sylvie goes off to the kitchen for a brush and pan, the others investigate a table half-hidden behind an ornate oriental screen.

Don picks up the piece of paper that's been left for them and reads.

'In order to standardise the equipment used for recording, you are all asked to deposit your mobiles in this locked box. They will be returned to you on the last day. There are an equal number of brand-new phones which I want you to use during the next week. Extra chargers are available on the right-hand side of the table. Don't let me down on this, it's important.'

'Yawol' mutters Becca, waiting for someone to comment. No one does. Becca frowns. All her life she has nurtured the secret belief that people don't listen to her. It's partly why she makes so much noise. She had hoped this group would be different.

Martie takes out his mobile and drops it into the box. It doesn't make a noise, so there must be something soft inside to catch it. Sylvie follows and both take one of the proffered mobiles and switch them on. Becca hesitates and Attracta gives her a furious, conspiratorial frown. 'I'm not doing anything like that' says Attracta.

‘PS’ Don reads, ‘anyone found at the end of the week not to have been using the official recording devices will be docked half a week’s pay. No exceptions. My way or the highway.’

After some predictable backchat Attracta and Becca drop their mobiles into the box. So do Alix and Don. Alix remarks ‘It’s no biggie. I can break the lock on this box in a minute. Our phones are safe in there.’

The group experiments with the phones. They are quick to discover their fault.

‘Shit’ says Attracta, ‘This Simcard is weird. It records okay, but I can’t get a line. It’s like they’ve been doctored so we can’t call the outside world.’

‘So what?’ snaps Becca, ‘if we get to the point when we desperately need the outside world, then we’ll already be totally fucked. This is good. Makes us dependent and responsible on just this tight little group.’

This is a worthwhile comment and if anyone else had said it there would have been a general murmur of appreciation. As it is, Becca’s words crash to the ground and roll away into the gloom under the sofas. She moodily sips her beer.

‘So who’s going to get credit for the first official spookiness?’ asks Alix.

‘I’m going to record *everything*’ says Attracta in a tone clearly not looking for a debate.

‘Yeah you do that’ responds Becca. ‘Carl’s still not going to shag you.’

Attracta’s head snaps round and she is about to respond when she decides that since Becca seems to have looked right into her mind, better to let the remark slide and be forgotten rather than protesting too much.

'Okay so the shit has officially begun' says Martie. 'Why don't we check into the nearest Holiday Inn and at the end of the week make up a bunch of stuff? I mean, I don't know about the rest of you, but for me the downside of this week is I have no doubts as to the presence of the supernatural and I don't need any of it.'

'If that's what you want to do' says Attracta, 'go right ahead. Carl doesn't need so many multiple accounts of the same thing anyway.'

'But you'll tell on me, of course?'

'You'd leave me no choice.'

There's a brief silence before Martie speaks again.

'I know a great game to break the ice. Spin-the-bottle.'

'Yeah' responds Becca, 'And we all know who'll you'll be certain to sit opposite. Don, he's starting already.'

'We could rotate' says Martie.

'No one's rotating. Not unless it's the room spinning or a headless being is revolving in mid air. We don't need to break the ice. We're already engaging in what I spoke about earlier. This is Storming and Norming.'

'Storming meet Norming' says Becca. 'Boring will be along in a minute.'

'You can't help it, Becca' says Don. 'Just give in.'

'I'm sorry we slept the afternoon away' says Sylvie. 'We should have explored more of the house before we lost the light.'

'Did you know there's a fully equipped spa? In the basement' comments Attracta.

'Great' says Alix, 'after dinner I could do with a sauna and steam.'

‘The basement?’ asks Martie. ‘I don’t know about you but the one place I’m not going is down there.’

‘Nothing better than a steam at the end of a dirty day’ says Don. ‘Attracta, I’ll meet you down there.’

‘Well’ says Martie, ‘if *everyone’ll* be down there, what’s the harm?’

After some more casual talk – casual talk with an unusual degree of tension floating just below the surface – it’s decided that no one is going to be on their own, if at all possible.

‘If it works for the police, there are six of us, it should work for us.’

‘I’m not sure I want a nanny’ says Attracta.

‘Easy to say that in a room full of people’ responds Martie. ‘Me, I’m even going to take a shit in company. Or at least make sure the door’s unlocked and someone’s listening on the other side.’

‘If you’re so scared’ asks Alix, ‘why apart from the obvious did you volunteer?’

‘I don’t know, I wasn’t convinced, then I saw the rest of you and thought it would be okay. Now I’m here, I’m not so convinced.’

‘Don will protect you’ says Becca.

‘Becca, that’s getting really stale really quickly.’

‘Yeah’ says Don. ‘We need to move into the Performing stage before we settle down for the night.’

‘Long night’ comments Sylvie.

‘Dark night’ says Becca.

'Nights tend to be dark' says Martie. 'Although I know what you mean.'

Working out a daily schedule by two, it's decided that Martie and Attracta will prepare this evening's meal. Then tomorrow it will be Don and Sylvie. The following day it will be Alix and Becca.

'I'd sooner share with Don' says Becca.

'That's because you're a South African racist' says Attracta.

Becca frowns. 'It's not that at all' she snaps back. 'I just would like to have some quality time with Don.'

'And racists always say it's not that at all' notes Attracta to the air.

'We can switch later in the week' grunts Don. 'Let's not turn every decision into a debate.'

'I know one combination you're not going to propose this week' says Martie. 'Me and Sylvie. I know you think the two of us are the weakest here.'

'From your lips' says Becca.

'It's just I think it's funny that I've had many years of being picked on and being bullied. So I'm used to an unusually high degree of negativity around me. I think you'll be surprised at how much I can take. I've got a feeling I'm not going to be the one leaving early.'

'Yeah?' asks Don. 'You figured that out already?'

'I'm pretty sure I know who's going to run the first time they shut the bathroom cabinet and see a murdered corpse in the mirror.'

'You're wrong if you think it's me' says Sylvie, in a quiet, determined way.

'No, I don't think it's you either. I mean, you're not stupid, you're not clumping around making lots of rookie mistakes. I've watched you carefully scoping out the potential hot spots. I'm pretty certain I can name the first one to bolt, perhaps the first two.'

'Then spill' says Don.

'Not yet. I suppose we're not in the Performing stage yet. And, before you say anything, Becca, shut the fuck up.'

Becca, who had already taken in a breath for speaking, flushes red as the rest of the group bursts into only slightly forced laughter.

'You'd better not be thinking of me' she returns, in fury.

'Babes, I don't think of you at all' responds Martie. He catches Don's eye and he sees the twinkle of approval in it. At this he flushes and looks down.

'It'll have to be something quick this evening' notes Attracta. 'It's nearly eight o'clock.'

'Don't we have McDonalds on speed dial?' asks Alix.

'We don't have anyone on speed dial' responds Attracta. 'Weren't you listening earlier?'

A few minutes later, in the enormous vault-like kitchen, the walls gleaming with highly polished white tiles, Attracta carefully pours the contents of quick-and-easy pasta parcels into boiling water. From a drawer Martie selects a kitchen knife for cutting the lettuce. Putting down the ladle Attracta catches the gleam of the knife in the overhanging lights.

'Put that back!' she shouts. Martie's eyes snap towards her and, rattled, he is about to respond equally aggressively when he sees the look of sheer terror in Attracta's usually uncommitted eyes and stops. He is not to know that Attracta's experience of the supernatural includes a knife that flew across a kitchen.

'Okay. Sure.'

'Just tear the lettuce into shreds' says Attracta, trying to regain her normal speaking voice.

'Sure. Gonna be hard to tear the tomatoes though.' Martie again looks in Attracta's eyes, sees them wide with fear, so he smiles. 'I'll wait till you've left the room.'

Attracta nods, suddenly distracted. 'I'll tell them to come in. I'm not doing maid service.'

She leaves and Martie looks around. This isn't the sort of room he normally likes to be alone in. But it all looks so calm, so ordered. There are wooden shelves piled with plates, glasses, pots. A couple of genuine antique prints on a kitchen theme. The gleaming white tiles, the empty expanse of working surfaces and the giant sink with a gleaming pressure hose for removing tough food deposits.

'You're not in here, are you?' he asks the empty air.

He doesn't really want a reply, so when none comes he relaxes. He lifts the ladle and stirs the boiling pasta parcels. He slices the tomatoes and arranges them around the lettuce. He pours Balsamic vinegar from a new bottle onto the salad. He feels someone behind him, but he wants to finish the preparation so he finishes before he turns round, with a happy smile, to greet the first diner.

There's no one there.

'Crap. CRAP!' shouts Martie. After a moment Don and Becca enter at speed.

'What's happened!' shouts Don.

'Nothing. Nothing. Sorry.'

The others appear behind them. All stare at Martie with wide eyes, mouths half-open.

'Sorry. `I was finishing the salad. I thought one of you was behind me. I turned round and there was nothing there. Sorry. I didn't mean to cause a drama.'

'That's fine' says Don. 'We're in a haunted house. We're all going to overreact this week.'

'I wish you'd go away' says Sylvie to the air. 'Can't you see you're frightening us?'

'Shut up!' snaps Attracta. 'Are you actually trying to drive away the whole reason we're here?'

'Oh. Sorry. I wasn't thinking' says Sylvie simply.

'Yeah' says Alix, 'our situation here is delicate. We don't want to shit our pants, but we do want to turn in good report cards to Carl. Who knows what other shit he might have for us if we get this right?'

This thought is clearly something that at least some of the others have already nurtured to their discreet bosom. For some reason everyone looks at Attracta.

'What? WHAT!?' she snaps.

'Oh, nothing. It's just … I mean I googled you' says Alix. 'I saw your Page 3. You were a star. What happened?'

Attracta flushes scarlet. 'You have no right to look into my private business. No right at all. You're such a rude person!'

'What else have you found?' asks Becca. Being Becca no one replies.

'You know what else I found?' asks Alix as though starting an entirely new conversation thread. 'I found some very sexy pix of Don. Sorry I didn't download them, Martie.'

'Will everyone stop it!' snaps Martie, louder than he would like to, but still recovering from the strange incident he experienced. 'Okay, I'm gay. Don's hot. And that's it. Frankly I think this focus on me is to take us away from what's really going on here. I mean it's quite clear Attracta, who is the hottest of the women here, has her eye on Carl. Which means the field is clear for Becca to bang Don.'

'Can we just eat!' shouts Becca. 'I'm hungry!'

After the meal, once Attracta and Martie have collected plates and washed them, which is informally agreed will be part of the nightly cooks' responsibility, the group assembles in the giant library and chill out room.

'That's an awesome TV' notes Alix.

'Can anyone see the remote?' asks Sylvie, striking a practical note. A very long, tedious search for the remote eventually finds it hiding behind one of the shelves of books.

'Listen' says Attracta, as she and Martie, hands dried, join the main party. 'There's no way that remote being there is normal. I'm going to record it as another manifestation.'

'I found it' says Alix. 'But I don't mind you having the glory.'

'If this is the level of this week's glory' says Don, 'I'm concerned we're not going to have enough data to please our employer.'

'So what?' asks Becca. 'We didn't guarantee him anything except our presence here for a week.'

Alix, then Don, as the two members most technically gifted, attempt to get the TV to work.

‘Oh great’ says Becca. ‘Typical men all talk and no results.’

‘Can you do better?’ snaps Don. Becca reflects that this is one time she was heard.

Fifteen minutes later it turns out the answer is no. In the meantime, Alix has returned to his room and now brings out a bag.

‘So I guess it’s up to me to save the evening’ he says, presenting a plastic snap bag of white powder proudly.

‘What the diz?’ says Becca. ‘That looks like a grand of coke.’

‘Two grand’ says Alix. ‘I had to get it on credit so they’re charging me double.’

‘You’re not serious’ says Don. ‘We’re here this week for the purpose of recording supernatural phenomena and you want to open the gates of your perception with coke?’

‘There’s enough for everyone.’

‘I agree with Don’ says Sylvie. ‘It’s not why we’re here.’

‘Just exactly what are we doing here, then, ‘cause I signed up for a luxury week and so far it’s not happening!’

‘You want something to distract yourself?’ says Don in a new, edgy timbre. ‘How’s this. Part of my discussion with Carl threw up some interesting data on certain members of this tight little group. Specifically, that someone in this room is guilty of culpable homicide, also known as manslaughter. And someone else is a murderer.’

Nine. First Night

'Oh great' says Martie, in a deliberate Southern drawl. 'Is this your idea of Performing, Don?'

'Who is which?' asks Becca. 'Cause they should be separated from us others.'

'He didn't tell me who' replies Don. 'And we can't get to Performing until we're all done with Storming. It's been on my mind since last night. I knew I wouldn't sleep tonight until I could bring it to the group.'

'That sounds so sensitive, so New Man. So unlike you' comments Becca.

'And' says Martie, 'the reality is it's more likely that it's you rather than us. You've got that hard edge that goes with a carelessness around lives.'

'True' says Alix, 'but he brought the info.'

'A cheap trick' says Martie. 'Isn't this just Carl raising the stakes?'

'Yeah. We're supposed to be bonding. Now we're all distrusting each other. And two out of us six might want to harm the rest of us' says Attracta.

'Hmm' says Martie. 'I saw how frightened you are of knives, Attracta, back in the kitchen. Does it bring up memories of stabbing someone? Slicing someone's throat?'

'Only yours, you little shit' comes the instant reply.

No one feels like hanging out after dinner, so the party makes its individual way up the stairs to their respective rooms. They lock their doors, or place a chair against the door, or resolve to keep a passage to the outside world available by merely closing their door. They visit their respective bathrooms, then prepare for the night.

Sylvie and Martie exchange a look. Martie invites Sylvie to go first and waits in his room until Sylvie softly knocks on his door to indicate the bathroom is his. Martie approaches the door to the bathroom. He looks down the long corridor, closed doors that seem to stretch into infinity. He wants to call someone to help him find the light switch that would illuminate the rest of the corridor. Instead he scoots into the bathroom and slams the door.

By resolutely not looking in the mirror, just in case it discloses something behind him, he gets through his nightly routine of brushing and flossing. Sylvie has taken precisely half the room in the medicine cabinet, so Martie arranges his own personal requisites in the remaining space.

It takes Martie a while to get to sleep, but when he does it's a deep sleep, untroubled by the thoughts of the day. There's the sound of someone walking along the corridor about midnight. An investigation would have shown this was Alix, unable to sleep, thinking that a glass of milk from the kitchen might help him drift off.

There follows a couple of hours of complete silence, the stillness of the country night broken only by the slight sound of snoring from Becca's room. Around 1.30am, Don gets up to use his bathroom. At 2.20am Alix wakes because he thinks he can hear scratching. A brief investigation shows this to be ivy, blowing in the night wind, tapping against the thick diamond-pane windows.

At 3.27am the group is woken by a series of terrible, heart-rending screams.

'It's Sylvie!' cries Alix, appearing a second later in the corridor. Don, fighting sleep, adrenalin pumping through his veins, fumbles his way to the corridor light and staggers towards Sylvie's room.

'Sylvie!' cries Martie, emerging from his room opposite Sylvie's. 'It's okay! We're all here!'

'Shut up!' cries Attracta, her usually perfect blonde hair sticking out at all angles, giving her the attitude of some madwoman usually confined to the attic.

'You shut up' says Becca as she emerges, dragging on a dressing gown. 'Sylvie's screaming.'

Martie's the first to bang on Sylvie's door. 'Sylvie, we're here. Open up!'

Don and Alix brush him aside. 'I'll break it down' mutters Alix.

The door opens. Sylvie is still half-asleep. 'What's going on?' she mutters, and Martie registers that she sleeps with a mouth guard.

'Wait' says Martie to the group, 'if Sylvie sleeps with a mouth guard, how could she have been the one screaming?'

It takes a second for the meaning of this to sink into the group's still sleepy brains. They all register its meaning at the same time.

'Awesome' says Attracta, 'this is definitely another manifestation. I'll make a record of it.'

'We'll *all* make records of it, Attracta' says Becca sniffily.

'Whatever. I'm the only one documenting *everything* that happens.'

Attracta turns on her heel and returns to her room, slamming the door.

'Whoever thought that woman would be a good addition to a group…' says Becca, leaving the end of the sentence unspoken.

'If everyone's finished pounding on my door' says Sylvie, mumbling because of the guard, 'I'd prefer to go back to sleep. I'm never as tired as this in London.'

Alix and Becca return to their respective rooms, leaving Martie standing with Don. Once his panic had subsided, Martie had found the spectacle of the assembled group intriguing.

'So. Now we know what each of us wears to sleep.'

By this he means that Attracta wears bra and panties, Becca an over large t-shirt, partly covered by her dressing gown, and Sylvie an old-fashioned pair of pink striped pyjamas. Of the men, aside from himself who is wearing his underpants of the previous day and a t-shirt, Alix wears a t-shirt and nothing else and Don wears boxers. Relieved of his shirt, Martie can admire Don's single pierced nipple and the elaborate tattoo of a tiger that advances from his shoulder and down his chest. It seems he admires this a little too long because Don grunts and returns to his room.

The light remains on for a while in Attracta's room. She focuses on the best way to convey the maximum drama from the phenomenon. Would Carl be interested in what she was dreaming when she heard the scream? How the scream wove itself into her dream, and she woke ready for action? Should she explain how she always sleeps nude, but quickly donned pants and bra so she could go Sylvie's aid? How sad Sylvie looked in her mouth guard and cringy pyjamas? For a moment Attracta remembers Don, the natural charge-taker, standing nude except for his boxers. She's seen so many tattoos, some brilliant ones, so even Don's spectacular specimen doesn't do much for her. Yet she has to admit to herself that a single pierced nipple is something of a fetish.

With an annoyed grunt Attracta remembers who it is she's doing the recording for. For heaven's sake, don't talk about anyone. Just say you were sleeping in the nude and there was a terrible scream and it wasn't Sylvie.

It needs a few takes to get the recording to Attracta's high standards. She finds she's mumbling as the dark fingers of sleep keep pulling her back into the land of Morpheus. Finally she runs off a perfect recording, sends it, and puts the phone back on the side table with a sigh of satisfaction.

Sylvie, once woken, finds it difficult to go back to sleep. Instead she lies in the dark, her tongue gently touching the mouth guard. So, she thinks, it begins again. Once again I am in this strange half-real, half-mad world where the usual rules of life don't apply. I don't want to remember what happened the last time, it's too exhausting, too painful, and I've gone over it so many, many times. I came here on a hunch and a prayer. Now I know I'm in the right place. But what will happen is as yet entirely unwritten. And I would give anything, even the money we're supposed to get for this bizarre week, to know that at the end of it I will come out having finally been able to make peace with my tortured life. Oh, Hailey, my dearest darling, pray for your Mum in her hour of need.

Ten. Day Two

As a spontaneous example of Performing, Alix and Becca, the couple responsible for catering for the second day, have organised a breakfast buffet. They have also loaded the washing machine, so as the others assemble, they can hear the machine guaranteeing them clean crockery and cutlery for the day. Although no one says anything, they are somewhat grateful for this everyday, comforting background noise.

The group appears one by one, in various stages of wakefulness, and various degrees of clothing suitable for the day.

'Going to be hot' says Becca, commenting on Don's sleeveless t-shirt.

'I could totally pull off one of those' remarks Martie, as he reaches for the cornflakes and milk. 'If I had muscles. And more chest hair.'

'Honey' Becca responds, 'You're so pretty, you don't need any more than nature gave you.'

Martie smiles as though grateful to be reminded of how the world perceives him.

'Oh please stop' says Attracta, 'You'll only give him a big head.'

'That's interesting' says Martie. 'Is that what people used to say to you, Attracta? I mean, some version of that. I think it's sad when people put you down when you're a child. You do personal development, Don' he says, changing the subject and the tone of his voice, 'what's your take on that?'

Don, standing by the toaster, watching his toast turn even blacker, grunts.

'Oh you're not one of those life coaches, are you?' asks Becca. 'I mean, they do a weekend's course and suddenly they're telling people how to live their lives.'

'There's more to life coaching than that, Becca' says Don evenly, as he retrieves his toast and applies butter to the carbonised slice. In the introductions he was debating whether or not to call himself a life coach but didn't want to be drawn into a debate where his ignorance of anything more than the four 'ings' of group dynamics would become evident. Better to merely imply and appear expertly vague.

'Not much more' says Becca. Then she drinks loudly from her cup of coffee to change the subject.

Once the group is fully engaged in eating, Sylvie, who has been playing with a cup of weak white tea asks 'What are we going to do today?'

'If the weather stays this good, I'm going to be out on the lawn, catching a tan' says Attracta.

'Yeah?' says Alix. 'I mean, don't you want to investigate what happened last night? What happened yesterday?'

'Exacty how would we do that?' snaps Attracta.

'I dunno. But there's a whole library full of books. I'm thinking that maybe one of them is a history of this house. Maybe we can understand what's going on. And who the crap was screaming like that.'

This causes a moment's silence.

'Intriguing' says Don. 'You think the scream has a definite explanation?'

'Well, won't hurt to find out. I mean, Carl would be pleased, right?'

'I think I know what Carl wants' says Attracta, and then pauses, registering that she's making her agenda too overt.

'We don't want to waste the day' says Sylvie. 'I'm sure we can both enjoy this lovely weather *and* make some progress on our reason for being here.'

'I'm not sure that *is* our reason. We weren't asked to solve any mysteries. Just to record what happens.'

'It's in the nature of humankind to be curious' says Martie. 'I can't be in the sun too long, it brings out my freckles. I don't mind spending some time in the library. As long as someone else joins me.'

'I'm with Attracta' says Don, 'I'm here to soak up the sun.'

Since the idea of scholarship was Alix's, he joins Martie in the library. Sylvie goes for a long walk in the grounds. Every so often she looks up at the castle scanning anxiously the many windows, the picturesque battlements. After a moment she registers a new thought. 'Of course!' she gasps.

Attracta and Don, she in a pink bikini, him in an electric blue Speedo, take towels from their bathrooms and lie on a section of newly mown grass, next to a grandly ornate stone urn, nearly six feet high, from which early summer flowering plants cascade.

After a few minutes Attracta turns over from lying on her stomach and sees Don has been watching her.

'Can I help you?' she asks, not unkindly but also not encouragingly.

'You interest me' he responds. 'When I met you at Carl's, when I watched you picking out all the expensive accents in his rooms, I thought 'just another gold digger.' I've not entirely changed my opinion, but I do think there's more to you than your average former pin-up girl. Maybe you really will be the one who makes it big. The next Katie Price.'

'Thanks. I think. I mean, I'm fairly sure you just called me a media whore. I don't mind, when all you have is how you look, you can't get indignant when that's what people see.'

'See, that's almost philosophical' says Don. 'I hope your better self won't get in the way of your ambition.'

'Not a chance' responds Attracta. 'If I ever waver from my quest, I only have to shut my eyes and see the shit hole where I grew up. Back comes all my strength and determination.'

'Wow. So you and me are really not going to hook up?'

Attracta regards Don for a moment. 'Oh Don, you have no idea how much you ring my bells. But you're a penniless hustler and so am I. Seriously, we're much better for each other if we become friends.'

'Friends with benefits?'

'Don't beg. It's demeaning.'

The library at Strawberry Manor features blocks of antique books locked behind mesh, and open shelves containing everything from 60's novels to piles of magazines, none of which is less than eighteen months old. Martie remarks on this to Alix. Alix shrugs. 'I'm looking for the key to those mesh doors. That's where we'll find books to do with this house.'

'Seriously, don't you think it's significant that everything in here stops 18 months ago? What do you think happened then?'

'I don't know. Wonder how difficult it would be to bust open these doors?'

Armed with a ladle, it turns out the locks on the mesh doors are only decorative, and easily give up whatever secrets they hold.

Alix flicks through rows of old leather books.

'What are you finding?' asks Martie.

'Crap. Books on dogs … growing crops …here's one on rainfall in the area.'

'Okay, but at least it's about this area. What you want is something like 'Famous Local Ghosts and their Origins.'

'I know, but all I'm finding is …breeding better cattle…'

Alix gives up easily. After breaking open a couple more doors he gets bored and exits while Martie continues to carefully scan the open shelves.

Becca watches Sylvie as Sylvie appears at the side of the castle.

'Find anything interesting?' she calls.

Sylvie smiles and waves. 'We really should investigate the whole castle. It goes on for ages.'

'We'll wait till it rains. Going through this place when there's lightning flashing would be amazing.'

Sylvie reaches Becca. 'I don't want to sound condescending, but have you ever seen anything like this before?'

Becca nods. 'Not in SA, obviously, but when I got to the UK, going round the country estates that are open to the public was one of my things. I've seen most of the biggies. First time I've actually stayed in one, though. I mean, it's pretty mind blowing.'

'It's so funny to think that right now our little group is in charge. Yet this time next week we'll be gone.'

'Yeah. I was expecting something … I don't know, abandoned, weeds… when you hear of an uninhabited haunted house, you don't expect this. This is the sort of thing I've paid good money to tour.'

'He's clearly made a great deal of money from his art' says Sylvie.

There's no reply, so Sylvie turns to Becca. Becca is staring at the castle.

'What?'

Becca turns to her with panic in her eyes. 'Uh. Nothing.'

'What have you just seen?'

'Nothing. I swear. I was just … remembering …'

Becca begins to walk back to the castle.

'The longer we're here, the more I admire Carl's selection of our little group.'

Becca stops walking but doesn't turn around.

'I think we're all haunted.'

'Of course' says Becca, still not facing Sylvie. 'And I think it's time we started to share that with each other. I'm so tired of holding it inside.'

Becca and Alix meet up to prepare lunch. Becca becomes annoyed because Alix is allowing her to do most of the work.

'What?' snaps Alix.

'Don't what me, I'm only saying that we're both supposed to be doing this. That's the deal.'

'You mean because I'm black and you're white?'

'Oh don't, don't even go there. Don't listen to Attracta, she's a stupid cow. I'm not racist and I don't expect to have to give you special treatment.'

'If you're white you can't help being racist' mutters Alix.

Becca bangs a clutch of forks on the wooden table. 'No! We are not going to start talking politics and social equality now! We're supposed to be preparing lunch. So please open those two cans of asparagus. And if I have to tell you what to do then, please arrange them on that white dish there.'

When the rest of the group joins Becca and Alix it's clear the two cooks are not talking to each other. No one wants to push it, so comments are contained to how lovely everything looks, and how clever they are to have arranged the cold meats and cheeses into such intricate patterns.

Outside on the lawn, Sylvie is the only one looking at the castle as the other five find places on the mown lawn and begin eating.

'Does anyone mind if I say something while we're eating?'

'Will it interfere with my digestion?' asks Martie, chewing an asparagus.

'I suppose it might' responds Sylvie, her apologetic tone indicating that she wished she had not said anything.

'Wait till we're finished' says Don. No one contradicts him.

Sylvie waits until everyone has finished before she speaks.

'It's just that I thought of something which I think is important. Why it is that the house is so … well, splendid, although there's no one living here.'

'Coz Carl is well loaded and he believes in mainter with her mouth full of cheese.

'I think there's been two things. At least two. I think happened in the past. And another that happened recently.'

'That makes sense' says Martie. 'And I can give you a date. The most recent magazines in the library stop eighteen months ago.'

'I'm thinking … I don't think Carl did all this, all the decoration. I think the previous owners did, perhaps they inherited the castle, perhaps they bought it. Eighteen months ago something happened. Perhaps that's to do with the screams last night. I think Carl bought it, probably bought it cheaply with all the furnishings et cetera.'

'That also makes sense' says Alix. 'There's cupboards full of old books. Antiques. The kind that take a long time to get together. Unless you bought everything at the same time.'

'So we've got two time lines. Whatever happened in the past, and whatever happened 18 months ago.'

'This morning' says Don, 'I took a look at the basement spa. I turned on the sauna and steam heating. And the jacuzzi. It's fantastic. So whatever happened 18 months ago, it was enough to drive out whoever spent a fortune making this place first class.'

'I'd kill for a steam' says Becca.

'I'd murder for a jacuzzi' returns Martie.

'So which of you is our murderer?' snaps Attracta.

'Stop it!' cries Sylvie. 'Can't we please just get on with each other? Every time someone opens their mouth it's like a trap.'

There is a brief silence. 'You okay?' asks Becca. 'You looked a bit fraught when you came back from your walk around the castle?'

‘Can everyone please look at me?’ asks Sylvie. ‘And please keep looking at me when I tell you something. For the last five minutes I’ve been looking at the castle, and there’s someone looking out at us.’

Five heads simultaneously flick round. To Sylvie’s annoyance the face in the window not so much turns away as it melts into the window’s surrounding blackness.

‘Shit! I saw it!’ shouts Attracta.

‘I couldn’t find the window’ says Don. ‘Where?’

‘I saw something for a moment then not’ says Alix. ‘Did it disappear?’

‘I saw it’ says Attracta. ‘She had flat hair, ringlets, some sort of high neck, black dress. Earrings? Sylvie did you see earrings?’

Sylvie pauses before speaking. ‘Yes. Pronounced earrings, they looked like black jet.’

Don leaps to his feet. ‘Which room?’

Martie jumps up as well. ‘From the centre, second window on the second floor.’

‘Isn’t that my bedroom?’ asks Becca. ‘Because if it is, I need to change.’

‘Come on’ says Don, glancing at Martie, ‘no more pissing about.’

Of course, by the time the party gains entrance to Becca’s room any spectral presence has long since departed.

‘They’ve ransacked the room!’ Sylvie reports, taking in the clothes casually strewn over the bureau, the chairs and the floor.

‘No, I just haven’t finished unpacking’ mumbles Becca.

'Don't you have hangers and cupboards in South Africa?' asks Attracta.

'Yes. Plenty. How about you in rural Ireland?'

Attracta's mouth snaps shut and she glares at Becca.

'So do we connect the scream last night with the woman just now?' asks Martie.

'I don't think we're supposed to connect anything. This isn't an episode of *Ghost Watch*.'

'I never watched that. Any good?'

'I have no idea' snaps Attracta.

'I'm not sleeping here' says Becca.

'Well no one's likely to want to change with you. And the other rooms either don't have bathrooms, or they're in the next corridor, a long way from this one.'

'Shut up, Don, no one made you leader.'

'I'll change with you, Becca' says Sylvie.

'What? You must be mental' says Attracta.

'This is what we're here for' says Sylvie, simply.

'Fine. Give me ten minutes to grab my crap and the room's yours' says Becca, hastily, as though before Sylvie can change her mind.

'Aren't you forgetting something?' asks Alix. Becca regards him questioningly.

'The little matter of clearing up and washing up.'

'Oh. Right. Yeah, Sylvie, I'll bring my stuff over later. Do make yourself at home as soon as you like.'

Downstairs in the kitchen, having gathered the remains of lunch from the lawn, Alix and Becca are efficiently dealing with cleaning and organising.

'Why do you think that woman's haunting this place?' Becca asks. Not receiving a reply, she turns to Alix, and realises he is deliberately ignoring her.

'What's the problem?' she says.

'Racist.'

'Oh come on, you can't hold – seriously, Alix, I am *not* racist. Some of my best friends et cetera. Now put the leftover asparagus back in the fridge and cover it with plastic.'

Alix ignores this directive.

'Last I looked slavery was abolished' he mutters.

Becca stops and looks over to where Alix leans against a counter.

'Alix' she says softly, 'you want me to prove I'm not racist?'

Alix clicks his tongue. 'How you propose to do that?'

'Shut the door. And drop your pants.'

Alix's eyes widen and he carefully examines Becca's face for clues as to whether she's having him on. Then he closes the door. He moves to where Becca stands. Alix presents himself to Becca and she efficiently unbuckles his belt. She slides his trousers down to his knees and fishing around in Alix's boxers produces his semi-erect penis. With a graceful grunt Becca goes down on her knees. A moment later there is a sigh of satisfaction from Alix.

For ninety seconds Alix continues to react to the warm mouth around his genitals. Becca discovers that Alix is a grunter, using a series of different moans and groans to indicate without words to Becca what he likes and likes not so much. Becca is getting ready to bring off the happy ending when the moans from Alix change in intensity and mood. She takes a moment to gather this new information, by which time Alix's body has become locked frozen and what's emerging from his mouth is a series of choked, terrified bleats.

Wiping her mouth and pulling her hair back in a single hand gesture, Becca stands up. Behind her she can see a white china dinner plate. Floating in mid-air. As she sees it the plate begins to spin and gaining speed hurtles itself with great force at the wall behind them. They both shout out, waiting for the next piece of crockery to defy gravity. When nothing more happens Alix hurriedly buttons his pants and flicks his belt buckle closed. The two stare at each other.

'We have to tell the others.'

'I don't want anyone to know!'

'Becca, think, they need to know it's down here too. We don't have to tell them what we were doing.'

'Oh. Ya, of course. Make sure you don't tell them by *inference*. I mean if you do, I'll throw plates at you myself.'

'We can finish up later' says Alix.

'Forget it. I've done enough washing up.'

'I mean finish me up.'

'Read the room, Alix. Can't you tell when the moment has passed?'

Eleven. Second Night

'I wish we lived in Iceland and it was the height of summer' says Martie.

'Why the fuck?' asks Alix.

'Because the sun never goes down in the summer. Here it's like the shadows are just waiting for the sun to go down so they can appear and scare us shitless.'

'That's not logical' says Don. 'Today we've had two manifestations in the sunshine.'

'None of this is *logical*, Don' responds Martie.

'If you're so chicken' says Becca, 'why did you volunteer for this in the first place?'

There is a pause.

'Good question' says Martie. 'I suppose this could be my cue to explain.'

The group is sprawled on various sofas in what they have adopted as their main chill out room, the library. Dinner has been served and enjoyed and today's cooks are pleased that tomorrow someone else will be doing the catering.

'Do you want a little stage? A spotlight?' asks Attracta.

'No, I suppose I'm just waiting for everyone's permission.'

'Given. Get on with it.'

'So, who's beer is this?' asks Alix, taking the spotlight.

'No one's' says Becca.

'What, so this is the ghost's? The woman with earrings? She opens it but doesn't drink?'

'Okay, it's mine' snaps Becca. 'I opened it and changed my mind. Is that a crime?'

'So do you want to hear, or what?' asks Martie.

'Please tell us. Alix, I'm sure Becca won't mind if you drink her beer.'

'Would you want to?' asks Attracta. 'I mean, do you know where her mouth has been?'

'Now *you're* a racist!' claims Alix.

'Just shut up Alix!' cries Becca. 'Can't you see she's winding you up?'

'Thanks, Alix' says Attracta. 'You've just confirmed what I've been wondering all day.'

'Seriously, are you listening?' asks Martie.

'Go on, sweetheart' says Sylvie.

'Right. I moved to London from Wolverhampton. Like you do' says Martie, defensively. 'Got a single room in a shared flat through this gay housing site. That's not actually relevant. One night I was in Islington, visited their gay pub. I usually stand in the darkest part of the pub. And I realise this guy's standing next to me. He starts to talk to me but it's so loud I can't hear him. He's nice, tall, short hair, well-dressed. He suggests we go somewhere we can hear each other.'

'Cut to his bedroom' says Becca.

'I'm not going to go on if you're not taking me seriously.'

'Sorry, darling, go on. Very interested.'

'Okay, so we get back to his, which is a small, double-storey house in a row. Nicely decorated, bit old-fashioned but that's on trend now. He makes tea, I sit in the lounge, admire his pictures. Beautiful fireplace, green tiles, green painted surround. So we talk about this and that, and we go to bed.'

Martie looks round, defying anyone to comment.

'Okay, so we make love, and it's … comforting. I felt looked after, understood. No sweat, no freaky moves, just very, very happy. In the morning he's off out quickly, so he makes me a cheese roll and I eat it on my way back to the tube. When I get there, I discover I've left my tube pass which is in a red plastic folder and sometimes falls out my pocket. So I turn round, run back to his in the hope he's still there. I get to the right street and I see that rather than a row of houses … there's these open walls. Bomb damage. You know how you see pictures of where a bomb landed and there's a space and it's opened the guts of the houses next to it. Shreds of wallpaper on the wall. Different walls painted different colours. All crumbling, peeling, open to the elements.

As I get to his I feel I'm walking slower and slower. I get to his… it's like the rest of the row. There's houses behind, but where his house was it's just the memory of the house that was bombed. I stand there, looking at the colour of his bedroom. The painted skirting board. And saddest of all, the flat part of a fireplace, tiles gone, but still painted green.'

There's a moment of silence, then Alix laughs.

'You're telling fibs, bro. That never happened to you.'

'It did. You don't have to believe me.'

'I can believe you because in the last couple of days we've experienced a number of phenomena we can't understand. But…' says Sylvie. 'If I understand you, it's not like some of the rest of us have experienced. I mean, your experience was a *whole*, like those two women who turned the corner at Versailles and found themselves back in the 18th Century.'

'True.'

'I hope you're ready for the scary sort.'

Martie thinks, nods. 'I'm tougher than I look. I think.'

The party breaks up into individuals. Don walks past Attracta. 'I'm off to the spa. The jacuzzi's been bubbling since lunch time.'

'I hate jacuzzi's says Attracta, confidentially. 'They make my skin smell.'

Some minutes later Don is lying face downward, nude, in the steam room. He enjoys the hiss of steam coursing up and down his body. He feels the door open and that someone's come to sit next to him. He's too tired and relaxed to lift his head. The other remains silent. Don starts to drift off, then comes to, remembers where he is, opens his parched mouth to speak.

'Attracta?'

The figure moves slightly.

'Attracta?'

'No. It's Becca.'

Don smoothly turns over and sits up. His manhood flops, half-aroused, he doesn't cover himself since the thick steam acts like a layer of clothing.

'How did you know I was here?'

'I heard you inviting Attracta. Or rather, I heard her turn you down.'

Don laughs. 'I would have invited you but you were talking to the others. I wasn't inviting the others.'

'Shame on you. Thought we were supposed to be in Performing?'

'That's for business. This is pleasure. Where are you?'

Don reaches out a hand and discovers Becca is wearing a bathing suit. 'You don't need that.'

There is a pause, then Don hears the suit being discarded. He makes room on the bench, draws Becca across. Now he's close enough to see her. He's pleased that under her clothes she has the firm body of an athlete.

'I'm impressed. You look like you lift weights.'

'Mainly swimming, running. Not so much since I came to London. Early ballet training, that's what gives you muscles.'

'I thought what I wanted most, right now, was an ice-cold beer. You've shown me I was wrong.'

In another fluid motion Don drops to his knees. He pushes open Becca's legs, which part willingly, and he moves his mouth down. She grunts as his tongue encounters her intimate flesh. She leans back, to give him greater access. After a minute the door to the steam opens again. To hell with them, thinks Becca. If they don't like it they can leave. Don seems to be entirely unaware of the newcomer.

A steam room works in shifts. First it fills up with the hot steam, then after a few minutes the steam dies down and you can see out of the glass. Becca, still wrapped up in Don's ministrations, watches as the clouds of steam melt into nothing and visibility returns. There is a figure sitting with head bowed on the other bench. Becca frowns. It can't be Don, it's obviously not Alix and it seems too big for Martie. The wrong colouring too.

Don shifts his practiced hold on Becca's thighs and thrusts even deeper with his tongue. The steam hisses and the glass box again quickly fills with concealing steam. After a moment it seems the other figure stands and makes their way out of the steam room. Becca hears the door slam.

'Don…'

'Ssssshhh … enjoy …'

'Listen. There was someone in here. They just left.'

'I know, I felt them. Must have been Martie.'

'It wasn't Martie, this guy was … bigger. And it wasn't Alix.'

Don removes his head from Becca's middle.

'Shit! Why didn't you say something earlier!'

'Don't blame me! I was – I was lost in the moment, if you must know.'

Don gathers his towel around his waist and pushes open the steam room door.

'I didn't hear the outer door slam. But it's closed. So where's he gone?'

'Don't blame me, I'm pretty sure I left it open.'

'This place is beginning to get on my nerves' declares Don. 'What the hell is going on?'

'Could have been worse' remarks Becca. 'Could have wanted to join in.'

'Shut up. Don't say crap like that.'

'Don't tell me to shut up, Don. I'm not your girlfriend.'

'My girlfriend, if I had one, wouldn't talk crap.'

'Actually' says Becca, gathering her clothes, hugging them to her as she makes for the door, 'it doesn't surprise me you don't have a girlfriend!'

'Where do you think you're going!'

'Oh what, you're such a stud you can just go back to what you were doing?'

'No. But do you want to go out there on your own?'

Becca hesitates and Don sees the look of fear on her face. He wouldn't like to be looking into a mirror right now, he's pretty sure his expression is similar.

'Just give me a minute to shower, we can go together.'

'Are you sure it's me you're protecting? Not you?'

'Fine. Go if you want to, Becca. Don't blame me if it's out there.'

Becca also has a shower then the two get dressed.

'So what? Now we know there's a woman who looks through windows. And a man, someone who doesn't look like Alix or Martie, who's up for a spa? I'm glad it's not our job to make sense of any of this.'

Outside the spa the corridor leading to the stairs and the ground floor has somehow lost its guiding light.

'Did it turn off the bloody light?' asks Becca.

'I'm not waiting to find out' says Don, and he moves carefully towards the stairs. Becca reaches to turn out the spa light. Instantly the area is plunged into darkness, except for a dim light coming from the steam room, and the lights from the jacuzzi.

'Leave it on!' snaps Don.

'Listen I know it's not our electricity bill, but I'm ethically against leaving a whole spa on the whole night. It's too decadent.'

Don swears, but he returns to the spa and switches off the facilities. Then, glaring at Becca, forbidding her to turn off the main light, they make their way to the stairs.

'Let me go first' says Becca.

'For fuck's sake.'

'I can see you are no gentleman.'

'Oh, only seeing that now? Not when I was eating you out a few minutes ago?'

'Is that what you were doing. I thought you'd lost your chewing gum.'

There's a silence and Becca wonders if she's gone too far. Then she hears Don chuckling.

'You South African girls, shameless' he says. The stairs are flooded with light as Don pushes open the door to the entrance hall. They enter the hall, blinking in the light, relieved no one is there to witness their humiliating defeat.

'We don't talk about this, okay? Too complicated.'

'Of course not' says Becca, already composing in her mind the detailed description she will be sending Carl. Detailed but censored, of course. He doesn't have to know their private business.

The two climb slowly up the grand staircase.

'What would you do if you met that thing again? Sliding down the bannisters?'

'I don't even know if what you saw was spectral' says Don. 'The ghosts I remember… they were a lot more violent. These seem to be refined, very English ghosts. If you get me.'

'I suppose so. They don't seem to approve of sex, I know that from two incidents.'

'What's the other incident? Oh… Alix. That's what Attracta was talking about this evening.'

'I don't know what you see in her, honestly' says Becca, in an honest tone of questioning.

'I think it's the unobtainability. I don't like a girl who's too easy.'

'Oh' says Becca, as they reach the top of the stairs. 'Now he tells me.'

Don laughs and kisses Becca on her forehead. 'Good night.' He moves towards his room.

'Don' says Becca, walking towards her room, the one closest to the gloom stretching endlessly along the corridor. 'No woman on this planet likes to be kissed on the forehead.'

'Serious? All my girlfriends liked it.'

'They were being polite.'

Don laughs again, bids Becca goodnight and closes his door. Becca stands outside Attracta's room but doesn't knock. Then she stands outside Sylvie's room but again she doesn't knock. Finally she knocks on Martie's door. After a minute it's opened. Martie's eyes are wide, although relieved to see his visitor is someone he recognises.

'Have you got a minute?' asks Becca.

'Sure. Nothing but time tonight and the rest of the week.'

'Thanks. Can I come in?'

Martie sits on the dishevelled bed clothes while Becca takes the most comfortable chair.

'Are the ghosts getting to you?'

'Not ghosts. Men. A man.'

Later, once Becca has cried, Martie has comforted her and both have agreed that Don is a piece of exploitative shit, Becca thanks Martie for his time and goes across the corridor and into her own room. Martie lies awake, his thoughts bound up in images from the day, embarrassment over his sharing that didn't go over well, and Becca. He decides that a late-night visit to the loo will prepare him for sleep.

He puts his feet on the floor.

Something under the bed reaches out and grabs both his ankles.

The scream that summonses the others has something in common with the scream of the night before. This time it's not so much a random, desperate cry, more a very clear 'Help! Help! HEEEELLLLLPPPP!!!'

Becca, only just drifting off herself, is the first one to come to Martie's aid. She gasps. He's crouched at the top of the bed, clinging onto the carved bedhead as though it's a life raft. His eyes are so large they seem to take up the whole of his head. His mouth is open in a travesty of a laugh.

Alix, still wearing only a t-shirt, appears, with Becca and Sylvie behind him. Forewarned by Alix's previous night wear she has brought a towel, which she gives Alix without a word.

Don, fighting off sleep, staggers out of his bedroom, again in boxers. His eyes snap open as he sees the terrified, frozen figure of Martie, clutching the bedhead.

'Martie, what's happened, what did you see?'

'It's under the bed!'

Five pairs of eyes investigate the void under Martie's bed and are able to reassure him that whatever it was has gone.

'I put my feet on the floor. IT WAS UNDER THE BED!!!'

'Martie. Stop that. Let go of the bedhead.'

'Nooooo!! It grabbed me. It wanted to pull me under the bed!'

Don yawns so deeply it rocks him. He walks over to where Martie huddles and gently pulls Martie's grip away from the bed head. He lets Martie transfer his terror onto him, like a monkey embracing a caring zookeeper.

'Come on. You can sleep in my room. There's a big enough chair.'

Held in Don's arms, Martie calms down. 'No, it's okay. Really. I'm sorry, it was just – I wasn't expecting it. It grabbed my ankles!' Really, I'm fine. I just … I'll sleep with the light on. I'll be fine.'

'Seriously?' asks Becca. 'You're giving up the chance of sleeping in Don's room?'

'Yes' says Martie firmly. Someone more awake might conclude that he doesn't want to be further confused and traumatised by being geographically close to Don.

Sylvie volunteers to stay with Martie until he falls asleep. She sits in the comfortable chair recently vacated by Becca. The others all wish each other goodnight. A few minutes later Sylvie asks Martie in a whisper if he's still awake. When she receives no reply, she silently moves to the door, and switches out the light.

Sometime later in the night the door of Martie's room creaks open. Only half awake, Martie grunts questioningly. 'Sssshhh' comes from the stygian darkness. Then Martie feels the bedclothes softly parted, and a body slips under the covers next to him. Martie knows the difference between how a black man's skin feels, and a white man's.

'Don… oh my darling, you came to me…'

'Ssshhhh. Don't say anything.'

When Martie wakes up, it's morning. He turns hopefully to the other side of the bed but it is empty. He reaches over and touches all that remains, a slight indentation on the other side. He could get up, but right now all he wants is to recall, as much as he can, the night's exertions.

Twelve. Day Three

'So this is Performing in action' comments Alix as he watches Don and Sylvie assembling the breakfast buffet, unself-consciously co-ordinating their efforts for maximum benefit. Becca laughs. The group, minus Martie, has assembled, still sleepy, glad to have got through the night.

Attracta stretches and looks out the window onto the rear courtyard. 'You know' she says to no one specifically, 'we should investigate the outbuildings. When we had a ghost …' she stops, then continues, 'when we had a ghost I one day went into the old shithouse in our garden. Just for a joke, you know, I thought I'd have a wee. I couldn't even get my pants down, the atmosphere in that tiny space was so insane. That's where the ghost hung out when it wasn't giving us grief.'

'That's interesting' says Becca. 'I didn't know people actually said 'wee' any more.'

'Oh yeah' says Attracta, off-handedly, 'and we say 'bitch' and 'ho' as in 'keep your bitchy attitude out of my face, ho.'

'I was only commenting on your use of an old-fashioned word. You don't have to jump down my throat' Becca replies, flushing.

'Honey, there's no room down your throat.'

'Seriously, there was no negative inference.'

'Maybe it's your accent. I can never tell what you mean' says Attracta.

'Then that's your problem' snipes Becca.

'Don't you mean 'your negative inference?'

‘Can we enjoy the lovely summer morning, please’ calls Sylvie, concentrating on arranging the flat ware.

Martie sidles into the room, his eyes seeking out Don. He walks up to Don, who’s flipping fried rashers of bacon onto a vintage platter.

‘Morning… Don’ he says in an intimate whisper. Don looks at him in surprise, grunts, removes the scrambled eggs from the skillet.

Martie joins Sylvie. He decides that this is how Don wants to play it. Nothing overt, nothing that Becca or Attracta can make fun of. So what? They can flutter around Don all they like: he knows what Don likes in bed.

Eating on their own, or in intense groups of two, the six consume the morning offering.

‘This bacon is just how I like it. Crispy not too burnt’ says Becca.

‘I saw a film from the ‘70s called *Burnt Offerings*. Everyone in it died’ says Martie.

‘Not until I’ve had my coffee’ says Sylvie.

‘So, who wants to explore the outbuildings with me?’ asks Attracta.

‘I’m lying in the sun ‘til the sun goes down’ says Becca. ‘Not that you were hoping I’d say yes anyway.’

‘I’ll go with you’ says Martie, since no one else has spoken. Attracta has her mouth full, presumably that’s the reason she doesn’t acknowledge him.

‘I want to explore the battlements’ says Don and instantly Martie, Alix and Becca realise that’s what they want to do as well.

‘I’ll join you on the outbuildings exploration’ says Sylvie, quietly, to Attracta. Attracta gives her a tight smile in acknowledgment.

‘How do we get up there?’ asks Martie, sending a sidelong smile to Don which Don finds puzzling. Then he remembers how he rescued Martie from the bedhead. If the little guy wants to hero-worship him, cool.

‘There’s a map in the library. Very detailed.’

‘Does it indicate secret passages? Hidden rooms?’ asks Martie, eagerly.

‘You so fucked, little man’ laughs Alix. ‘None of that shit is real.’

‘Actually, there’s a priest’s hole and there may be secret passages. At one time the servants would use them so they could get around the house almost invisibly.’

‘You think someone’s in them now? That’s what we’ve experienced?’ asks Becca.

‘No. Maybe the woman at the window.’

‘Maybe the guy under Martie’s bed’ says Becca.

‘I’ll meet anyone who’s interested in the library in fifteen’ says Don.

Most of the group shuffles out to get ready. Sylvie and Don organise the washing up.

‘Third day and as yet no major injuries.’

‘Oh, Don, don’t say that. Don’t tempt fate.’

‘I really respect you, you know, Sylvie. You seem to be the most vulnerable, yet you don’t complain, you just get on with whatever.’

‘Thank you, Don. I don’t like thinking about me. I prefer to … well… be as invisible as a servant.’

Don observes Sylvie as she stretches up to replace a bowl on a high ledge. She has a vibe of being in her 40's but her body is still tight, her breasts are firm. She's probably no more than 35. A real woman. Returning to her normal stance Sylvie is aware Don is watching her, and she gives him a quiet smile.

'It's bizarre to think this is only our third day. The outside world seems … another galaxy.'

'I have dreams in which I'm on my phone. Then I get in my car and visit … London, New York … it's like my subconscious can't work out where I am.'

'I don't miss my mobile' Sylvie reports. 'I often think the world moves far too fast … and for what worthwhile purpose?'

'I'm not sure what purpose it serves to keep a castle like this. I mean, how much does this cost Carl in maintenance?'

'I was thinking about that. Perhaps what we're here to do is document the extent, the *gravity*, of the ghosts. Then Carl's going to compile our evidence into a brochure so he can prove to whoever that the place is liveable.'

Don smiles. 'I don't know if I'd want my wife and kids in a place where there are mysterious screams in the night and clutching hands under the bed.'

'That's interesting' says Sylvie. 'I had no idea you thought in terms of wife and kids. You strike me as a natural loner.'

There is a beat before Don continues. 'I was being... general.'

Fifteen minutes later, when Don appears in the library, Martie, Alix and Becca are already examining the map. As Don approaches the library table Martie gives him a particularly intimate smile. Don slightly flinches.

'Look, Don. There *is* a secret passage. There's a panel in the hall and it goes … right up to here on the first floor. It's not my room, though, looks more like Attracta's.'

'Don't tell her.'

'Yeah? I thought we really should.'

'Unless you want to change rooms again?'

'Oh. Crap no.'

'So… we reckon if we walk to the end of our corridor, and take the stairs, then there's some sort of iron staircase, and then we should be out on the roof' says Alix.

'I think we should explore the rest of the rooms in our corridor first' says Becca. 'In fact, I don't know why we're on day three and we haven't already.'

'Perhaps something is subconsciously telling us not to' hazards Martie. 'I, for one, am fine with keeping to the known areas.'

'You can join the girls checking out the outbuildings if you like' says Don, a little harshly. Martie blinks. This is taking cool too far.

'I'm right with the rest of you' says Martie. 'Only I'm the one who's actually been grabbed. You could be more sensitive to my feelings.'

'Oh fuck' says Don.

'No, seriously' says Martie. 'I know you've taken some sort of professional development training, that Forming, Storming stuff. Didn't they teach you about Empathy?'

Don sweeps up the map and folds it. 'I'm going up to the roof. Anyone who's not having a breakdown can join me.'

Don, Becca and Alix immediately leave. Martie feels hurt and remains. Then he realises he doesn't want to be in the house on his own, so he runs up the staircase to meet them.

Alix finds the switch that illuminates the whole of the corridor.

'There must be twenty doors off this corridor' says Becca solemnly.

The little party silently walks its length, towards the stone arch at the end, rattling and opening all the doors. Not all will open and those that do prove fairly unspectacular. A bed, a washstand, a carpet. Curtains either open or closed as though the last chatelaine couldn't be bothered to organise a uniform look. After each room is examined, they close the door. Finally they reach the stone arch. From here they see that there is another corridor, stretching to the left.

'More corridor?' asks Alix, rhetorically. 'What did the builder have in mind?'

'There are calendar houses: 12 entrances, 52 staircases, 365 rooms. One for every month, week and day of the year' says Martie.

'What do they do on Leap Year: build an outside privy?' quips Becca.

Being Becca, no one replies. She just doesn't understand it.

The group is now tired of examining a plethora of virtually identical bedchambers, so they concentrate on finding the staircase up to the roof. Becca listens as their footsteps echo around the narrow, spiral, stairs.

'If we meet some ghost coming down…' but she can't think of how to finish the sentence and apparently neither can anyone else.

At the top of the stone stairs they look around. It's a broad area, with more doors.

'More doors' remarks Alix. 'I fucking hate doors.'

Martie laughs. 'Don, which should be the door to the metal staircase?' Don has been examining the map. Now he silently points to a particular door. He tests the door, which swings open easily. Inside there is an empty area with a metal staircase.

With cheerful ringing noises the party ascend the stairs. At the top Don stops.

'Don't tell Alix. It's another door.'

Martie laughs and Alix punches him in the arm. 'Ow!' cries Martie.

'Girls, girls…' mutters Don as he tests the door. It swings open easily. Possibly a little too easily for one so rarely used.

The four shamble out. Someone, presumably the same person as the one who employed the decorator downstairs, has paid out a considerable sum of money to repair the ancient roof.

'At least we won't fall through a hole' grunts Don. The four fan out, examining how, from this angle, the seeming hodgepodge of additions, made over the centuries by a series of owners, fits seamlessly into a logical footprint. Those who dare walk over to the battlements and look down at the ground some 60 feet below them.

'Don't move. There she is' says Don.

For once, the others obey. They slowly turn their heads in the direction indicated by Don. Indeed, there she is. The woman is dressed in grey and black. She wears a mantilla on her head. She seems to be about 25. She seems cloaked in a profound sadness. At first the four think she's looking at them, but as she nears they realise they are not her intention. Martie flinches as the spectre walks a mere few feet from him before continuing. She comes to rest at the battlement, and looks over, her arm firmly grasping a hold on the curved grey stone. When they've recovered the four slowly move towards the battlement, wondering what it is she sees.

Below them, beyond the mowed grass area where they took lunch the previous day, the see the figure of a man. He appears to be around 30. He also wears clothes of indistinct cut in grey and black. His hair appears to be fair. He is not looking at the woman, though. Instead he is looking further along the arboretum. As though he is waiting to be joined.

After a moment the woman turns and again the group freezes. From her mouth or perhaps from the air around her they hear a distinct moan. She turns back, again looking down at the man. The group realises that now he is not alone. He has been joined by another man.

The woman turns away from the battlement. Now it is as though for the first time she sees the group. She opens her mouth and emits a series of terrible screams. Then she runs along the roof and partway along dissolves into nothing. Becca and Don have the presence of mind to see if the men are still below, but down below the grass is clear of figures.

'Three of them' says Becca. 'Shit.'

'Thanks, Becca, you really should do this professionally' snaps Don.

'Piss off, Don. I'm allowed to have my own opinion, you know.'

'Do you think they'll come back? Do they do this every day?' asks Martie, his voice trembling.

Don turns to him and at the sight of Martie's terrified face something soft gives in Don and instead of sneering he lightly touches Martie's arm in a gesture of comfort. Tears appear in Martie's eyes, which is too much for Don to cope with, so he moves towards the exit door, expecting that Becca will give Martie what he needs.

Which she does. Traversing the way back, down the stairs, along the corridor, and down into the sunshine outside takes a few minutes. By the time their shoes are crunching over the gravel all of them have resumed their usual demeanours.

'To answer Martie's question' says Don. 'No, I don't think they do this every day. I think they did it for us. It was a show for us.'

'So if Carl thinks he can flip this place, he's wrong' says Alix. ''Cause those spooks will put on a total shitshow for any prospective buyers' and he laughs hugely at this thought.

'That's not our problem' says Becca. 'I'm going to make a report while I can still remember exactly how it happened.'

'Fuck that' mutters Don. 'I want sunshine.'

'But what if they're out there?' cries Martie. Don regards him soberly.

'Get a grip, Martie. This is only the third day. They put on a show for us, that's all.'

'You didn't have your legs grabbed' responds Martie, miserably. 'I don't know if I can do this.'

'Sure. Split' says Becca. 'We'll ask Carl if we can have your bucks.'

Martie frowns. 'You know I was so much crapping myself, I forgot. Six hundred quid a day. I suppose I can crap myself a bit for that sort of pay out.'

Don laughs and punches Martie in exactly the same place as Alix had.

'Ow! FFS!'

Meanwhile, Attracta and Sylvie are exploring the outbuildings. The first one was the castle's forge. There is a massive central work island, composed of wooden railway sleepers. On it is a complicated iron wall bracket.

'Look' says Sylvie, picking it up. 'This must be the last thing the smithy was making. It's beautiful.'

Attracta takes it off her. 'Yeah. Souvenir.' She keeps hold of the bracket.

'What's back here?' Behind the workshop is the forge.

'If I was a restless spirit' says Attracta, to draw Sylvie's attention, 'I would hang out right there.'

She points to a windowless room beyond the forge. The two women attempt to make out any shapes in the dark.

'It's like staring into a black hole' says Sylvie.

'And it can stay a black hole' says Attracta, turning back to the entrance, still clutching her swag. Sylvie follows her as she returns to the courtyard. There are a number of further rooms, some locked, some without doors, what the Spanish call *dependents:* those rooms associated with the main residence. They explore the areas previously reserved for horse-drawn carriages. And the stables. 'This is bullshit' Attracta concludes. 'I wish I'd gone up to the battlements.'

'At least you can make a report to Carl' Sylvie reminds her.

'Are you kidding? He's a world-renowned artist. He can't be bothered with boring shit like this.'

'At least you got a souvenir out of it' responds Sylvie.

'God, must you relentlessly find the good in everything?' asks Attracta as though desperately weary.

'I don't think that's fair' says Sylvie, her voice trembling. 'I don't think I'm like that at all.'

'Yes you are. Believe me you are!' cries Attracta, walking back towards the main entrance.

Sylvie stands for a moment, looking round as though bidding farewell to the disappointing *dependents.* 'Believe me I'm not' she says to herself, grimly. 'And if you weren't such an obvious pinhead you'd know that.' Don, she remembers, actually does seem to get her. Which was a surprise.

Thirteen. Third Night

Attracta is even more irritated when she discovers that the others have achieved a major scoop with no less than three ghostly sightings. She glares at Sylvie the whole evening, apparently having forgotten that the outbuildings were her idea. When Sylvie, in her usual unobtrusive manner, puts Attracta's evening meal in front of her, Attracta moodily pushes the plate away.

'I think if we're going to be at our best we need some control over the menu' she announces. 'This is the third dinner we've had and I'd appreciate some bloody variety!'

'You don't get it' replies Don. 'You were cook first day, so you only had to heat up what was there. We have to cook from scratch. And this is basically all there is.'

'Shit' says Attracta. 'So what's in the rules stopping us from ordering takeaway from McDonalds?'

'Only good taste, dear' murmurs Sylvie, characteristically not loudly enough for Attracta to hear. Although Don does.

'How are you going to order takeaway? We don't have working phones.'

There is a brief moment before Attracta's answer flies across the room, in the form of her plate. The food falls off en route so it's only the plate that smashes against the panelled wall.

'Fuck it! You child!' shouts Don, angrier than anyone has yet seen him.

'No fuck you!' shouts Attracta back, the coarsest tones of her native land rich in her voice. 'I can't take this shit anymore. I want my friends. I want my phone. I want to go out and get a McDonalds when I want it!'

'First you shouldn't eat takeaway because they buy up the cows who've died of old age or disease. Second you're being paid six hundred quid a day to be here. If you can't do without your crap and your phone for a few days …' Martie shrugs and doesn't finish the sentence.

'Shut it you snotty little poofter' screams Attracta.

'Oi!' responds Alix. 'Leave the kid alone.'

'Oh what are you fucking his bum then?' cries Attracta.

'Shut up you little cow' says Don.

'Attracta, are you a natural bottle blonde?' asks Martie. 'And what's with your lips, did a bee sting you several times?'

'I can't stand this! I want to go home!' cries Attracta.

'Good! Go!' Martie answers. 'We'll give your love to Carl.'

With a sickening jolt Attracta remembers her grand plans for the week. How she was going to shine. How she was going to leverage her reports into partnership with Carl. How, if she leaves, she will be dishonouring Evita, Madonna and Carrie.

'Just leave me alone' she cries to the room generally.

'Who would want to touch you anyway? Skank' says Martie. Alix laughs.

'Oh shut up Alix' says Attracta, seizing the soft target. 'Everyone knows if I dropped my pants you'd be sniffing my girl parts in a heartbeat.'

Alix briefly considers the veracity in this. 'True. But you're too much of a stuck up skank to be interested in me. So why don't you sit on a cactus and swivel?'

'I think Attracta needs to apologise to Martie. I can clean up the plate' says Sylvie.

'No' says Don in a no-nonsense tone. 'Attracta will clean up her own shit.'

'You're not the boss' says Attracta, but her voice signals defeat.

'Just do it.'

There is an uncomfortable silence as Attracta fetches a clean cloth from the kitchen and cleans up the mess. She scoops the broken pieces of plate into her hand.

'Ow. Cut myself. Don't suppose anyone cares.'

Sylvie is about to go to her aid when a look from Don stops her. In silence Attracta takes the detritus and returns to the kitchen.

'That's my man…' murmurs Martie. A little too audibly.

'What was that?' snaps Don.

'Nothing' says Martie. Honestly, the man is unreadable.

With nothing else to do other than seek out each other's company it's not long before the ugly moment is forgotten. By all except Martie. Nevertheless, over coffee, cheese and fruit, the dynamic of the group becomes more expansive and accepting.

'So we know about me' says Martie, pointing to the others as he names them. 'I still know nothing about what Becca, Alix, Don and Sylvie have experienced, speaking supernaturally.'

There's a silence.

'Sure, I don't mind going first' says Becca. She finds a spot where she can address the whole group without them having to move. 'Okay, so in South Africa I was visiting a little town in the Cape called Graaff-Reneit. A beautiful little 1830s settlement. Old corrugated-iron roofs.

So unspoiled some of the roads are still not tarred, they're just dirt. I had visited the only bar in town and I was walking back to where I was staying with friends. They were still in the bar, South Africans can really sink a pint. I could see a couple of people walking towards me, on the other side. On both sides of the pavement there were tall trees, blue gums, like they have in Australia. They make a creaking noise as the wind catches their branches.'

Someone sniggers. Becca stops. Attracta speaks up. 'Sorry, you were being *so* poetic. Like this is a party piece you've worked on a lot.'

Becca glares at Attracta, then continues. 'Ya, I suppose I have told other people this story. Is there a law against it? So I'm a little sleepy, but I'm walking okay, and I see two people coming towards me … and it's like the same as we saw on the battlements this morning. They're both wearing old clothes. The woman's holding a parasol which is eccentric for late at night. I'm about to say hello when something … about them… I stop and they walk past me. Then they just … like the woman this morning… they just disappear.'

'Oh right, so basically you've just recycled what you all saw this morning. Convenient' remarks Attracta.

'Piss off, skank' returns Becca.

'There's only one skank in this room and I'm looking at her!' snaps Attracta.

'You're such a hypocrite!' howls Becca.

'At least I'm not a slut!'

'Stop it!' shouts Don.

'Oh shut up, Don, of course you're defending your girlfriend. Sorry, fuck buddy.'

‘If this unpleasantness is going to continue, I’m going to bed!’ says Sylvie. There is a collective sigh from the group.

‘Seriously’ says Sylvie. ‘If we’re going talk about our experiences, we have to know we will be respected by the group. Or we might as well spend the week in our bedrooms.’

‘So why don’t you go next?’ asks Becca.

‘I will. If you’re finished?’

Becca frowns then she nods. From around her neck Sylvie takes a small, antique, locket. She opens the gold lid and shows the group the tiny photograph inside.

‘This is my daughter. Hailey. She’s aged about four in the picture. I chose it because it was such a special time, taken when we went to Colwyn Bay for the week.’

Chastised, Attracta makes a point of saying ‘She’s lovely. What a pretty locket.’

‘When Hailey was five … I still don’t know how it happened. She was playing in the little back garden. One minute she was there, and then when I looked again the back gate was open. I never, never left it open!’

The group is taken aback by the fury and bitterness in Sylvie’s usually placid voice.

‘She was missing 42 hours exactly. Before the police found her body.’

There is a taut silence.

‘You don’t have to tell us if it’s painful’ says Martie.

‘The police were clueless. Stupid and unhelpful. They trampled my flower bed and came up with precisely nothing. When they told me they’d found her body, I thought I would die.

'I didn't die. I had to keep on living. The second night after she was murdered, I heard a noise from her room. I opened the door. Hailey was there, she was sitting up in bed, as she always did. I felt no fear, only an infinite relief. I sat on the bed. I held out my hand and she put her little hands in mine.

'It was so wondrous. I had a chance. I told her how very sorry I was that I had not joined her in the garden. I told her I should have put a proper lock and chain on the gate. I told her I wanted to die, to be with her. She listened to all this, and she, it was as though she had been blessed with infinite wisdom. She could listen to me as though she was the mother and I the child. I begged her forgiveness. I wept and she brushed away my tears.

'And then she told me who had taken her.'

The room is so tense that if someone had cried 'boo' everyone would have jumped.

'It was the man, Harold Duff his name was, from two doors away.'

Sylvie is still, her calm face hiding the tumultuous emotions within.

'I watched him. I got to know every minute of his daily routine. I waited.'

'Did you see Hailey again?' asks Martie.

Sylvie looks over to him and smiles sadly. 'Every night I hoped she would return to me. It never happened. Instead my days were full of Harold Duff. The police told me they had no leads. I couldn't explain about Hailey, I didn't want them to think I'd become unhinged, so I told them I had seen Duff sniffing around the lane behind my back garden. Duff, though, had by that time concocted an elaborate alibi. I remember the gormless look on the policeman's face as he recited what was clearly a complete lie. I was so angry, if I could see through it why couldn't he?'

Sylvie pauses in her narrative.

'Have you told anyone else about this?' asks Don gently.

'No one. And now I'm trusting all of you' Sylvie replies. 'Well, I suppose you can guess what happened next. I waited. I waited seven long, tortuously long months. Finally the day came when I knew enough time had passed. I opened the door to Duff's front garden, making sure I wasn't seen. I rang his bell. I asked him if I could come in. When he had his back to me, making coffee in the kitchen, I took the knife from my purse and stabbed him a number of times.'

The room stretches even tighter. No one breathes.

'The official count was eleven times. I don't know at what point he stopped breathing. I think I must have gone into automatic because I have only vague flashes of what happened. I remember washing off the blood. I remember wiping down the sink where I had rested my hand. I remember backing out the door, standing by his front gate, leaving it open. Going home. Taking a shower. All the time I was talking to Hailey, telling her it was all right now. Mummy had killed the bad man.

'It took a couple of days before the postman decided to have a look round and found the body. I stayed inside, watching the usual vultures collecting outside. There was talk of a serial killer. There was … sufficient connection between what that monster did to Hailey and what I did to him for the police to be looking for a single suspect. They didn't even call on me. At least, at one point I opened the door and there were two policewomen outside my door. I began to scream, and they went quickly away. The screams were genuine, I needed to go away for a few months after that. I went to Colwyn Bay, where the woman who owned the guest house remembered Hailey and was exceptionally kind to me.'

The room is silent.

‘I have to ask’ says Martie. ‘Are you sure you could trust what the ghost said?’

Sylvie stares at Martie for a moment before nodding. ‘There was something the police had missed. Something of Hailey’s he’d hidden.’

‘That’s nothing to do with us’ says Don. ‘I can’t see that anyone in this room has any business with it.’

‘I agree’ says Attracta. ‘If you’d given me his address I’d have offed the bastard myself.’

Becca doesn’t speak but she goes to Sylvie and hugs her. Martie also hugs Sylvie, who is crying silent tears which course unheeded down her pale face.

After a minute Sylvie wipes her eyes and says, fiercely, ‘I’m not crying for myself. I’m crying for my daughter.’

‘It’s okay’ says Alix, in a voice so soft it surprises the others. ‘We understand. We all love our Mums and our Mums love us.’

Sylvie excuses herself to wash her face. The group flicks glances round, each examining the others.

‘So that’s the killer’ says Attracta. ‘Who wants to own up to manslaughter.’

‘Enough’ says Don. ‘Tomorrow’s another day.’

Attracta shrugs. ‘I fancy a spa. Anyone?’

Becca and Don exchange a secret smile. ‘Yeah, have a great time’ says Becca.

‘I’ll join you, Attracta’ says Martie. Then he sees that Becca, unseen by Attracta, is shaking her head furiously.

‘Uh, I’ve just remembered, steam brings me out in hives.’

Alix does volunteer to accompany Attracta and the two peel off from the group to collect towels and bathing suits.

'I know we shouldn't go to bed so early' says Don, 'but these country nights. I'm dead tired and it's only nine thirty.'

'Short days and long nights. Bad recipe' says Martie. 'Reminds me of this film *And Soon the Darkness.* At the end everybody dies.'

Don laughs, which lightens the atmosphere and Martie sends a look of complete hero worship at Don. The look is caught by Becca, who inwardly smirks.

During the night Sylvie stirs in her sleep. She believes she heard a noise by the door. It seems that she has woken just as someone has come into the room. 'Hailey? Hailey darling is that you?' She holds her breath but she can hear nothing, see nothing, and a minute later she falls back to sleep.

Later during the night the door to Martie's room creaks open.

'Don? I'm awake.'

'Ssshh..' The figure slides into bed next to Martie and takes Martie in his strong arms. This night's lovemaking is even more urgent than the previous night. Martie deftly inserts another difference. When kissing the neck of his partner he gathers his lover's flesh in his mouth and discreetly bites it. Martie's ability to make love bite welts is something of a joke among his circle. As his partner pulls away, as his lover's head moves with kisses down Martie's body, Martie smiles inwardly. Tomorrow Don will no longer be able to hide the truth. It will shine from him in the form of livid purple bruises.

Fourteen. Day Four

The day dawns with unpredicted rain. The day's cooks, Martie and Attracta, set up breakfast in a room off the entrance hall. It features full-length, bevelled-pane windows and a round, informal table with matching wooden chairs. As the group assembles, wearing jerseys or other additional clothing in acknowledgment of the colder morning air, Martie is annoyed to see Don is wearing a high-collared shirt under his jacket. His calculated plan will have to wait.

'Who did the sausages yesterday?' Becca wants to know. Don, chewing a mouthful of scrambled egg and toast, nods in acknowledgment.

'These sausages are much better.'

Attracta laughs.

'Anyone who wants to do two days cook shift is welcome' grunts Don.

'Yeah' notes Attracta, 'typical male.'

'I don't mind cooking Don's sausages' says Martie. 'I quite like the sizzling sound.'

Martie shoots a look at Don, who resolutely ignores it and reaches for the bottle of brown sauce.

There is the kind of silence that descends naturally when a group of people are eating.

'I think it's stopping' says Sylvie.

'Thanks, Mum' mumbles Alix.

Becca laughs. 'Yeah, I've just realised. We're sort of a family now, aren't we?' Being Becca, no one acknowledges this.

Pushing away his plate, Don stands and walks to the window. 'It's definitely stopping. Blue breaking through the clouds.'

'Great' says Martie. 'So, everyone in their swim gear on the lawn in an hour?'

There's general confirmation of this idea. Martie smiles inwardly.

'Right now I'm going to use this time to explore more of the castle' says Attracta.

'Want company?' asks Alix. Attracta lets the question hang in the air just a moment too long.

'Sure. Becca?' The women exchange a smile.

'Anyone else want to explore the castle?' asks Alix, in what is an obvious bid at face-saving.

'Sure' says Martie. 'Soon as I've done the washing up.'

'I'll bring a blanket. The grass will be wet' Sylvie notes.

Don turns back from the window. 'Look at us. Sylvie's the mum. I'm the dad. You four are the unruly but basically loveable kids.'

'Piss off' says Attracta. 'I've already got one fuckhead for a dad.'

'I'm not sure I'm comfortable in the role of mum' says Sylvie, without aggression.

'Suck it up, you're a natural' responds Becca.

'No, really. I'm not.'

'Hey, Dad' says Martie, 'want to come ghost hunting round this cool castle?'

'Yeah, why not?'

‘Wait, doesn’t that mean we’ll be leaving Sylvie on her own?’

‘You go ahead’ says Sylvie, ‘I don’t mind.’

‘Gee thanks Mum’ says Martie.

Sylvie says nothing. She helps with the plates and gathers the disposable serviettes. Then she seems to realise this is exactly what a mum would do, so she looks annoyed. She walks out without a word.

‘Mum’s pissed’ says Becca.

‘Dad, go after her’ says Attracta.

‘Leave it kids’ says Don. ‘Your mum’s got a lot on her plate.’

‘Seriously, should we go after her?’ asks Martie.

‘What do you think, junior?’

‘Don’t call me junior.’

‘Why, will you start crying?’ asks Attracta.

‘Blub blub’ says Becca.

‘You two bitches really are dumb bitches’ Martie responds, and taking a pile of dirty plates he quits the room. Behind him he hears, from Don, ‘Becca and Attracta, don’t bully your brother.’

Martie smiles grimly to himself. He’ll soon wipe the smirk off Don’s face.

The two groups of explorers meet in the entrance hall.

‘Basically it doesn’t matter which way you go, wherever you look there’s bloody castle’ comments Attracta.

'Yeah but we went along our corridor yesterday' Martie reminds his group of Don and Alix. 'Bags we go down the other corridor. Bet there's some deep shit down there.'

'Ooh, I can see you're no gentleman' remarks Becca. 'Don't you know it's ladies first?'

Martie brays a laugh. 'Sorry, I don't mean to state the obvious, but the only lady around here is Sylvie. She can't help it, while you two are just helpless.'

'Piss off' says Becca. 'Come on Attracta.'

The two women, carrying torches, move towards the staircase. Alix and Martie exchange a silent look then they both thunder up the staircase, gaining the first floor and entering the further corridor. Attracta and Becca can hear particularly irritating cries and yelps of victory.

'We want the other corridor' says Becca in a direct appeal to Don. Don laughs.

'Sorry. Two against one.'

'Piss off' says Attracta. 'You're all about as useful as a condom full of holes.'

'Not that my sister Attracta knows what a condom is' remarks Becca.

'Good luck on your search. Document whatever looks promising' says Don.

Attracta and Becca shake their heads. 'Pitiful' mumbles Becca.

Don joins Martie and Alix, who are already opening doors and peering into new rooms.

'We should have brought the map' notes Don. 'There's a staircase up to some sort of schoolroom. Perhaps the grey woman was a teacher?'

Sylvie, sitting quietly in the library, hears a noise and looks up.

'Is that you? I won't be frightened. I just want to talk to you.'

'Can you imagine why anyone would want this number of rooms?' asks Attracta to Becca. They have just passed the staircase that leads up to the roof, and turning a corner find another long corridor of closed doors.

'Maybe they kept an army here?'

'Wouldn't mind meeting some hot squaddie ghosts' notes Becca.

'Yes you would. You'd shit yourself' says Attracta, casually.

'I wasn't scared when I saw that couple in Graaf-Reneit' notes Becca.

'But what if they came up right next to you and…' and Attracta waves her arms wildly and screams directly into Becca's face. Becca shrieks and the two laugh and hug and scream till they can no longer squeeze any more frivolity or hysteria from the moment.

'Thank heaven you're here' says Becca. 'I'd have had a shit time on my own.'

'Yeah, likewise. The men on this weekend are strictly no fun.'

'I gave Alix a blow job in the kitchen' notes Becca. Attracta looks at her and the two again burst into deliberately hysterical laughter, enjoying how their banshee cackling disturbs and challenges the thick silence.

'Look' says Don quietly. Having found a modest staircase leading to a plain door, the three are in some sort of schoolroom. There are two single school desks with integral seats. A blackboard on the wall. Someone has left a pile of books with colourful covers, which have fallen over so some are splayed over the floor. In the corner there is what seems to be the shape of a person.

'She's here' whispers Martie.

The three men become aware of chills running up and down their legs. It's cold in the room, but not that cold. Alix glances at the window, seeing the sunshine outside and the gloom within. The figure in the corner shifts.

'We don't mean to hurt you' whispers Martie. 'Can we help you?'

For a moment the figure lifts its head and Martie gasps. Then it melts into the simple whitewashed wall.

'That was intense' notes Alix.

'And unexpected' says Don. 'We came looking for a female teacher. And found a man.'

'Yes' says Martie, his voice strangely hoarse, 'it was definitely a man.'

In the library Sylvie stays still. She can feel the air around her being disturbed as something invisible appears to walk right around her.

'Hailey? My darling? Can it be that it's you?'

She is aware of holding her breath. Nothing must disturb the moment.

Suddenly Sylvie cries out, as she feels a great blow on the back of her head.

'Stop it! Stop it! Leave me alone!' Sylvie cries, dropping to the floor. She hears footsteps but sees nothing. After a moment the door bangs shut. Sylvie rubs the back of her head where it's tender. She half-walks, half-staggers to the hallway, and sits on the lowest of the stairs. She breathes deeply and raggedly. She lifts her head and cries out 'Help. Help. Help me!!'

Returning from the school room the three men are silent.

'So one of the spooks from the lawn yesterday was like the schoolmaster?' hazards Alix.

'Shh' says Don.

'Fuck you, man, you're not my daddy'

'I'm trying to piece it all together' says Don.

'I got a 1000 piece jigsaw puzzle once. Couldn't work out what it was about.'

'Yeah, shut up Alix' says Martie. 'Can't you see something incredible's going on? I mean do you have to reduce it to chatter?'

Alix clicks his tongue and strides forward, leaving the other two. Don looks at Martie. Martie smiles hopefully.

'It's sunny outside. I'm going to change' says Don.

'I'll join you' says Martie. Finally, Don seems ready to acknowledge, or rather, incorporate their nightly intimacy into the day. As he dumps his cold-weather clothes on the floor and reaches for his other Speedo, Martie almost regrets the trick on Don that's about to be exposed. He hopes Don won't make a big deal about it.

Alix hears Sylvie's calls for help as he turns into the corridor that leads to the staircase. He starts running and calls out for her to hang on, he's coming. Thundering down the staircase he reaches the bottom and throws his arms around Sylvie. She is shaking, sobbing, her usually organised hair is a rat's nest, as though she's been pulling it out strand by strand herself. From deep in his throat Alix begins making a keening noise, like a father comforting a terrified child. He's shocked by how greedily, how desperately Sylvie grasps his powerful body. By the time that Martie and then Don, now dressed for sun worship, appear at the top of the stairs Sylvie has moved to one of the wooden hall chairs. Alix stands protectively to her side, frowning sternly at the newcomers.

'What the fuck?' asks Martie.

'She saw something' mutters Alix.

'I didn't *see* anything! I felt something walking behind me. Then it hit me on the back of my head … I have a mark.'

Don examines the back of Sylvie's head and clicks his tongue. 'Sylvie this looks bad. The skin is broken. That must have been a hell of a wallop.'

'I don't feel well. I'm going to lie down.'

'You think?' asks Martie. 'Wouldn't you be safer outside with us?'

Sylvie doesn't reply to this. Instead she asks 'Where are the others?'

Attracta and Becca, exhausted from laughing hysterically at the slightest provocation, traverse a yet further corridor, arms amiably linked.

'You think we should go back at some point?' asks Becca.

'If we keep going long enough, we'll probably find ourselves back in the hall. Or maybe we'll join our own corridor.'

'Okay, that's one way of thinking about it. The other way is that we're in a maze, we're trapped in a maze, going round and round and we'll never get out.'

'Oh what, like *Blair Witch Project* when they go round and round and can't get out the woods?'

This reference causes them to stop.

'Seriously, could you even tell if we've been along this corridor before?'

They look carefully at the corridor's identifying features, the odd picture, the chair or coffer. The endless doors.

'Should we retrace our steps?'

They turn round and behind them the vast expanse of anonymous corridor does not seem welcoming.

'I'm not going to freak, right?' says Becca. 'That would be the worst thing to do.'

'Like drowning, when you die because you struggle. Apparently' agrees Attracta.

'What do you think would happen if we … if we just turned round and went back?'

Out on the lawn the grass shimmers as the sun's warm rays cause the droplets of rain to evaporate. From the lawn the whole castle seems to glisten.

'Feeling better?' asks Alix. He has brought out some antique cushions and dumped them on the grass for Sylvie to sit on.

'Yes, but we really shouldn't have these out here. They're going to be ruined.'

'Tough' notes Alix. 'No one said they were only for indoors.'

'I wonder what's keeping the others?' asks Martie of Don. As he does this, he deliberately shucks his t-shirt and exposes his bare torso. He's hoping that the gesture will cause Don to do the same, since Don is still wearing his high-collared shirt.

'I suppose I'd better look for them' mutters Don, clearly reluctant to step away from the soothing warmth of the sun.

'Where would you look?' asks Martie, practically. 'Hmm, feel that warmth on my skin. So good.'

'I feel responsible somehow.'

Martie laughs. 'Don, you're not *actually* their dad. I mean that's just some weird fantasy shit we all got into this morning because we're going stir-crazy. Castle crazy. Ghost crazy, whatever.'

'I'm afraid I can't see the joke anymore' says Sylvie. She touches the back of her head delicately. 'I'm sorry, I think I have to go home now.'

The others express concern.

'I think my whole reason for being here is, well, hopeless. I don't think Hailey's going to come to me. And I'm frightened. I don't need the money so much that I'm willing to continue to be frightened.'

At that moment Becca and Attracta, swimsuits under wraps, appear and cross the gravel to the grass area.

'We thought you'd got lost!' shouts Don.

'We thought you'd got eaten' shouts Martie.

‘Shut up’ says Becca, automatically. ‘We explored what must have been a hundred and fifty rooms. There’s nothing there. Just rooms and shit.’

‘Sylvie not so happy’ says Alix. The expressions of the two new arrivals morph into genuine empathy.

‘I felt something. It hit me. I’m sorry, I don’t know if I can go on.’

Martie watches Don, his frustration at the lack of stripping off mounting. ‘Sylvie, feel how warm and comforting it is out here. We already knew we shouldn’t be on our own. Now we’ve got proof. So from now on we’ll just have to take double care not to be alone. But right now, let’s get some sun!’

Finally, thinks Martie, shooting a quick look at Don, finally he’s getting the point. Martie watches with a smirk as Don, concentrating on Sylvie, automatically undoes the buttons on his shirt and peels it off his skin. Now it comes! Thinks Martie. Don makes a pillow of his shirt and prepares to lie on his towel. And no one says anything. No one comments on the angry purple bruises on his neck.

Because there are none.

And, come to think of it, thinks Martie, internally flushing, the chest of the figure in the night was entirely smooth. Don has some chest hair. And one pierced golden nipple.

‘Shit!’ explodes Martie. ‘I don’t believe it. Shagged by a ghost! *Again!’*

Concentrating on Sylvie, it takes the group a moment to adjust to Martie’s drama.

‘In fact’ he says, addressing no one and everyone, ‘counting the other time, that’s *three*!’

'What?' asks Becca, ready to be either supportive or aggressive, but right now just confused. 'Who's been shagging ghosts?'

'Nothing' says Martie. Then he glances at Don. Don has been trying to make sense of Martie's seemingly arcane utterances. He suddenly nods and smirks.

'Okay. Okay I think I know. And let's just drop it' says Don.

'Drop what? I'm not dropping nothing till I know what I'm dropping' says Becca.

'Attracta, isn't it time you got lunch organised?' asks Don.

'If we must' responds Attracta. 'Come on useless' she says to Martie. Martie is ready to peel away from the bigger group and goes without an argument. He pulls on his t-shirt. As they crunch back along the driveway, Attracta calls to Becca over her shoulder.

'And if you can find out what shit Martie was about, tell me. Privately.'

Alix looks questioningly at Don. 'Leave it' says Don. And he smiles again.

Fifteen. Fourth Night

The dinner discussion, like that of the lunch, centres around the identity of the male ghost in the schoolroom. Although, as Attracta apparently never tires of telling the group, solving the mystery is not what they're supposed to be doing.

'I'm sorry' says Don, when she again drops her joy killer into the general debate. 'We're here. We're bored. We're going to figure out the mystery. If you don't want to join in that's fine.'

'Although' says Martie, having recovered from his earlier disappointment and realisation, 'those many reports you're sending Carl will look curiously uninformed.'

'Don't listen to them darling' says Becca. 'Men.'

'Thanks darling' responds Attracta. 'I never do.'

'As Oscar Wilde wrote' says Martie to the air, 'women rarely ever call each other 'sister' until they've called them a lot of other names.'

'What I've been thinking' says Attracta, looking only at Becca, 'is I've got a pretty good memory for faces.'

'I'm sure you have' coos Becca, 'it's a sign of intelligence.'

'So what we should do tomorrow is see if there's a portrait of the woman we've been seeing on the battlements.'

'Brilliant!'

'If we can identify her, we'll probably be able to identify the two men.'

'Not a bad idea' says Martie. 'I think I can pick out the man in the schoolroom too.'

'Martie, drop it. Enough ghost talk for the day.'

'Yes, Martie, don't give away all our advantages' says Don.

'Sorry' says Attracta, 'are we still competing? I thought we'd arrived at an understanding?'

There is a pause.

'This is what I understand' says Don. 'Woman on the battlements. Man in schoolroom. Another man in the garden. If we say the one in the steam room is one of the two men, then it seems like three specific spectres.'

'What hit me on the head?' asks Sylvie, resentfully.

'I've been thinking about that' responds Don. 'Were you trying anything on with it? I'm thinking, and don't have a go at me if I'm wrong, were you speaking to it as though it was your little girl? Hailey?'

Sylvie is silent.

'So maybe it wasn't malevolent' says Martie, gently, 'but it was hacked off.'

'Thank you Martie' says Sylvie grimly. 'I can make up my own mind.'

'So what are we dealing with?'

'If we could go online we could search for the castle's past.'

'But we can't. Any actual practical suggestions?'

'We could ask locally.'

This novel notion causes a stir.

'Isn't the idea that we don't investigate?' asks Attracta, hoping that her question now fits the moment.

'Shut up Attracta' responds Alix. 'You're like a broken record.'

'So who, tomorrow, wants to canvas the locals?' asks Don.

'I agree with Attracta' says Becca. 'This isn't an episode of *Ghost Watch*. And we don't want to attract attention to ourselves.'

'What about the locals who prepared the place for us?' asks Martie. 'What makes you think they don't already know?'

'What makes you think it was locals? Carl could have used people that know nothing of the history.'

'What, just to spite you?'

Sylvie stands. 'Thank you for dinner. I have a terrible headache. Goodnight.'

'Someone walk Sylvie to her room.'

'We'll walk with you, Sylvie. Attracta's promised to condition my hair. Apparently her conditioner brand is divine.'

The three women exit, leaving the men to finish off the bottles of wine.

'Seriously' says Martie. 'What do you see in them?'

Don laughs. 'Oh Martie, if only you were a girl.'

Don pulls himself up and walks slightly unsteadily to the door.

'Did he just say he fancies me?' asks Martie eagerly of Alix.

'Dunno wasn't listening' replies Alix, making himself comfortable in the sofa cushions.

'No way! Don't go to sleep down here. What if that thing takes a shot at you while you're asleep?'

Alix's eyes open wide and he springs to his feet.

In the night Sylvie, sleeping fitfully, hears what she makes sense of as a scratching at the door. She opens her eyes wide, hoping to make out vague shapes in the country darkness.

'Who is that…?'

She hears a rustle of material close to the bed, and reaches out a hand. Tiny fingers grasp hers and she gasps in joy.

'You *are* here! You *did* understand!'

Later in the night Martie also hears a noise in his room. He half-rises.

'Is that you?'

From the inky gloom, a sound: 'Sssshhh…'

A moment later Martie feels the covers being gently tugged. He cries out, and switches on the torch he's been holding while sleeping. For an instant he has an image of a naked male body, a handsome face with unfashionably long hair, then with a grotesque sigh like nails being drawn down a blackboard the vision fades into the shadows of the room.

'Piss off' shouts Martie. 'You dead twat!'

Sixteen. Day Five

The day dawns fair and sunny. The cooks, again Becca and Alix, aren't talking to each other. Martie, not sensing the atmosphere, walks up behind Becca and sniffs deeply.

'Hmm. Yeah, that conditioner really is divine.'

Being Martie, he gets away with it. He takes a plate and begins heaping it with the morning's offerings. He watches Sylvie enter, wearing a track suit and a happy smile, and indicates she should sit next to him, which she does.

Becca sits and Attracta loads up a plate for her.

'Thanks babe' says Becca, 'just the right amount. You're a star.'

'Have we died and gone to Lesbos?' asks Martie into the air. Don and Alix enter, already in conversation.

'Here's a debate we can have without it descending into tears. What are you going to do with your ten grand?' asks Martie.

There's a pause then everyone starts talking. Over the babble Sylvie can be heard.'I don't know if it's just me, but I've forgotten money exists. We're here, we're fed and watered, it's a completely unexpected week at a luxury hotel.'

'I need ten grand plus' notes Don.

'Gambling debts?' asks Martie. 'That's glamorous.'

'You think so? You want to give me your ten grand?'

'No but I admire you for trying it on. I've got it earmarked for new furniture and if there's enough left over, a widescreen TV.'

'I'm definitely going on an extended stay back to SA. London's too bloody hard for me. Coming, Attracta? My friends will love you.'

'Listen to us' says Don. 'Acting like we can see a future beyond Strawberry Manor.'

The group stops talking.

'Why shouldn't we?' asks Alix. 'Only two more days.'

'Doesn't it strike anyone as odd' Don continues, 'that someone as presumably cool as Carl Raeburn would pay us all ten grand to piss about for a week?'

'See' says Attracta, 'you all laugh, but that's why I send my daily reports. Twice a day most days. I'm earning my bread.'

'What makes you think he reads them? Maybe all he wants those for is to find out which of us is still alive.'

There's a general outcry.

'That's rubbish. We've been here five days and the worst is Sylvie got smacked on the head because she pissed off one of the ghosts.'

'There's nothing wrong with this house' says Sylvie, in a distracted voice. Martie looks at Alix. 'Why's she suddenly channelling Mystic Meg?'

'I've got a routine I like' reports Don soberly. 'I'm done with trying to work out what's going on. I'm going to spend the day in the sun, evening in the library and the night with my door locked. I just don't care anymore.'

Alix looks at Martie. 'We can still explore the castle.'

‘How about *not* exploring the castle’ says Don. ‘Don’t you see? The more we interfere with the castle, the more whatever’s behind the woodwork interferes with us.’

‘That’s not exactly true. I mean I didn’t ask whatever …’ then he stops. ‘No, screw it, you’re supposed to be my friends. I didn’t ask whatever’s been getting into bed with me the last three nights to do so.’

‘But Martie,’ asks Becca in a tone which lets slip that she thinks she already knows the answer, ‘who did you think it was?’

Martie pushes away his plate and stands. ‘I thought it was Don. Okay? And just in case you think I’m completely delusional, last night he said to me ‘Oh Martie, if only you were a girl’. I don’t know what that meant, but it was certainly interesting.’

The others look at Don, who smiles the smile of someone used to owning whichever room he inhabits. ‘I meant it. If Martie was packaged in the sort of body I fancy, I’d be right there. Unfortunately, he isn’t. It was something of a compliment, although it also expresses the impossibility of our finding happiness together.’

Martie exits the room, calling out ‘Whatever, Don. Keep telling yourself you’re entirely heterosexual. I’m sure someone will buy it.’

Attracta looks at Don with a smirk. ‘Seriously, none of us cares.’

‘Piss off, Attracta’ says Don. ‘You and your Irish Virgin act don’t impress me.’

‘Excuse me’ says Becca, ‘Attracta is only being herself.’

‘Yeah? I know what Page 3 girls get up to, and it’s not distributing food for the parish poor.’

Attracta walks around to where Don is sitting and, since he is talking to Becca and has his profile to her, gets in a resounding slap so loud it echoes. Don jumps to his feet.

'Don't think because you're a woman I won't hit you' he snarls.

'I don't think that at all. I knew exactly what you were, that first time you came sniffing round me like a dog in search of its own balls.'

Don's reply is low and even. 'Get out Attracta. Now.'

Becca moves to her friend. Don pushes his chair back and walks out.

'What is it with the boys this morning? Can no one just walk out the room normally?'

'Please don't provoke them. We're all under pressure. We see the sun and we think it's all right. It's not all right' says Sylvie.

'Whatever, Mum' responds Attracta.

Sylvie stands, wipes her mouth on her serviette, drops it in her plate, nods to the cooks and exits.

'Honestly Becks,' says Attracta. 'I think you and I are the only sane people in this house.'

'Hello I'm here you know' says Alix.

'I think you're right. How's your hair feel this morning?'

'I'm totally changing my brand to yours.'

With a muttered oath Alix stomps out.

'Did you hear something, darling?' asks Attracta of Becca.

'Only the wind, tapping against the window-pane' she responds and they both dirty laugh.

After an hour in the sun Attracta turns to Becca. 'You know, there's a whole spa going begging here.'

‘Yes darling’ responds Becca, ‘but the last time things got a little … steamy.’

Attracta laughs and signals to Alix. ‘Alix, can you look after a couple of sweaty chicks?’

Alix grins confidently. ‘Thought you’d never ask.’

Don watches as the three walk back across the driveway and into the castle.

He addresses Sylvie.

‘Something else I’ve been thinking about, in terms of Carl’s selection of us. None of us have close personal relationships. I only remembered such things exist just now, looking at those two.’

Sylvie stares intently at Don. ‘You mean … we’re all loners? Individuals?’

‘That’s part of it. More it’s we don’t have people we’re in contact with every day. No one in the outside world is wondering where we are.’

‘Oh I’ve got friends monitoring my progress.’

‘How?’

‘Uh, I don’t mean this week, I mean generally. On Insta and Twitter. I mean.’

‘But no one who’s going to call the police if they don’t read any new online posts?’

‘I’ve got a couple of ex’s who would be concerned’ says Martie.

‘So, as I was saying Sylvie, we’re all loners.’

‘But aren’t we forming our own family unit here?’ pushes Martie.

‘We have moments. We’ll see’ replies Don.

Sylvie stands. 'I didn't come here to find a new family' she says firmly.

'Sure, but you're here for something more than the money, aren't you?'

'I think if we're all such loners, we should respect each other's personal space.'

Martie watches Sylvie leave, then turns to Don.

'I'm sorry about what I said this morning. I did appreciate what you said last night.'

Don nods. After a beat, Martie puts his hand on Don's leg. When Don doesn't move, Martie slowly strokes it. After a few seconds Don speaks.

'Martie. Stop it.'

'But… '

'I mean it. Don't push it. I'm not interested. I don't want to hurt you, but I will.'

Attracta and Becca reach the spa first. They keep their bathing suits on as they ooh and aah their way into the steam room. As though excited to have guests to pamper, huge enveloping clouds of steam gush out of the metal vent. Becca fumbles for her friend's hand and helps her sit on the tiled step. A small amount of time drifts by before they hear the door to the spa being opened.

'Don't disturb us, Alix' says Attracta. 'Find your own seat.'

The figure, glimpsed only slightly in the fog, obediently sits some distance away.

'I could get used to this life' reports Becca. 'This week is the first decent time I've had since I arrived in bloody London. It's no place for a white woman. Sorry, Alix, no racism intended.'

'Think we could make a career out of it? Get hired to go to huge country estates and hang about doing nothing?'

The two women cackle. The figure in the corner stands up.

'Alix, I do very much hope you've kept your costume on' says Becca.

'Alix, I do very much hope that you're going to keep to your side of the steamroom' says Attracta.

The figure moves towards the door. They hear the click of the door opening and watch the steam swirl as the figure steps out and shuts the door.

'Twat' comments Attracta.

'Gave him a blow job' comments Becca. 'You should give him a try.'

'No thanks. I mean, I've seen him flaccid and he's impressive. But I've got my sights on Carl. Don't want any gossip getting back to him.'

'Have you told Carl any gossip about me?' asks Becca quickly. Attracta's denial comes too fast and Becca is about to follow this up when the door opens and Alix pushes his way through the steam.

'For pissing sake, what did you forget?'

'What do you mean? I had to take a major dump. Must have been the breakfast.'

'So … you weren't here a few minutes ago?'

'No way. Why, weren't you alone?'

There is a momentary quiet.

'Seriously, Attracta, this place is going to give me a breakdown.'

'I think that's what Carl thought it would' says Attracta thoughtfully.

'So you tell your boyfriend we've had enough of his creepy castle' snaps Becca.

'I would, but he's hardly my boyfriend, is he? I mean I have zero influence.'

'I wasn't being serious. Can you get out my way, okay? This steam room is no place for a good South African girl.'

As Becca pushes past and makes her way to the door, Attracta shouts 'You forgot *white* girl.'

'Fuck you! Skank! Virgin skank!'

Alix and Attracta sit back in the steam.

'So I guess you're not BGF's now?' he asks.

'Shut up' says Attracta. 'I didn't spend an hour conditioning her hair to lose her as a friend now' she says, loyally.

The door opens again.

'I swear' says Attracta into the clouds of steam, 'if that's another bloody ghost I am going to lose it big time.'

'No' reports a sad voice, 'it's just Martie.'

In the evening, after complimenting the cooks on not having burned the dinner this time round, the group assembles in the library.

'I never knew how many hours in the day there could be if you couldn't watch TV, get online, or talk to friends' remarks Becca.

'I never knew …'

'Stop it' says Don. We've got only one more night after this one, then we're the fuck out of here and we never have to see each other again.'

‘That can’t happen soon enough’ notes Attracta.

‘It will happen when the little hand has been fully round the dial twice’ responds Don.

‘You know, if you weren’t so attractive the truly vile nature of your personality would be obvious’ says Attracta.

‘Oh, I know. Whereas in your case, although you are definitely very attractive, as many a pervert who has seen your naked body will confirm, the sheer agony of your pathetic personality has long been fully exposed. To anyone who cares to look.’

‘Really, Martie’ says Attracta, ‘I just don’t know what you see in Don.’

‘Stop it’ says Sylvie. ‘I don’t care if you’re all going to call me Mum. I want it to stop. We should be using this time to … I don’t know, have some sort of special experience. We should tell each other things we’ve never told anyone else.’

‘Oh, you did, dear’ drawls Becca. ‘How many stab wounds was it? Nine? Twelve? I forget.’

Don points a rock-firm finger, on a steely hand, at Becca. ‘Shut up. I mean it.’

‘If either of you were a real man, you wouldn’t let him talk to me like that’ says Becca to no one in particular.

‘Good job we’re not real men, then, isn’t it, bro?’ asks Alix of Martie. Martie smirks.

‘We still don’t know who’s the one guilty of manslaughter’ says Attracta.

‘We all know who’s got the biggest gob, though’ Don responds.

'Okay. Okay. You want to know … I'll tell you' says Martie, rising to his feet. 'I'm the one. Surprise. Manslaughter. Never convicted. Never ever charged. So easy. I kept thinking my tongue would start speaking and betray me. It didn't. I sat still, shrugged, looked bewildered and innocent. They went away. They never thought it could be me.'

Martie refills his glass. The others glance at each other. Don shrugs.

'So now we know' says Martie. 'And I'm not prepared to say anything more.'

There is a silence.

'A thought' says Don. 'How do we know the manslaughter Carl knows about is the one Martie's owning up to?'

Sylvie rises, her frail body shaking with emotion. 'Oh stop! Stop! I can't take any more. I thought I was with a group of adults! I'm going to bed.'

There is more silence as they watch her walk to the door and exit.

'I can be perfectly adult' reports Becca. 'I know if I wasn't so freaked in this place, I'm sure I'd impress you all with my gravitas.'

'Yeah' says Alix. 'None of us have to prove ourselves. Being here is all the shit we need.'

Martie speaks. 'Let's ask questions. Kind of like *University Challenge.* Except for people who are shut up in a castle and can't leave while a bunch of ghosts can do whatever they like to us, whenever. And why are we here? Because we don't have enough money. Because we're this desperate. Because I so want to get far away from this place, I might have to do something desperate so Carl will have to come and get me.'

There's a silence and Becca goes to Martie and holds his shoulders.

‘Martie’ says Don. ‘I came here by car. If you really want to leave, I’ll take you.’

‘I can’t’ says Martie speaking slowly and dividing the words carefully, ‘I don’t have any money. I need to leave my crappy job. Do I have to go on?’

‘So you could crash with me’ suggests Becca. ‘You’re easy to live with.’

‘Thanks, but … I think I’m past those sorts of band aids.’

Martie pushes away from Becca and goes to the door. ‘I mean, I’m not going to off myself. I’m not going to end up on the gravel. I just, I just really wish I didn’t have to go on living.’

Martie goes. Attracta turns to Don. ‘Go after him.’

‘Me? No way. He’ll expect me to fuck him.’

‘So why don’t you?’ demands Attracta. ‘You said yourself he’s pretty.’

‘Piss off, Attracta. Seriously they must have sucked out your brains and injected them in your tits.’

Attracta snatches up a wine glass and throws it at Don. It breaks as it bounces off his forehead. He cries out but with a visible effort does not retaliate.

‘Leave him’ says Becca to her friend, ‘he’s not worth it.’

The two women exit, leaving only Don and Alix. Don touches the blood that slides down his face.

‘You’ll need a stitch in that’ observes Alix.

‘Let it bleed’ says Don. ‘All the more to show Carl the day after tomorrow.

In the night Sylvie lies awake. She suddenly feels an imprint on the pillow next to her. A little body is lying on the pillow next to her.

'Hailey, my darling. The rest of my life is nothing, you know, nothing. Only these moments with you.'

At around 3am Attracta, heavy with sleep and the alcohol she continued to consume, in her room, with Becca, feels something shifting on the bed, and tries to force herself awake. A rough hand clamps over her mouth and a powerful shoulder pins her down. The second hand pulls at her bra and pants. She cannot move, can barely breathe. The weight of the intruder presses down on her body. Struggling to breathe, trying to make out the shape on top of her, Attracta grunts with pain as she feels something thrusting eagerly into the space between her legs.

'No… no' she cries out in her mind, but the hand across her mouth prevents her from crying out. The thrust, expert, callous, continues. Now the full weight of the intruder on top of her begins to crush Attracta, as the relentless pumping causes waves of agony to break over her helpless body.

Seventeen. Day Six

Don and Sylvie being the day's cooks means that when the others arrive, one by one, in the kitchen they are greeted by a cheerful jug of garden-picked flowers, and a foaming pitcher of champagne mimosas.

'Impressive' notes Alix, the first to sit down. Martie arrives, ignores Don, says pointedly to Sylvie 'thanks for this, it's a fantastic spread.'

Becca arrives, looking more dishevelled than usual.

'You look like you were partying with Kanye West' notes Martie, chewing a piece of pancake. 'Did you leave any booze for the rest of us?'

'Don't start a drinking contest with the Irish' observes Becca, 'they'll drink you under the table and keep going.'

'So we needn't expect to be blessed with the presence of Attracta?' asks Don.

'I'll take something up to her. When I've eaten enough to soak up the alcohol' explains Becca.

'I'll take her something. You eat' says Sylvie. She efficiently puts together a harmonious breakfast tray. 'Anything I should concentrate on, that you know she likes, Becca?'

Becca, eating to feel better, trying to keep from throwing up, carefully shakes her head.

'Well, I'll take her a bit of everything' says Sylvie philosophically.

'You won't get in' notes Becca. 'She locks her door.'

'So use the secret panel' says Martie. His eyes are shining. 'I've been dying to use it.'

'Bull' mutters Don. 'She can have her food cold.'

However, Becca and Alix are also eager to explore the panel and the three hurriedly finish and leave the table. Don and Sylvie are left to clear up.

Consulting the map, the trio are slightly disappointed to discover how easy it is to access the secret way.

'I was hoping it was one of those you have to press a button and that works a lever and then something drops down and finally the door creaks dramatically open. This is just a door built into the panelling.'

The door opened, it reveals a narrow stone flight of steps leading upward.

'There's even a light. What a shame' notes Martie, flicking the switch. Their way illuminated, it takes only as long as it usually takes to mount a flight of stairs for them to arrive at a small vestibule, with a single, wooden door. Martie knocks on the door.

'Attracta?'

'Yeah, if she's not awake *that's* going to please her.' Becca leans one hand on the door and it springs open.

Attracta lies sprawled on the bed. The bed clothes are tossed about and she is naked. There's something very wrong about the tangle of arms and legs.

'Get out' says Becca quickly. 'I'll deal with this.'

'Shut up' snaps Martie, 'she's unconscious. Alix, unlock the door.'

Alix goes to the door while Becca and Martie throw a sheet over Attracta's body.

'She's not …'

'No, she's breathing.'

'So maybe she just had a wild night?'

Coming to, Attracta finds three people in her room. She begins to scream.

'No, she's definitely not okay' says Alix.

'Get out you two' snaps Becca, gathering her friend in her arms, and this time the others do what they're told.

'I'll get Sylvie' says Alix.

'Run her a bath' says Martie at the door, 'that always helps.'

'Get out! Geeettt ouuuuttt!' shrieks Attracta.

Some time later, having given Attracta a couple of sleeping tablets she was keeping in case of her own emergency, Sylvie looks at the others, seated in the breakfast room.

'So. What? Happened?' asks Sylvie, casting the question out generally.

'It looks like one of two things' replies Martie. 'Either she was raped by a ghost – no, let's be real here – or someone, one of us, entered her locked room through the passage and raped her.'

'And by one of us Martie, since your predilection is so well known, you don't include yourself. You mean it was either me or Alix.'

'It wasn't me' says Alix. 'I swear on a bible.'

'What do we do?' asks Don. 'We can do one of two things. We can walk to a phone booth and dial 999. Or we can get in contact with Carl. Ask him what we should do next.'

There is an unhappy silence.

'I think we have to call the police' says Martie. 'Surely no one thinks that shouldn't happen?'

'No, of course not' says Alix.

'It's the end of the experiment, of course' says Sylvie. 'The police are going to have a hard enough time understanding what we're doing here, even before we explain that either one of us, or something supernatural, raped our colleague.'

'Technically it's not an experiment. Technically it's Carl's art' notes Don.

'Yeah, that's when they're going to start making 'screwy' motions behind our backs. Of course they're all going to be looking at me.'

'Why you only?' asks Don. 'I've also got a penis. And yesterday Attracta slapped me and cut my forehead with a flung glass.'

'And what if,' says Becca, 'having been spurned by Don the great heterosexual, Martie decided to try straight sex for once? And Attracta fought him off?'

'That is crap!' shouts Martie. 'Come on. After all the prejudice and bullying I've endured through my life, *surely* it makes me above suspicion in this case!'

Don stands and moves to the door. 'I'm going to make a phone call.'

In the doorway he meets Attracta. She looks pale, shaken, vulnerable. She wears an outsize t-shirt of Alix's.

'No.'

Attracta walks passed Don and back into the breakfast room.

‘We’re not going to talk about this. We’re not going to tell the police. Or Carl. Nothing. It didn’t happen. I’m not going to let it destroy our work here.’

‘Come *on*, Attracta! You’re not thinking right.’

‘I’m fine. I’ve had a bath. I’ve had time to think.’

‘Attracta’ says Alix evenly, ‘you have just gone through a horrible experience. You can’t trust one of us. Whatever you think, we really do need to call the police.’

‘No.’

‘We’re going to.’

‘Then I’ll deny it happened. Prove it.’

Don cries out in frustration. ‘Attracta we’re only trying to help.’

‘You can help me more by forgetting you saw me like that. It’s not how I like to present myself.’

‘I think you’re wrong’ says Sylvie, without emotion. ‘I think you may come to regret it.’

‘There are no rules here’ says Attracta. ‘Who knows. Maybe this was my initiation. Maybe this is what shows the difference between me and you all.’

‘Attracta’ says Don, ‘all I can repeat is that now you cannot trust one of us.’

‘I can live with that. And if it was you, Don, I’m sorry. I behaved badly.’

‘Oh come on!’ cries Becca. ‘What are you apologising to him for?’

‘I was baiting him.’

'It wasn't me, Attracta, I swear it' says Don.

'Yeah, that's what they all say' says Becca.

'Stop it' says Attracta. 'It's over. We'll go on with the day.'

She turns and makes her way out into the kitchen.

The others look at each other.

'So help me' says Becca to the room generally, 'if I ever find out it was one of you, I will gut you with a kitchen knife and make you swallow your dick.'

She then leaves to join her friend. From outside they hear Attracta loudly dismissing her friend. 'Go *away*, Becca, I'm not changing my mind!'

'And on that note' says Sylvie, 'the incident would appear to be closed. For now.'

For the rest of the day the only one in the group Attracta can bear to have near her is Martie. They sit on a green wooden bench in one of the shady arbours that dot the grounds. Discreet enquiries, mainly from Becca, return only a wooden silence. Becca is forced to stand behind a hedgerow so she can hear some of what is being discussed. She gathers that Attracta keeps returning obsessively to the shards of memory she retains from the previous night. The evidence, the key which Attracta seeks to find by going over and over not only her memories, but what Martie can share of his own nocturnal assault, may be discovered in trying to separate out what could be the work of the supernatural with what could be a human being helping himself to a sleeping victim.

During the day Attracta occasionally feels herself overwhelmed with fear and terror and has to leave the shade of the arbour for the more reassuring rays of the sun. At times she can't even bear to have Martie with her. Yet all through the day the one constant is she does not want Carl to find out. That, she tells Martie to tell the others, is because she does not want to draw the wrong kind of attention to herself. They can laugh at her, but she needs this opportunity more than the rest of them. And she is prepared to set her own feelings aside rather than rock the boat.

'You realise' says Sylvie dryly, on hearing this, 'that she's basically repeating the behaviour of every vulnerable woman who comes up against a man.'

'But we don't know' replies Martie.

'How ever far we think we progress' observes Sylvie, 'we are still no further on than the whim of the next man more physically strong than we are.'

'I know' says Martie simply. 'I just wish I could help.'

Don volunteers to swap rooms with Attracta. So does Alix and Attracta chooses Alix's room, and doesn't bother to explain why to Don.

Eighteen. Sixth Night

Attracta sits on her own in one of the deeply cushioned armchairs dotted about the library. She sips a brandy.

'I made my report on the day' she notes to the air. 'I kept it short. Interesting how we didn't have anything happen last night.'

'Did you put down what happened in the spa yesterday?' asks Becca, hoping this titbit will cause Attracta to respond more warmly to her again.

'You can. You were also there.'

'Okay. I'm not going to push you' says Becca. 'Anything I can do, tell me.'

'What time tomorrow are we expecting Carl?' asks Sylvie. 'Normally I would be clear about these sorts of details, but at the start of the week, well, I was so excited and nervous I let it slide.'

'I think he's going to come here. I suppose I can remind him' replies Don.

'Yeah. Because you're the Alpha Male' responds Becca.

'I can feel a headache coming on' mutters Sylvie.

'I'll send him something now. Of course, he can't reply so we'll need to be ready to leave round about lunchtime tomorrow.'

'Wouldn't it be funny' says Martie, although he's already sensing the room is not ready to break into happy laughter, 'if he's disappeared? And we don't know it?'

There is a reproachful silence.

'It's cool' says Don. 'I've got my car parked round the corner, remember?'

'We've got a whole minivan' notes Becca. 'And I still remember how to drive.'

'You didn't by any chance leave a spare mobile in your car?' asks Martie.

'If you want to look' says Don, 'my keys are in my bedside drawer.'

Fishing round the bureau in Don's room Martie finds a box of condoms. He is aware his hand is shaking as he picks up the box.

'Please don't let it be opened' he whispers. It is not. The cellophane wrapper still protects the contents from the desires of the outside world. Martie sighs. He never really thought the rape was Don, but this is a sign that supports the hope.

Walking down the drive, away from the lights of the castle, towards the country dark that hangs heavily around him like thugs in a laundrette at midnight, Martie wishes he'd asked for company. Still, after what he's experienced this week, could seeing a shadow be any worse?

He pushes open the iron side gate next to the great entrance doors, and turns left, as per Don's instructions. With his torch he can make out the road, and he follows the wall till it turns left. He grunts when he sees Don's car.

He turns the key in the door, and slides into the passenger seat. He flicks open the glove compartment and fishes around for the promised mobile. He can't see anything. In frustration he stares out the window into the darkness. Something stares back. So suddenly does the face come up to the window that Martie cannot engage his intellectual mind, he cannot logically remember that he has experienced the supernatural right up close in the last few days. Instead he screams and screams, the tensions of the week finally breaking through his reserve. A second face appears in the window, a middle-aged woman.

Martie jumps out the car. It's now a toss-up who is more terrified; him or the middle-aged country couple just out for a nightly stroll and wondering what the strange car was doing parked on a dark road.

'Are you all right?' the man asks, rather a stupid question as Martie continues to scream.

'Has he had a fit, do you think?' asks the woman in a forced conversational tone.

'I'm fine' Martie gasps. 'Fine. I was – you scared me.'

'You scared us' says the man with rural logic.

'I'm looking for something' says Martie. He still can't find the mobile.

'Have you lost something? I think he's lost something' says the woman to her husband.

'Where are you?' asks the man. 'Are you at the manor? Have you seen something you can't explain?

'Is that why you're overwrought dear?' asks the woman.

Martie takes a deep breath. He can't find the torch so he might as well interview the locals.

Sometime later, minus torch, Martie reappears in the sitting room and drops Don's keys onto a highly polished mahogany table, where the grooved edges leave scratches.

'No mobile' he reports.

'That's crap' retorts Don. 'I put it there myself.'

'Well, it's gone. Go see for yourself. If you meet Helen and Peter, give them my love.'

'Who's that?'

'Local couple who scared the shit out of me' says Martie, pouring himself a glass from one of the ever-present open bottles of red wine. He knows they're all watching him. He drinks.

'Did you find out… anything about the house?' asks Attracta. Martie turns to her and says gently that he did.

'Eighteen months ago someone took on the castle after it had suffered years of neglect. Russian millionaires seeking the simple life in a castle. They spent a great deal of money and stayed, apparently, two nights. Suddenly the wife discovered she didn't like living outside a city vibe.'

'What did they tell you about the history of the house?'

'It was built nearly three hundred years ago, so there's a hell of a lot of history that's been lost. But sometime late in the 19th Century, a new couple bought the house. They had a child they wanted educating. They found a nice young man. One day the milk cart arrives as per and discovers the body of the woman of the house in the driveway. A Victorian police search throws up the body of the schoolmaster in the bushes behind the central fountain. Plus the body of the child in the schoolroom. And the body of the husband, they didn't say where.

'Thereafter it was used during the two world wars for a bit, although none of the soldiers liked to hang around a minute after they had to. Then it was bought as a sanitorium, but it drove all the inmates crazy, so they closed it down and locked it up. Until our Russians appeared with their decorator swatches and bottomless pockets.'

'So it may be the problems began in the late 19th Century?'

'Unless there was an existing haunting. Perhaps they were spooked by whatever was already in the house.'

'What are we going to tell Carl?' asks Attracta.

'I'm going to say thanks and give me my dosh' replies Alix. 'The rest of you can stick around. I'm packing for the Caribbean.'

'And no one's going to … talk about me?'

There is a grouchy silence.

'It's your call' says Alix. 'We'll follow you.'

Attracta thinks and then nods.

'Look I've got something to tell you' says Alix, and he's taken aback by how swiftly and tensely the group train their eyes on him. 'Nothing about *that*, WTF? No, I thought since we're never gonna be in the same place again, all of us together, I want to tell you how I got these…'. He indicates the scars on his cheeks.

'We can hardly see them' says Becca.

'Bull' says Alix. 'You think I don't know when people are looking at my scars instead of looking me in the eye?'

'I think they're sexy' mumbles Becca.

'I'll tell you how I got them. Okay, my dad was in and out of my mum's life. When I was 15 he started coming round often. One day I'm at school and he comes to meet me at the gates. I'm all like 'oh cool it's my dad' to my mates. They're watching me. I go up to him and he says 'Alix I'm never gonna see you again. Goodbye' and he goes.'

A murmur of empathy runs round the group.

'See, I was used to him doing my head in. He took me by surprise. And I was so shocked, I started crying. And all my mates they started laughing at me. I don't know why, I couldn't stop crying and they were laughing.

'It went round the school and they all called me queer boy and shit. They told me they were gonna beat the shit out of me, only I was such a girl they didn't wanna touch me. The worst was someone told my mum and she got really upset.

'One day I couldn't take no more. I got my mum's scissors, and I stood in front of the bathroom mirror.'

'Oh no, please, Alix' murmurs Martie.

'It didn't hurt so much. Not after the first few. I stuck the scissors in and kinda twirled them about.'

Becca puts a supportive hand on Attracta's shoulder, thus causing her to jump.

'I went to the hospital and all. I was off school for five weeks. When I came back I had these amazing scars on my face. No one ever called me a girl again.'

There is a silence.

'I thought you were going to say your scars were somehow tied up with your supernatural experience, Alix. Not that that matters. I'm so sorry.'

Alix smiles sheepishly. 'Yeah, that. Okay, so I've never actually seen nothing spooky. Never been in a haunted house. I just really needed the skrilla. I hope no one's going to judge me.'

Don chuckles. 'So now you *have* been initiated. How do you feel?'

'There's weird shit everywhere. This way I'm getting paid' says Alix stoically.

'You know' says Becca, 'we've not heard about your experience, Don. Are you also running a con?'

'No' says Don. 'And I don't mind telling you about it. But not now. This is Alix's moment. Want another beer, bro?'

Alix smiles.

'I never heard that Forming Storming shit before, but I want you to know I consider all of you my friends. We few, we happy few' says Martie. Then to Alix 'it's what the first world war soldiers said to each other: 'We band of brothers.''

'And there goes the misogyny' says Becca.

'Do we know everyone's story now?' asks Attracta. Her recent experience has inflated her status in the group, and everyone wants to prove their support.

'Sorry I bullshitted you all, okay?' asks Alix.

'I will tell you. But not yet' says Don.

'We don't know the details of Martie's manslaughter' says Becca into the air.

Martie takes a deep breath. Then he shuts his mouth. 'Actually, I'm fine. I think I've already deep shared enough.'

'Well I want to know sometime' says Alix. 'Or I'm gonna follow you and haunt you!'

'That's a point' replies Becca. 'Wonder if we're gonna be taking any of the house away with us?'

'Crap' says Attracta. 'I'm leaving all this behind real soon.'

‘Yes’ says Sylvie, who has been particularly quiet all day. ‘It’s true. They come back. There’s always time to tell them what’s been eating you up inside.’

Martie and Don exchange a look. Don nods. ‘Sylvie, is there something you want to tell us?’

Martie asks ‘Have you … has your daughter been visiting you?’

Sylvie’s face shuts tight. ‘I have nothing to say.’

‘Because … consider this carefully … there’s a least one child in this house. We know there was a school room. And a tragedy involving a child. All I’m saying is don’t get fooled.’

Sylvie’s eyes blaze and she stands up. ‘None of you have ever understood how I suffer! Now you want to deprive me of my only consolation!’

‘No Sylvie’ says Attracta. ‘Don’t go. Talk to us. If what happened to me is that something supernatural raped me, don’t you think you could also be in danger?’

‘You don’t understand! You have no idea! You’re all so cold, you’ve never truly suffered!’

Sylvie runs from the room. Martie begins to go after her. She half-turns. ‘Don’t any of you follow me! I don’t trust any of you!’

They hear her footsteps as they pound rapidly up the wooden stairs.

‘So what’s going on there?’ asks Becca.

‘I expect the same thing that’s been happening to me. She’s been visited. She thinks it’s her daughter. I think Don’s right, if it’s anything it’s the child who died here.’

‘So what do we do?’

'Nothing' says Don. 'She's an adult and it's her decision. If connecting with whatever's in this house gives her some sort of happiness, it's not up to us to interfere.'

'These spirits are terrifying' says Attracta and the rest of the group looks at her.

'I'm so, so glad it's the last night. We never have to be in this house again.'

'Yeah' says Becca in a deliberately flat voice. 'After all these fancy rooms and brilliant food, I can't wait to get back to the smelly single room I sublet. I can't tell you how much I'm excited.'

'I just want my bucks' says Alix. 'My mum needs a sea cruise.'

'I wonder if the police would be interested in Carl's art experiment. I'm thinking of 'reckless endangerment' for a start' says Martie.

'You signed an airtight contract' says Don. 'To me it looked like the sort of deal all those reality shows use.'

'You think there's hidden cameras? I've seen movies about that, turns out there's some old dude behind a one-way mirror jacking off' asks Alix.

'Carl's a highly respected Brit artist' notes Don. 'I doubt he'd put all this organisation into duplicating what's already appearing in a trashy film.'

'Although we don't know what he's going to do with the reports we're giving him.'

'Most work' says Don, 'is irrelevant. I've worked on campaigns that cost huge amounts of money and effort. They went nowhere. Sometimes people experiment. If you have the money, whatever crazy thought you've had, you can make happen.' Don knows this sounds impressive. What he doesn't add is the one time he broke into big money consulting the firm went bankrupt before he got paid.

'So you think we should ask for more money?' asks Becca. 'I mean, Attracta for an obvious example. And Sylvie got her head bashed. And Martie had all kinds of stuff going on he thought was coming from Don.'

'Yeah' says Martie into the air, 'it's interesting how everyone thought my experience was a bit of a joke.'

'Be honest' responds Becca, 'So did you.'

Martie frowns. 'Perhaps there's more to me than being the butt of jokes. Butt, ho ho. No pun intended.'

'You're okay, Martie' says Don. 'No one has said anything disrespectful.'

Martie thinks and then smiles shyly at Don.

'Baby' says Becca, 'you've really fallen hard for Don, haven't you?'

'Shut up' says Don, with irritation.

'It's fine' says Martie, 'by tomorrow night I'll be back in Soho and none of this will matter.'

'Meanwhile' says Alix, 'we've still got to get through tonight.'

'Look, I know everyone's winding down, but shit' says Becca, 'I'd really like one more visit to the spa. I mean, I know there's something down there, but it hasn't done anything, right? It's just kind of a weird public steam room. And I'd really like to use the jacuzzi. Any takers?'

'Why don't we all go?' asks Don.

'Even Sylvie?'

Ten minutes later the group, minus Sylvie, is stripped to swim wear and enjoying the spa. In the jacuzzi Martie turns to Becca. 'Let me say, whatever happens from now on, in this moment I am supremely happy. I have bubbles going up my arse and my body feels totally chilled.'

'You're welcome. Just stop playing with my tits' responds Becca.

'Are you nuts? I'm not doing that' says Martie. He stands up in alarm. 'Is something doing that?'

Becca laughs. 'Relax, I'm messing with you.'

'Funny.' Martie moves from the jacuzzi and opens the door to the spa. He shuts it and Becca realises she's alone.

'Not that there's anything wrong with that. You just keep away from me' she says into the empty space.

In the spa, Martie sees Don and sits next to him.

'This steam is insane' says Martie.

'Shut up' says Don. 'I'm meditating.'

'Cool beans' mumbles Martie.

He peers through the gloom and sees Attracta, her hair wrapped in a towel, her body also.

'This was a good idea.'

'I'm watching what's coming in and what's going out' Attracta notes.

'I wish Sylvie was here. The group should stay together.'

'She knows where we are' says Alix, invisible in the thick, swirling steam.

The door opens and then shuts.

'Becca?'

Silence.

'Becca you have to identify yourself. Now.'

More silence. Then 'No, it's me. Sylvie. Becca's in the jacuzzi.'

'Thanks for joining us' says Martie.

'It was easier than being up there on my own' says Sylvie, honestly.

'Can you guys go outside if you want to talk?' asks Don.

'Actually no' says Martie. 'This is a fucking steam, not a meditation room.'

Attracta laughs.

Outside Becca decides to get out of the jacuzzi.

'You've been incredible, but I'm becoming a prune. Gotta go now.'

She attempts to stand on the plastic floor, yet can't. Each time her feet fumble for a foothold, it's as though there is something under the water, something she keeps standing on. She begins to scream.

Not much noise finds its way into the spa. The glass walls are thick.

Becca again tries to climb out, using her arms rather than her feet. Something bangs her head hard on the plastic rim of the jacuzzi and she scream again. The noise of the unit seems to become louder, drowning out Becca. Drowning. Becca feels herself beginning to slip under the bubbly water, steam rising, so inviting.

Then the timer activates and the jacuzzi turns itself off. The water stops churning. Becca screams again. She can now see down to the bottom of the translucent water. There is nothing. Nothing stopping her. She screams again and this time there is insufficient noise to prevent those in the spa hearing her. As Becca hauls herself onto the dry floor, Martie and Don, followed by Alix, Sylvie and Attracta, spill out, steam billowing after them.

'Sorry!' says Becca. 'My own fault! There was something under the water. I couldn't get out.'

'So now you're out?' asks Martie.

'The timer went off and it stopped.'

'Oh wow. We were waiting for the guy who likes to steam with us, we didn't think to look in the haunted jacuzzi!' remarks Alix.

'This place is too much' says Becca. 'I just want to go to sleep and tomorrow get my bucks.'

There isn't a lot of enthusiasm for continuing to enjoy the spa, so the group dries themselves and quits the basement. As they climb the stairs to the ground floor and then up to their bedrooms, they toss casual thoughts out to the group.

'I'll tell you one thing' says Becca, 'if someone told me eight days ago that seven days from then I'd be telling you that something invisible in the water was trying to drown me, and now I just want to forget about it, I wouldn't believe them.'

'Yeah' says Don. 'It's like in a war. Things happen that would blow your mind completely if they were dropped into everyday life. But when you're getting used to all kinds of shit going on, it's amazing what the human psyche can adapt to.'

'Do you think we'll all suffer PTSD when we leave?' asks Sylvie.

'What's that?' asks Alix.

'Post Traumatic Stress Disorder' says Becca.

Alix laughs. ‘I know what PTSD is, stop being so racist.’

Becca punches him affectionately on the shoulder. ‘Don’t set me up. I was trying to be helpful.’

‘Yes, that’s interesting’ says Don, referring to Sylvie, not Becca. ‘We’ve gone through a highly dramatic, traumatic few days. Like people who’ve survived a plane crash. It’s only afterwards we’ll be able to see the effect it’s had on all of us.’

‘Nothing changes me’ says Martie. ‘I’ll forget you in a cocktail glass.’

‘Bull’ says Attracta, putting her arm around Martie. ‘You’ll never forget this week.’

‘I know’ says Martie, ‘it’s just that we have to say goodbye tomorrow, and I totally hate goodbyes. Really. I’d sooner you look in my room in the morning and I’m gone. Goodbye baby and amen.’

‘Yeah, if that happens, we’ll have to search the castle to find you. I presume Carl will want to see you in person. You know, to give you your ten grand?’

‘Oh right. Okay but don’t anyone expect any big hugs. Just a quick wave *ciao*.’

As Sylvie opens the door to her room, Martie walks over to her.

‘Sylvie, I can guess what you think is going on with you. I’m not trying to interfere. But don’t trust something you think you’ve got covered. This place doesn’t play by the rules.’

Sylvie stares intently into his eyes. ‘What you don’t understand, dear’ she says gently, ‘is I’m already dead.’

Martie’s eyes widen and he cries out.

'Oh, I don't mean like that. I mean inside. So you see, nothing that happens can have any effect on me.'

Summoned by the noise in the corridor, Don appears, already stripped down to his boxers. Sylvie sees him, moves quickly into her room and shuts the door.

The two men face each other.

'Sorry, Sylvie said some shit about already being dead and it spooked me.'

Don doesn't understand but he nods. He doesn't move. Martie begins to raise his hand, to very tentatively reach out to touch Don's exposed chest. Then he pulls his hand back and moves to his door. At the door he turns. Don is still watching him.

'You're a bit of a bastard, you know, aren't you?' asks Martie.

Martie steps into his bedroom and closes the door. For a moment Don stands, as though waiting, expecting some further development. Then he heads back to his room.

In the night Attracta thinks she hears something at the door. She sits bolt upright, she brings from under the pillow the knife she purloined earlier in the evening. Her breath comes in ragged whispers. Nothing. She lies back on her pillow with a deep sigh and is soon asleep.

In Martie's room he lies awake. He's fairly sure the visitor will not disturb him again. He wonders what the whole ghost thing is about, what they are trying to tell the group. It may be noticed, if you are an insomniac, that in the space between awareness and sleep there is a dark zone where thoughts emerge out of *spiritus mundi.* There is a zone inside us, or perhaps it is outside us and in the dark zone we can touch it, where we can understand things intuitively, without having to work them out, without needing information and fact. So it is that while Martie lies in the dark, eyes open yet also briefly closing, that he has a vision of who the ghosts in Strawberry Manor are. Not so much their physical form, which they already know, but their relationship to each other. Even their relationship to the group. What it is the ghosts have been trying to convey to the group from the beginning.

'Of course' whispers Martie. Soon he feels himself drifting towards sleep and this time he doesn't do anything to stop it.

Sylvie turns one way and then the other. She sighs. She flicks on the light, then becomes aware she's doing it wrong and flicks it off again. She calls 'Hailey…' Nothing. Tears prick the sides of her eyes. She reaches for the box of tissues she always keeps on her bedside table. For a moment she wonders if, as she reaches out her hand, a tiny hand will take hers. Sadly not. She pulls a few individual tissues from the dispenser and wipes her eyes. She begins to keen. Softly crooning, making audible the terrible pain she always feels in the area that used to be her contented heart.

'I don't care what you are. You make me so happy' she says into the darkness.

'Please. Just one more time. Please. We're going home tomorrow.'

Nothing.

She sighs more deeply, a flurry of grief.

'I would give anything to hold you in my arms again' she whispers. 'I mean it. Anything.'

Don thinks he hears a noise and wakes. For a moment he has the crazy thought that it's Martie, defying his dictum, braving his fists. He snaps on the light.

'Attracta!'

'This isn't sexual' she says. 'I just need to be with someone. Not sexual!'

'I understand I think' says Don, making room for her. She wears her usual bra and pants. He wants to run his hand down her body but knows he must not. Must not.

'I won't say anything to Carl' he notes.

'Thanks. I knew you'd understand.'

Attracta arranges herself just far enough from Don not to collide with him in sleep.

'I'm glad of the company' says Don.

'Goodnight' says Attracta.

After she has gone to sleep Don listens to her gentle breathing. He wonders what it would be like to put his pillow over her face. He grunts. Where did that come from? This place… it infects our thinking, our behaviour.

None of us are responsible for what this place makes us do.

Alix has nightmares. He is held down and a cruel hand screws steel bolts into his cheeks.

Becca has a great night's sleep. She dreams she goes back to South Africa an international star and is interviewed for local television. 'SA is just as good as overseas' she tells the gratified interviewer.

Nineteen. Last Day

Don wakes to find he's alone in the big bed. Figures. Before he showers he packs, it's something he's always done as a precaution: you never know when your luck will run out. Having dried and dressed he makes his way down the stairs where he's wryly amused to see that everyone else has also packed and there is a neat pile of luggage by the front door.

'Parting is such sweet sorrow' he mutters to himself. 'Can't wait.'

Walking into the vast kitchen he sees the other five sitting round the table. He's come into a discussion.

'Morning. How did everyone sleep?'

He intercepts a glare from Attracta and nods imperceptibly.

'Nothing' says Martie. 'Nearly died of boredom.'

'I had a fantastic dream' says Becca.

'Yeah, she's now Beyonce's BGF' says Alix. 'I had a shit night.'

Don realises that worse than other people's holiday photos is asking about their night. He throws out a huge yawn, enjoying the way his t-shirt rides up at the front. He trusts at least half the audience will appreciate the view.

'We've been working out the story of our ghosts' says Sylvie.

'Okay, so this is what we've come up with' says Becca.

Attracta literally pushes her to one side and begins talking rapidly. 'Okay. We know there are three spectres. Husband, wife, tutor. So what happened is:

The wife fell in love with the tutor.

The husband found out.

The husband killed the child in revenge.

The wife killed the husband in revenge. Then she threw herself off the battlements.

The tutor killed himself.'

Don nods. 'Not bad … Let's walk around the theory… kick the tires… take it for a test drive. What if:

The tutor falls in love with the wife.

For a while she goes with him. Then she feels guilty because she's a mother. Also her husband's rich and tutors, especially in the 19th Century, were very poor.

The tutor kills the kid out of revenge.

The husband kills the tutor.

The wife kills the husband.

The wife throws herself off the battlements.'

'Any other variations?' asks Don. 'Might as well test drive all the theories, however nuts.'

'The wife kills the kid so she can run off with the tutor' says Becca. 'The husband kills the tutor out of revenge. They did that a lot in olden days. The wife kills herself and the husband kills himself.'

This appears to have exhausted all possibilities.

'Unless' begins Sylvie, 'it's all about the child. The wife and the tutor are in love. The husband kills the child. This stops the wife leaving with the tutor. The tutor then kills the husband, and the wife throws herself off the battlements.'

'That way the tutor remains alive?'

'The tutor is on the battlements one day and the ghost of the wife pushes him off.'

'Nobody killed anyone' says Don. 'They were an entirely innocent household. And, as often happened in the old days, since they had lots of money ruffians from the village broke in, killed everybody, and made off with the valuables.'

'Oh' says Becca. 'Yeah. That would explain why they're confused but not, I don't know, murderous.'

'Yeah' says Alix. 'I mean if they wanted to, they could take us all out right now. While we're sitting at this table.'

There is a noise from the hall. Everyone stands and several of the group cry out.

After a moment Carl strides into the kitchen.

'Carl!' cries Attracta.

'Play it cool' says Becca to her as an aside. Martie smirks.

'Hello gang. Thought I'd surprise you.'

'We weren't expecting you till lunch' says Becca.

'That's why it's a surprise' says Attracta in withering tones.

Carl wants to look round some of the castle, so the group finishes breakfast and follows him. Somehow Attracta manages to link her arm amiably in his and they lead the way.

'Be nice' says Martie, noticing the daggers Becca is sending to the back of Attracta's head.

'She's supposed to be my bestie. Carl arrives and she just drops me!'

‘She can’t help it. She’s desperate.’

Carl enjoys Attracta’s droll commentary as he inspects the bedrooms, the various public rooms, and even takes a walk up the secret passage. Thirty minutes later they’re back in the kitchen and Sylvie and Becca are making tea. Alix and Martie are coordinating the washing up. Don is talking to Carl and Attracta is hanging on Carl’s every word. Carl, used to both domestic staff and managing the lesser people who actually create his artwork, waits until he has a full quota round the table before speaking.

‘Thanks for the many, many reports. I was beginning to think you guys weren’t taking a dump you didn’t tell me about.’

The table dutifully laughs. Attracta is the last to gurgle to a stop.

‘So what did you make of our ghosts?’

Don outlines the various theories, with some help from Sylvie and some interruptions from Attracta who wants to be sure Carl understands how much she’s valued the week and how she’d love to come back again when it’s just the two of them.

When Don has finished Carl leans back in his chair. He seems to be mulling over the information.

‘Hmm… there is an actual story, you know. There are diaries…private, that came with the house, I’m the only one who’s read them… sadly none of your theories match with what’s known historically.’

The group looks severely put out.

‘Or’ says Martie and waits till he has everyone’s attention.

‘This began as the story of a faithful wife. She wanted her child educated. Her husband suggested a tutor. The wife thought carefully. She didn’t want a woman, there were far too many stories of governesses giving birth to illegitimate children. So she chose a male tutor. She also thought about the *other* stories she'd heard about, where the wife falls in love with the male tutor. This is where the faithfulness comes in. She examined her conscience most scrupulously and concluded that she loved her husband and child and there would be no problems.

The tutor was hired. The child was happy. And then something unexpected happened: the husband fell in love with the tutor. And the tutor with the husband. For a while the castle was a combination of a great deal of unhappiness and the odd ecstatic tryst, carried out in one of the many, many spare bedrooms.

Eventually the wife, driven mad by the situation, smothered the child.

The husband threw the wife off the battlements.

The tutor found the husband, inconsolable with grief and guilt, in the garden.

The husband shot himself.

The tutor, wracked with grief and impossible love, killed himself.'

There is a pause. Then Carl makes a gun out of his fist and pulls a finger trigger at Martie.

'I don't know how you knew' he says, 'but that's exactly right.'

Martie attempts to conceal a huge smirk.

'No one likes a show-off' remarks Becca.

'Sorry. It took a long time to work it out. With some supernatural help' says Martie.

'Only it doesn't get you any more money, does it, Carl?' asks Attracta, 'because you didn't set us the task of solving the ghost mystery.'

'Yeah, true' says Carl, 'but I'm impressed you have.'

'So where's our scratch?' asks Alix. 'I'm asking for a friend.'

Carl laughs. Then he stops laughing and becomes serious.

'Your money's safe. It should be in your bank accounts by now.'

'Can we have our mobiles back now?' asks Becca.

Carl laughs again. 'You guys! Did you actually leave your mobiles in the box? I thought you'd have broken through the lock. You guys are the best!'

Carl gives the key to Martie, who opens the box and lays out everyone's mobiles.

'My battery's down' says Attracta, with irritation. Others in the group switch on their phones and begin running through their texts and emails.

For a while Carl does nothing but watch.

'This is so interesting' he says after a time. 'People deprived of the benefits of the tech age re-discovering the joy of instant communications.'

'Never again' breathes Becca, 'I'm never gonna let go of my phone again.'

'That's a shame' says Carl, knowing his words are being carefully listened to. 'Because I have another art experiment for you.'

'That sounds wonderful! says Attracta automatically.

'Only thing is, it can't be just two or three. You all have to want to get involved.'

Don frowns. 'Shit, Carl, can you give us time to reorient? It's been a hell of a week.'

‘I know. You’re spaced out, your nerve endings are on fire. That’s perfect for what I have in mind.’

‘Spare your breath’ says Sylvie firmly. ‘I’ve had more than enough.’

Carl switches to a look of sympathy. ‘Hey, how’s the bump on your head?’

Sylvie looks down at her phone and doesn’t respond.

‘Any of you interested in hearing my proposal?’

Becca and Alix shout yes, Martie looks wary, Attracta puts her hand on Carl’s leg and avers ‘Carl, you’re incredible. I’m with you.’

For a moment Carl gives Attracta a searching look, as though if he could, he’d make an exception for her. Then the look fades and he gives her a cold nod in acknowledgement.

‘This isn’t my only property. This week you’ve had the chance to get to know each other. And that’s been hugely successful. I’ve been watching all of you since I arrived. You’re a team. You breathe as one.’

‘Yeah’ drawls Martie. ‘There’s been a whole heap of Performing. Not much Fornicating, bit sad really.’

Carl snorts. ‘You’re a card, Martie. I’m really glad you’re in this group.’

Martie looks modest, flashes a glance at Don and Attracta. It’s interesting, he thinks, how certain people become the ones you look to when it’s called for.

‘You must exclude me’ says Sylvie. ‘I only want to go home.’

Carl looks intensely at Sylvie. ‘So you don’t mind letting your friends down?’

The group doesn't exactly stare at Sylvie, but she's aware they're all waiting on her reply.

'I don't like to be the centre of attention.'

'I felt the same way' says Don, 'all I wanted to do was go home and chill. Now I'm curious. We've had an insane few days together. I think we should at least hear Carl out.'

'Thanks, Don. Okay, take it or leave it, here's the pitch. First I must congratulate you on your many and varied reports.'

The group exchange happy smiles although some of them are guarded. The 'but' seems to be coming.

'As far as they go. I'm 100% happy with your performances this week. Only…'

He deliberately pauses so the others can calibrate their attention to whatever criticism he is about to drop on them.

'Only… it's not enough. As you know from my art, I need to be edgy. It's where the market is, I am a slave to the market. Marc Quinn with his ice sculpture made of five pints of his own blood, for example, that was a game-changer. Nowadays, if someone presents a shark or a cow or any sad animal floating in formaldehyde everyone yawns. The market is greedy. The most outrageous example is the *Body Worlds* concept. Dead bodies frozen in plastic, the veins, brains, muscles and organs opened up to the world.'

'I think *Body Worlds* is revolting' says Sylvie. 'Those poor people think they're being immortalised. Instead every snotty kid with entrance money laughs at them. If that's the sort of notoriety you're planning, Carl, you will definitely have to leave me out.'

Carl nods, as though seriously considering her feedback. 'I'm after something much more vital and alive. Artwork which goes right to core, to the limit, of what human beings are. The essence of humanity is the essence of life. The essence of the planet.'

'So we're the essence?' interjects Becca.

'You could be. You could, while being very much alive, be part of an art concept that takes the limits of human experience and stretches them to the maximum.'

'That sounds lovely doesn't it Attracta?' asks Martie innocently. 'You'd love Carl to stretch you to your maximum.'

'It's inspired' breathes Attracta to Carl, while deliberately not hearing Martie.

'So. I have another property. It's not like this one.'

'Oh good' says Becca. 'This one's haunted, did you know?'

Carl nods several times in quick succession. 'In fact it's derelict. There's water coming down from the roof. The paint's peeling, vandals have stripped some of the rooms of their wooden panelling. No comfy sofas. No en-suite bathrooms.'

'Are we supposed to do it up, like *Restoration Home*?'

'These hands weren't made for wielding hammers!'

Becca asks for the whole group 'What on earth makes you think we would stay there? At least this place was luxurious.'

'Let me finish. It has as bad a rep. as this place. You'll see there've been attempts to renovate and restore, but no builder can put up with the place long enough to bring it into the 21st Century.'

'I have to say with each word you make it more and more unlikely that I will be going there' says Sylvie to no one in particular.

A snuffling noise draws their attention and they turn to see Alix snorting coke from an antique hand mirror. He looks at them, a little white powder caught on the side of one nostril.

'What? I'm off the clock.'

'I would't mind a little of that myself' says Don and moves across to Alix.

'I'm terribly sorry' says Sylvie 'but if everybody's going to take drugs at this time of the day I am definitely leaving.'

'Not everyone' says Don, partaking in Alix's stash, 'just need something to focus my attention if Carl's gonna blow my mind.'

'I wouldn't mind a bit of that' says Becca, casually. 'Save me some?'

'You guys made free with the contents of my booze cabinet this week' notes Carl, without rancour. 'Perhaps I'll toss in a kilo of snow in the new house.'

'Not going to be a new house' says Sylvie with grim determination.

'I think it's an incredible opportunity' says Attracta. 'And here's my 'but'. But why should we go from this house to this other one which sounds worse and worse the more you describe it. I mean, I know we're missing something.'

'Yeah. Where's the happy ending?' asks Martie.

Carl hesitates before the big reveal. Once the atmosphere is appropriately electric he continues.

'I will supply basic needs. Food, camp beds and sleeping bags. You'll be expected to make recordings as you have this week. There's no time limit on this one. You'll understand why in a moment. It will be tough. But this week you've all proved you are tough. You've shown you can come together as strangers and forge an incredible sort of bond with each other. I wouldn't let you go to the new place if I hadn't already listened to the progress of all of you this week.'

'So now you've bought us dinner and taken us dancing, when do you fuck us?' asks Martie.

'There's no equal shares for everyone. It's a different ball game. But I will give the last person to leave the house… three million pounds.'

The group gives a collective gasp. The figure runs round the room, going from person to person. Inside each they are reacting to the idea of never having to worry about money again.

'Now, a sensible person' says Carl, 'would, say, spend £500,000 on a decent flat and invest the other £2.5 million in buy-to-lets. This would then ensure you wouldn't have to work for the rest of your life. On the other hand, you could hit Las Vegas, coke up, and get through the money in two glorious drug-hazed years. Up to you. Whoever's the winner.'

'What about the rest of us?'

'A firm handshake goodbye.'

'But won't that set us against each other?'

'I didn't say that. You might find that's what happens.'

'Seriously, wouldn't that make us all into enemies?' asks Becca.

'Darling, I love you like the sister I never had' says Attracta, 'but if you come between me and three million I'll strangle you myself.'

'This is appalling! You said yourself we've formed an extraordinary bond with each other. Now you're callously going to tear us apart!'

'I'm not doing anything. It's up to the group to decide how you want to spend your time in the house.'

'You call it a house' asks Don, 'so it's not a castle like this one?'

'I call it a house because it's called Borley House. It's the same sort of dimensions as this one. You can call it what you like.'

'Borley House' says Martie. 'I've heard of Borley Rectory. That had a rep. for being the most haunted house in England.'

'This is Borley House' answers Carl. 'Different place.'

'Kind of a coincidence' Martie remarks.

'Life is full of coincidences' says Carl.

'Three million. Pounds. Not South African Rand' says Becca. She looks at Attracta and they both nod.

'Excellent. I believe two of you have signed on. However I'm serious. It has to be all of you. This week I have amassed recordings from all six of you. It would damage the integrity of the project if one of you is missing.'

'Come on, Sylvie' says Martie. 'You could do something amazing. Start a foundation in Hailey's name…?'

Sylvie says nothing yet neither does she leave the room.

'Okay' says Alix, looking at Carl with unnaturally bright eyes. 'Sign me on.'

'If I was going to sign on' says Don, 'I'd want to know more about whatever's in the place. This time we were amateurs. We came in blind. Now we're professionals. You have to give us more.'

Carl contemplates Don intensely, then shakes his head.

'No can do. You'll understand why. If I spoon feed you there won't be the excitement as you discover the house for yourself.'

'I think we've had enough excitement for a long while' states Sylvie flatly.

'I mean the excitement of the art piece' responds Carl.

'So this is all for art. And you're not at all concerned about us? We're just cattle?'

'No, you're not cattle. I wouldn't give a cow three million quid. I'm being entirely transparent here. That's the deal. I'm not promising you a rose garden. I don't know what you'll come up against in there. I tried speaking to the locals but they were all so nutty it sounded like aliens and a portal to a distant galaxy. Because there's no scientifically ratified evidence I can't give you anything. And even if I could, seriously, hasn't part of this week been about discovering for yourselves?'

'But we're so tired, we're exhausted' says Attracta. 'Can't you send us away somewhere tropical for a week, we can rest, chill, and then go to the new house?'

'I need you exactly as you are now. You'll never be in better psychological shape than right now.'

'I'm a mess' says Sylvie, and she places a protective arm across her breast.

'So sleep. In your provided sleeping bag. Think of it like this. If as you say you're already exhausted, it won't be long before most of you quit the house. Leaving the last one standing with three million quid. Who knows, perhaps I'll be putting the bucks into your bank account … this time next week.'

'But' says Don, 'What is the primary motivation for our leaving? You said yourself, despite what Strawberry Manor threw at us, we haven't left. What's Borley House packing that nearly all of us would voluntarily quit?

There is a pause.

'I have no idea' says Carl simply. 'That's what you, in your reports, are going to tell me.'

'I'm in' says Sylvie suddenly. Martie moves to her and puts his hand on hers.

'Are you sure?'

'I have a boring little job and a boring little life and no one to go home to. I should take this adventure for myself. If I was brave I would. Instead I'm in because if I'm not in then none of you are in. And I've grown very fond of you all, in quite different ways, this week. I want to do my bit to give one of you a golden future.'

'If you put it like that' says Martie, 'I'm definitely in. Although I can't say I've grown very fond of all of you, even in different ways. Sometimes you get on my tits. For three million big ones, though, I'd spend time with Boris Johnson who I hate more than anyone in the world.'

Don says 'how long will it take to set up?'

'I don't understand?' asks Carl.

'Organising the provisions, even if we're camping out, we have to camp on something.'

Carl smiles, the cat given the key to the cream cupboard. 'It's all here. There's a truck at the top of the driveway.' He fishes in his pocket and produces keys. He throws them to Don.

'Fetch?' he asks.

'He's not driving' says Martie. 'He's flying.'

'I can drive a truck' says Becca.

'Excellent' says Carl. 'And I'll need the keys of that car that's parked round the side.'

Don fishes for keys. 'Might as well, I can't drive anyway.'

'Wait, wait,' says Martie, 'are we really going to leave here as we are and go somewhere else and do the whole thing again?'

'Yes and no' replies Carl. 'I really don't think you'll call Borley House a repetition of your week here. In fact, I guarantee it.'

'So you'll show us around?' asks Don, more aggressively than is his usual delivery. Martie realises he has to make allowances for the coke.

'Sadly no. I have back-to-back meetings with foreign buyers. Spoiler alert: I'm in negotiations with several international art galleries for the new piece.'

'The piece that's basically us?' asks Alix. 'I mean, are we gonna get credit?'

'Three million is a lot of credit' Carl says soberly.

'But what's to stop us… when we get there' probes Martie, 'from five of us turning round, leaving the sixth one in the house to collect the three million. Which we split six ways?'

Carl thinks before answering.

'That's a five-star question. I think you won't do that. I think I can trust you to enter into this new artwork with integrity and honesty. And since you brought it up, I'll insert a clause in the contracts that no one can claim the prize within less than say four days.'

'But on the fourth day…?'

'I'm being entirely transparent with you. If on the fourth day you pull the scam you propose, I will say nothing. I promise I will pay out three million. And if you've formed a cabal against me, well I'm a big boy, I won't cry.'

'By the way' says Martie, 'we worked out who the murderer is and who is guilty of manslaughter.'

It takes Carl a moment to catch up, then he laughs. And laughs. 'You guys, you're too much. I don't have that sort of detail about you. Don was pushing me for additional info. I made that up to mess with him!'

The group exchange annoyed glances.

'I bet if I asked you to find the hidden treasure you'd do that too. You're priceless!' laughs Carl.

The group gathers outside to wave Carl off. Don frowns as his car, driven by Carl, bites deeply into the gravel and sends it flying as it speeds on its way.

'You can stop waving now' says Martie to Attracta. 'He's halfway to London.'

Becca drives the truck to the entrance and they swarm around it, investigating what Carl has provided. Then the group watches silently as Don shuts and locks the front door. The key he leaves to be found by the cleaners. Then, rather than getting into the truck, the group stands as though unable to believe they can simply just leave Strawberry Manor. Martie spontaneously runs out onto the lawn and turns to look at the castle.

'I wonder if they're going to appear, to wave us off?' he asks.

'Haven't you seen enough ghosts this week?' shouts Becca.

'I'm kind of going to miss my gentleman caller!' responds Martie.

'You're hilarious!'

It finishes up taking longer than it needs to for the group to load into the front passenger section of the truck.

'It really feels like we're saying goodbye to something fantastic. I mean, there were lots of times this week when I wished I was somewhere very far away, but now that we're actually leaving ...'

'I keep thinking that if I look one more time at the windows, I'll see her face.'

'Maybe now we know their secret, they don't have anything else to tell us?'

'That's a positive thought' says Don. 'That's a good one for us to leave on.'

As his last action for the group Carl had taken away their ordinary phones, noting that he would return the winner's to them personally, while the losers would get theirs returned via FedEx.

'I can't decide whether I want to burn it out of here, or go really slowly, like it's a wake.'

'No one's died. Burn it.'

Becca turns on the engine, slowly engages the truck in a three-point turn, and when the truck is facing the driveway, she gently manouvers it in the direction of the gates. Then onto the open road. And the start of their journey that will eventually take them to Borley House.

Twenty. Borley House. First Day

'Civilisation' comments Becca as she steers the truck through a village called Upper Enderby. The group has been staring intently out the windows, drinking in such prosaic scenes as cows chewing grass, couples walking, tractors lazily moving through fields of ripening corn. Now they take in housewives shopping, kids lounging outside takeaways, men gathering to talk about what's in the news.

'Strange to think all this normal stuff is going on. I suppose that's how heroin addicts feel when they come down and it's the same shit world' says Martie, looking at Alix for insider confirmation. Alix frowns.

'Why you looking at me, white boy?'

'Sorry, I just thought…'

'I'm only pulling your wire.'

'Becca stop!' shouts Attracta. Becca does, looking round wildly.

'Half decent clothes shop' Attracta explains, pointing to a shop that rejoices in the name *Apparel by Dawn and Gail*. 'I hate everything I brought with me.'

'Divine, doll' says Becca, deftly turning the truck into a bay marked 'Disabled Only.'

'We should stop for lunch anyway' notes Don. 'You'll find us in the pub. It's got a beer garden.'

A short while later Attracta and Becca, laden with brightly coloured shopping bags, appear on the pub's rear lawn, where the rest of the group is enjoying a pub lunch, with alcohol.

'Sorry Sylvie' says Becca, 'we forgot to ask if you wanted to come with.'

'Perfectly fine' says Sylvie, composed as usual, 'I did some washing last night.'

Having ordered refreshments and food, Attracta and Becca drag extra wooden chairs over to the group and sprawl in them, enjoying the sun. Beyond the eating area, the beer garden's grass drops down to a smoothly running stream.

'This is paradise' sighs Becca. 'I could stay like this forever.'

'You think?' asks Martie. 'You clearly don't need the three million.'

Becca pulls herself up and frowns. 'Thanks. I was trying to be normal for a bit.'

As the publican brings out Attracta and Becca's orders, Don regards the group coolly. 'Eat, drink and be merry. In an hour we'll be at each other's throats.'

'Oh not so!' says Sylvie. 'We don't have to do anything we don't want to.'

'I want to' says Attracta, picking her way through a cobb salad. 'I love you all and Becca's the sister I never had, but when we arrive at the front door of Borley House you're my deadly enemies.'

'Now stop it' says Sylvie, genuinely crossly. 'We do not need to attack each other.'

'I think you'll find we do' says Don. 'Carl's a clever bastard. The last few days we've become a single, supportive unit. Now if we support one another it might blowback on us. I value everyone but I'm with Attracta. You'd better get your shit together going in because I'm not saving straggling lambs.'

'I agree with Sylvie' says Martie. 'Don't forget we have to be there for a minimum four days. Therefore we still need to look out for each other.'

Don eats his chips and doesn't reply.

'All I can think about is the look on Mum's face when I tell her I've got three million quid. And no one needs to look out for me ever' avers Alix.

Becca rests her arm on his. 'Your life must be very different to mine' she says gently.

Alix laughs. 'You're so easy to wind up!'

Scattered fragments of conversation keep the energy in the group while they consume the first lunch in a week they haven't had to make themselves.

'My treat' says Don, dropping his credit card onto the small plastic tray provided by the publican. 'I figure you deserve something for your time at Borley House.'

'You're so full of crap' figures Becca.

'I hate long goodbyes' says Martie. 'This lunch, this is us saying goodbye to each other. When we get to Borley House, no one should make a big deal about going. Just go. We'll work out you've gone when you're not there at the next meal.'

'Oh I don't like that' says Sylvie. 'What if someone's hurt and they need to go to hospital? What if they're crawling up the driveway and none of us know they're there?'

'We can glance out the window from time to time' says Martie lightly. 'Just to check no one's crawling up the drive.'

Attracta and Alix laugh and Sylvie, feeling the sympathy of the group against her, says nothing more.

Returning to their truck Becca is unsurprised to see she has a ticket. She pulls the flapping paper from under the windscreen wiper, balls it and tosses it over her shoulder. The group boards, Sylvie shaking her head disapprovingly, and Becca pulls the truck back into the passing traffic.

‘We should sing songs’ notes Martie. ‘Help pass the time.’

But there’s no enthusiasm. It seems that after the meal that symbolised the last time they would be a single unit, each member of the group has become lost in their own preparations for Borley House.

Martie speaks. ‘So, Borley Rectory used to have a reputation for being the most haunted house in England.’

‘Used to?’ asks Becca. ‘Did it clean up its rep.?’

‘No. It burned down.’

‘Then Carl calling this place Borley House is either a *homage* or a private joke’ notes Don. ‘I wonder at whose expense?’

‘You shouldn’t talk about Carl like that’ says Attracta.

‘I think it’s so sweet you defend Carl when it’s obvious he has no special interest in you.’

‘Shut up, Becca’ returns Attracta. ‘You’re not too old to slap. Even though you are pretty old. No wonder you need all that make-up.’

There’s a moment’s awkward silence then Attracta and Becca laugh and hug each other.

‘But we’ll be okay, right?’ asks Alix. ‘I mean we’re all experienced around spooks, right?’

‘I think we should stay together for four days, then draw straws to see who’s the last to leave’ says Sylvie.

‘But that’s a cheat’ notes Don.

‘No, it’s following our contracts to the letter.’

‘Look, he’s playing fair, being transparent, okay? He needs our unabridged, unrehearsed reactions to whatever we experience. If we bullshit him for four days … don’t you think it goes against the spirit of his art?’ asks Attracta.

‘I don’t understand art’ says Alix. ‘And I’m not pulling your wire.’

‘I hate modern art’ says Martie. ‘There’s one guy who makes sculptures out of elephant shit. I mean, yeah, he’s the first to think of it but so what?’

‘Decadence and vanity’ says Sylvie.

‘Sylvie, don’t talk like that. You’re part of an amazing, trailblazing art project’ says Attracta.

‘I think we should just give the three million to Attracta’ says Martie. ‘We all know she’s going to be the last one still standing.’

‘Thank you Martie’ says Attracta. ‘I appreciate that.’

‘Oh, no, don’t, I was only pulling Alix’s wire.’

Don’s map reading is precise and Becca soon brings the truck to a halt outside the magnificent wrought iron gates of Borley House. The group climbs out the truck and looks around. The odd car drifts down the road behind them but otherwise they are entirely alone.

‘No birds are calling’ says Sylvie.

‘It’s not bird calling time of year’ says Martie.

‘I’m only saying.’

‘That’s interesting’ says Don. ‘Even though the place is unoccupied, the gates are open. They’re even chained open.’

‘That’s a sign of welcome’ says Attracta.

‘Or maybe the house is daring visitors to enter?’

‘We’re official’ says Alix. ‘We’re on a mission.’

Don and Martie elect to walk up the drive while the others pile back into the truck and Becca steers it up the winding path.

‘They did this deliberately’ says Martie.

‘What?’

‘The architect and landscaper. Long, long driveways, with the house hidden behind trees. Then you turn a bend in the drive and suddenly the whole house opens out in front of you.’

Don grunts.

‘Are you nervous?’ asks Martie.

Don grunts again. ‘Aren’t you? Aren’t you crapping yourself? What’s in this house that we’re being bribed with three million pounds not to leave?’

Martie continues walking silently.

‘We’re pretty experienced when it comes to the supernatural’ says Martie, after a couple of minutes.

‘Yeah’ says Don grimly. ‘That’s what’s bothering me.’

They turn a bend in the drive and there is Borley House. In the weed-strewn gravel that makes the entrance court they see the truck, doors opened, and the group warily regarding their home for the undetermined future.

‘It’s not exactly Strawberry Manor’ says Martie.

The house is a bricolage of architectural ages and styles, with a central Gothic section, a Tudor wing on the left and a Georgian addition on the right.

'I don't know about architecture' says Martie, 'but then neither did whoever built this.'

'I love it' says Attracta in upbeat tones. 'I'm going to get Carl to bring it back from the dead.'

'Can we not speak of the dead' says Sylvie.

'You'd need a couple of million to start with' says Becca. 'That roof looks like the next storm the whole lot comes down.'

'I didn't imagine it would be this bad' says Sylvie. 'I'm quite disappointed.'

'Don't concern yourself with the outside' says Don, 'My hunch is the inside is going to be *much* worse.'

Alix walks up to the front door. 'Who's got the key?'

'There's no key' says Don solemnly. 'The front door is always open.'

'Aren't they worried about vandals?' asks Becca, her eyes sweeping the many windows that stare, sightless, out onto the group.

'I think it's vandals who would be worried' answers Don.

'Stop it!' commands Sylvie. 'Or I'll turn round right now and leave!'

'Sorry' says Don. 'Gallows humour.'

'I mean it! Stop it!'

The group retrieves their luggage, Attracta and Becca additionally laden with their spoils from *Apparel by Dawn and Gail.*

Alix pushes open the door with some difficulty.

'It's rusty' he cries to the others. They watch as he disappears into the gloom within. The three women are the next to enter, while Don and Martie linger outside.

'Is this a terrible idea?' asks Martie. 'I mean we could all just turn around and go home.'

'There are no terrible ideas with three million quid at the end.'

'But nothing for anyone else.'

Don thinks, then puts a hand on Martie's shoulder. 'Come on Tiger, it'll be fine.'

Don picks up his luggage and moves easily into the house. Martie stands watching him, then he smiles and follows.

The group have jettisoned their luggage and are staring at the sights within. Alix has discovered there is a key on the inside of the groaning front door.

'It's not like Strawberry Manor' notes Becca.

Facing them is a vast interior. A rotting wooden floor, with three staircases, one into the bowels of each of the three architectural periods.

'This was never a family home' says Don. 'It must have been built as some sort of institution.'

'What, institution like a mental asylum? Asks Becca.

'Maybe it was used for research' says Martie. Only Alix feels free to walk around the gloomy interior, to test the wooden treads of the three staircases.

'I'm guessing we don't have assigned bedrooms as we did at the manor?' asks Sylvie.

'That sounds right' says Don, running his eyes warily up each of the staircases, taking in the darkness of the landings above.

'There was a stage play called *The Dark at the Top of the Stairs*' says Martie.

‘Everyone died?’ asks Alix.

‘Didn’t see it.’

‘So which is the newest part?’ asks Attracta. ‘Maybe some bits are better than others?’

Don doesn’t reply. His eyes continue to take in their immediate environment.

‘Don, say something’ says Sylvie. ‘You’re scaring me.’

Don shakes his head. ‘Sorry, just thinking. Yes, Attracta’s right. There must be a more civilised part. I think we should check out the Georgian section. Eighteenth Century.’

Moving carefully up the right-hand stairs the group finds their way to the upper landing.

‘What’s that pong?’ asks Martie. ‘It smells like a thousand pigeons all crapped themselves then committed suicide.’

‘If it’s this bad we can’t stay here’ says Sylvie. ‘It’s making me nauseous.’

Don investigates the first rooms and returns shaking his head.

‘It’s bad. We don’t have cleaning materials for this. Go back down to the hall.’

‘What’ asks Martie, ‘were there really dozens of pigeon corpses?’

‘Yeah, that must be it’ says Don, but he doesn’t elaborate. ‘I’m guessing the Gothic section is Gothic Revival, therefore mid-19th Century. Might be in better nick.’

Back in the hall the group ascends the central stairs to the Gothic section.

'Oh, this isn't so bad' notes Attracta. 'It's even got a decent bit of carpet.'

The group arrives at the beginning of a long corridor. The first room on the left is mercifully empty and contains no foul smells. There is a single sleeping bag, crumpled as though someone has only just emerged from it.

'This is clearly the sleeping dorm' says Becca. 'I'm going to go for a window view.'

'Think' says Don in a voice that calls them to attention. 'Are we really all going to bunk down in the same space?'

'Bloody right' says Becca.

'No, Don's right' says Attracta. 'We can't rely on each other's support anymore. We have to fend for ourselves.'

'I don't agree' says Sylvie. 'Anyone who wants to can share my room.'

'Don't you think we should do that normal civilised thing of the men in one room and the women in another?' asks Martie.

Alix crows. 'Finally, Martie, you get to see Don in the raw!'

'Piss off. And just for that I'm sharing with the women.'

After some ill-tempered discussion it's resolved that Martie, Sylvie and Becca will sleep in the room. The room on the other side is taken by Alix and Don. Attracta insists on a room on her own.

'I'm surprised' says Sylvie. 'After what happened to you at Strawberry.'

'Yeah, the jury's still out on that one' says Attracta flatly.

Don bristles. 'What does that mean, Attracta?'

'It means anything you think it means' says Attracta lightly.

Sylvie and Martie help Attracta pick her room, although she tells them both she doesn't need their help and basically doesn't appreciate it. Don throws her sleeping bag into the room and doesn't hang around.

'Who's going to help me bring in the food?' asks Sylvie.

The kitchen is located behind the central staircase.

'This is disgusting' says Sylvie. 'Are there cleaning supplies somewhere in those boxes?'

'Hope not' says Alix. 'I'm hungry and I don't fancy filling up on cleaning supplies.'

'Here's something' says Martie.

'Oh thank heaven' says Sylvie, opening a bag. 'Washing up liquid. Windowlene. Bleach for the toilets.'

'You think there's toilets?' asks Martie innocently. 'I reckoned I'd simply stick my arse out the window. Like they did in medieval times.'

Sylvie thrusts the bleach into Martie's hands. 'I saw a toilet next to the staircase. Give it a scrub.'

Martie takes the cleaning items but doesn't move.

'What, Martie?'

'Why are we trying to bring civilisation here? Isn't the point that we're surviving like in the jungle?'

Sylvie frowns. 'They were supplied. Therefore we must be required to use them.'

Martie shrugs and moves to the door. 'Just wondering' he notes before leaving.

Don walks the entire corridor of the Gothic section, pushing open doors. Some are set up as offices. A couple might have been store rooms although he doesn't look at what may be left under fifty years of dust.

Returning to the entrance hall he walks behind the Tudor staircase on the left and pushes open the door to a vast reception room.

'Here's the sitting room' he shouts to no one specifically. After a minute Attracta appears.

'You shouted?' she asks.

'Nothing. This is the hang out room.'

'Anyone who wants to hang out here is welcome' responds Attracta. I'm going to find the attics and the cellars.'

'What are you trying to prove?' snaps Don.

'You're afraid, aren't you?' says Attracta, somewhat surprised. 'You're shitting yourself.'

'I'm cautious. I'm concerned Carl's not going to play fair.'

Attracta laughs harshly. 'You need to catch up, Don. There are no rules here.'

Nevertheless, the group meets in the kitchen, where Sylvie is doing her best to bring the values of suburbia to the years of stubborn grime. She has found a battered old-fashioned kettle, the kind you put on a ring to heat hot water. She has lined up an assortment of chipped mugs and now makes tea for the group.

'The damaged crockery is a nice touch' notes Becca. 'Nothing says you're living in a haunted house like chipped mugs.'

Being Becca, no one responds. Later Martie says much the same thing and the group spontaneously chuckles.

'So are we going to have cooks and formal shit?' asks Attracta. 'Coz I'm thinking we should all see to ourselves.'

'I think anyone who wants to function on their own is welcome' says Sylvie. 'But I am happy to cook for more than myself, if it's reciprocated.'

Martie, Becca and Alix agree to this, while Attracta and Don say they'll see to themselves.

There is a ruminative silence. Martie looks round the group, feeling suddenly sad that they are no longer a team.

'So, should we go round the group and say something they do which really pisses us off? You know, would that help with the alienation thing?'

'I'll go first' Attracta jumps in. 'Martie, I hate that you're such a twinkie twat.'

Martie laughs, then stops. 'Are you serious? Wow, harsh.'

'I think Alix raped Attracta' says Becca. 'I haven't wanted to say anything but now I guess this is my chance.'

Alix's face is thunderous. 'Maybe you raped her? You seem to fancy her enough.'

'Oh that's ridiculous' snaps Becca.

'Yeah? That BJ you gave me was about the worst ever. You definitely don't know how to please a man.'

'I am not going to sit around for this' says Sylvie. 'I'm going to go for a walk before it gets dark.'

'It's dark already' says Martie and they stare out the filthy window.

'You all heard Carl. It's a fight to the death against each other.' says Attracta. 'I'm the only one who's taking it seriously.'

'I'm taking it seriously' says Becca.

'Piss off Becca. You know what I hate about you? Whenever I turn round you've got your tongue up my butthole.'

Becca pulls back, genuinely offended. 'You're so two-faced. You think you're going to get Carl? He's laughing at you.'

'He's laughing at all of us' says Alix. 'We're a bunch of jokes.'

Don has been looking through the provisions.

'Is this everything?'

'Everything I could find in the truck' says Alix.

'There's not a lot here. Not like at the manor. It's like Carl's looked at us and calculated how many people per day. And each day we'll need less.'

'Yeah, well I don't mind starving for a couple of days when I've got a three million pay out at the end of it.'

'You know what I loathe about you, Alix?' asks Attracta.

Alix sighs. 'You can't say anything to me I haven't already been called at school.'

Attracta hesitates before speaking. 'You're always trying to fit in with the rest of us.'

'No I'm not' says Alix, 'I'm just being Alix.'

'Yeah' says Becca, 'he's right. You're very pretty, Attracta, and it makes me sick to see how men look at you. But you have the personality of a brick wall. A crumbling brick wall that boozers piss on.'

Attracta laughs harshly. 'Is that the best you can do?'

'No, I can do this as well.' Becca walks over to Attracta, her hand raised. Thinking Becca is going to slap her, Attracta lifts her hand to protect her face, and Becca punches her in the stomach. Attracta gasps and bends over. Don laughs. Sylvie grunts loudly in disapproval and she and Martie leave the kitchen.

Becca turns to Alix. 'Come on, Alix, let's go practice BJs'. They exit, leaving Attracta clutching her stomach and Don watching.

'She really hurt me.'

'So leave' says Don. He watches her from a seated position, his expression maddeningly affable.

Attracta shoots him a furious frown.

'You're not so clever' she says. 'If you were you wouldn't be with the rest of us.'

'True' notes Don. 'Only I do have the best chance of being the last to leave.'

'Not if I slit your throat in the middle of the night.'

'Attracta!' says Don. 'Can you keep it real?'

Attracta moves towards the door. 'All I can see is the money, Don. You have no idea how much I need that money. I will do anything. I mean it. So keep out my way.' Rubbing her hand over her stomach she grimaces as she leaves. Don takes his particularly chipped cup and throws it against the wall. The fragile pottery shatters into a dozen pieces and fall onto the floor. Don watches with something like satisfaction.

Although the whole group has gathered in the sitting room after the evening meal, the atmosphere is very different from that at Strawberry Manor. Alix in particular is angry with Becca because her suggestion of practicing BJs was her way of pulling his chain.

'Anyone experienced any supernatural phenomena?' asks Martie into hostile silence.

'I saw a flying coffee cup' says Don and there is a murmur. 'Only I was the one who threw it.'

'Can we be serious' snaps Attracta.

'Serious about what? There's been nothing.'

'Perhaps the negativity in this room is enough?' asks Sylvie. 'I know it's certainly more than enough for me.'

'What'll you do when it gets too much?' asks Becca. 'Off one of us like you did before?'

Sylvie doesn't reply although there is a sharp intake of breath from Martie.

'If I wanted to sit around bitching with a bunch of crapheads,' says Martie, 'I'd have visited my local gay bar.'

'Yes and that's something else I loathe about you' says Attracta. 'Always going on about being gay. Get over yourself.'

'Do me a favour, darling' says Martie to Becca, 'give her another punch in the guts for me?'

'Any time' replies Becca.

Don laughs. 'This is all very funny and very juvenile. But what's really going on?'

'We're waiting for the axe to fall' says Sylvie. 'And we're taking it out on each other.'

'Fuck off, murderess' says Attracta. 'If you don't like it, leave. We'll tell Carl you stayed the four days.'

'Yes' says Don. 'That's interesting. Why don't we agree, whoever leaves, the others don't say anything in their reports to Carl.'

'Can do. Won't he think it weird they've stopped making reports?' asks Alix.

'So if you leave' says Don, 'you have to leave your phone. As a last gesture of friendship. Or whatever you want to call it.'

'Leave a forwarding address' says Becca. 'And I'll send you a postcard from my villa on Ibiza.'

In the night Becca is dreaming that something is sniffing its way around the room. She forces herself awake and lies in her uncomfortable sleeping bag. By the faint light of the moon she can make out the crumpled shapes of Martie and Sylvie, dead to the world. Nothing else moves.

'Martie' she whispers. 'I'm dying for a piss. Come with me?'

She remembers the luxury of her en-suite at Strawberry Manor. Martie does not stir. She sighs, drags a cardigan around her bra and pants, staggers to the door and with snorts and giggles finds her way into the corridor. She can just about make out where the staircase is by the void in the middle of the bannisters. The only clean toilet, courtesy of Martie, is down the stairs, turn left, turn right before the kitchen. She grumbles.

Three treads down the staircase she becomes spooked by the stygian darkness below. She wishes she'd organised a torch. Also, the pressure from her bladder has become extreme.

With another giggle she dares herself to take advantage of being all alone in the middle of the night. She feels her way to the stair rail, pulls down her panties, and begins to send a stream of urine up and through the bannisters. It will land somewhere on the way to the kitchen, so she vaguely plans to rise first, so she can clean it up. If she remembers, and if she gets up first. Finishing she groans with relief and turns back up the stairs for bed.

Something blacker than the night seems to be in her way.

'Sylvie? I swear I'll clean it up in the morning' she mumbles. 'I'm a good girl from Jo'burg.'

The figure rushes towards Becca and before she can fill up her lungs to scream the force of impact pushes Becca far out and wide of the safety of the stairs. Then she plummets back down onto the treads with exaggerated force and tumbles downward swiftly. With each impact, each bang and jolt, there is less Becca left alive, so by the time she comes to rest at the bottom of the stairs she is only a rag doll, flopped out, limbs akimbo.

The figure takes its time joining her. There is no malice in the eyes, only a sense of doing what must be done. The door to the basement opens with an audible click. The broken body of Becca begins to move as the shadow drags it towards the basement, that hell hole with its potential way out through the windows, and its horrid contents.

Twenty-One Second Day

Attracta wakes in solitary less-than splendour and in the bathroom minutely examines her photogenic features. To her intense irritation one side of her mouth is beginning to lose its pout. She doesn't have the energy for a full warpaint, so it's a light mascara, rouge and lip gloss. When she enters the kitchen, warmly wrapped against the house's chill and its general hostility, she sees Martie, Sylvie and Alix.

'Becca's done a bunk' notes Martie. 'Buggered off and abandoned us.'

Attracta frowns. 'That's good isn't it?'

'I think it's sad' says Sylvie.

'One down and no argument' Alix chips in, playing with a cup of coffee. He gives the others a savage grin. 'Who's next?'

'Where's Don?' asks Attracta.

'He's somewhere in the house. The Georgian wing, to be exact' Martie clarifies.

'Once we get out of here' says Sylvie, 'I'm never going to go on a country house tour again.'

'I never have' says Attracta, with the honest attitude of one who's never seen the point of culture or anything that doesn't involve close proximity to wealthy sportsmen. She helps herself to the simple breakfast fare. 'Carl obviously puts all his energy and money into the first date. This is disgusting.'

'I don't usually bother with breakfast' says Martie. 'I'm only eating this toast and Marmite because I'm bored.'

'How can you be bored?'

'Because I'm missing all the comforts and benefits of civilisation!' cries Martie. 'And don't pretend you aren't either. Oh yeah, when the electricity goes out it's fun to sit with candles for half an hour. After that it's only a giant pain in the arse. At least at Strawberry we had a spa.'

'You don't know, maybe there's a spa here. Anyway, we've got the whole place to explore this morning.'

'Oh yeah, just as I wrote in my application: 'Loves country house exploration'' answers Martie sarcastically.

'What *did* we all put in our applications?' asks Sylvie. 'Serious question.'

'Serious answer' says Martie, 'who cares? We're here now.'

'You got out of the wrong side of the bed this morning' says Attracta, as she helps herself to coffee, carefully selecting the least chipped of the available cups.

'I didn't sleep in a bed' snaps Martie.

'And there's a mystery. When I came down this morning, there was a puddle of urine in the path to the kitchen.'

'That's interesting' says Martie. 'I thought I heard something sniffing around our room in the night.'

'But how could a dog get in?' asks Attracta.

'We could find out. Might be useful.'

'For what? If we start to keep pets?'

'If we have to get out in a hurry.'

'Why would we need to?' snaps Attracta.

'Actually I don't think I'm going to talk to you anymore' says Martie. 'You're turning into a real pain.'

There is a silence. Alix deliberately slurps his coffee.

'Sorry. It's Becca just going like that' says Attracta.

'You were the one who said no big goodbyes.'

'I didn't mean Becca' says Attracta quietly. 'I didn't think she could just go.'

There is another silence.

'So, what, we're acknowledging that the people here mean something to us?' asks Martie.

'Of *course* they do! You do!' says Attracta.

'Great. Some of us like you, too.'

At a noise at the door they look up and Don enters.

'You look grim' says Martie.

Don nods. 'Morning. I couldn't find her.' He takes coffee and a piece of toast.

'Where did you look?'

'All of the Georgian section. Half of the Tudor. Some of the rooms are really far gone, you need to be careful stepping onto those floors.'

'And you didn't find a spa?' says Martie lightly.

'There's the basement. I can't find a way down there.'

'Do we know there *is* a basement?'

'When we arrived, I saw half-windows that lined up with the level of the drive. There must be something down there.'

‘Okay so that’s today’s quest’ says Martie. ‘Find the basement entrance. Anything rather than have to braid Attracta’s hair.’

‘Do you know what happened to the front door key?’ asks Sylvie.

Don shakes his head. ‘The last I remember is locking up last night. I left it there in case someone wanted to … go stand in the moonlight.’

‘Well it’s got stuck.’

‘There must be other doors out.’

‘So that’s the second quest’ says Martie. ‘Find a door out.’

‘We were talking about Becca’ says Sylvie, leaving a space. Don nods.

‘Each person leaving will be a mystery. I’m presuming she sent a last report to Carl?’

‘Knowing Becca she’d have sent him a pic of her extended middle finger.’

‘Not if she wants her regular phone back.’

‘How do we feel about Carl having such power over us?’ asks Sylvie.

‘I guess that’s too late to think about now.’

‘I’m still curious. Why do you think Carl concentrated on a group of people who had already had supernatural experiences? Isn’t the usual group a blend of believers and sceptics?’

‘Maybe he wanted people who wouldn’t crap their pants the moment The Green Man appeared at the end of their bed?’ opines Martie.

‘Well, he slipped up with me’ notes Alix. ‘So much for his fancy criteria.’

‘We still don’t know one person’s experience’ says Martie. ‘Not that I’ve been keeping a book although I have. Don…?’

Don finishes his toast, knows the others are waiting, expectant, doesn't care. 'I'll tell you. When I feel like it.'

'Better do it before any more of us have had enough.'

The group splits into two parties. Attracta and Alix in one, the other three in the other. They comb the different periods of the enormous property. At one point Attracta nearly falls through a hole which appears to be a dark rug, and Alix has to grab her back to safety.

'Thanks! But you should have let me fall. Eliminate the competition.'

'Girl, I'd prefer to do that properly, not cheating.'

Martie taps the woodworm-ridden panelling of the Great Room in the Tudor section. 'If I had the time I'd investigate this whole room. I bet there's a proper secret passage somewhere in here.'

'Why don't you have the time? Asks Don. 'Thinking of leaving us?'

'I'm thinking of it' responds Sylvie. 'I don't think I can take another night lying on the floor in a sleeping bag.'

'There are some mattresses in one of the first floor Gothic rooms' notes Don, 'We could drag some into the dorms. Make it a bit more comfortable.'

'I don't get the feeling Carl wants us to be comfortable.'

'No,' says Sylvie in agreement. 'In my reports I'm stressing how terribly uncomfortable and unhappy we all are. I hope it's what he wants.'

'Sadist' mutters Martie, still tapping the panelling hopefully.

'Yeah, let's go overboard in our reports' says Don. 'Make him feel sorry for us.'

'I don't think he's that sort of person' Sylvie responds. 'I think he's one of those 'artists'. The sort that used to let their family starve and die while they got on with the business of art. If it's a Wagner or a Modigliani, whose children died basically because they had no money, then fair's fair. Most of today's lot – let's say they shouldn't bother starving, art is not going to thank them.'

Don laughs. 'So where does Carl sit in your judgment?'

Sylvie considers. 'I'm not a fan of 'conceptual' art. If you need paragraphs on a piece of paper to explain what the artist is trying to do, I'm left cold. I've seen a couple of Carl's earlier works that I thought *were* interesting. I suppose it's just the enormous weight of competition. Everyone's trying to be the first to outrage public opinion, that sort of thing.'

'They've got dead bodies on display' says Martie. 'What next?'

'Actually I don't think they're calling that 'art' anymore.'

'I agree.'

The group moves from the Great Room, along a gloomy corridor, then into a series of empty rooms with dirty barred windows. 'I wonder how much this place would cost?' asks Martie. 'Wouldn't it be incredible to buy it, do it up, live in it as a commune?'

'Would you like to live with all of us?' asks Sylvie, in a light, happy tone.

'It would be incredible. I've often tried to share with someone else. It's always been disastrous. But here we already know each other.'

Don is silent as they continue to walk the corridor, pushing open doors and where there are other doors inside, investigating those doors as well.

'I once shared a house with two other people' says Don. 'I'm amazed we didn't all kill each other.'

'That would have been technically difficult' Martie drops in.

Don looks at Sylvie. 'You want to know my supernatural experience?'

'Yes, but shouldn't you wait for the whole group?'

Don frowns. 'I'm in a mood to tell you right now. Can't guarantee how I'll feel later.'

Sylvie smiles. 'We're listening.'

By now they have got used to testing where they're walking, and it's only Martie who at one point puts all his weight on wood rotten and treacherous. As the group ascends the far staircase up to the second floor Don speaks, his voice disturbing the graveyard quiet.

'So there were three of us. My best friend from Uni. An ex-girlfriend of his. I didn't know her but we kind of hooked up just on the first night. We were happy. Things weren't good, though, the rhythm of structure was missing. Phone messages were apparently left but I'd find the piece of paper only days later. Money went missing. I'd lie awake listening to Tess walking round and round her room, keeping me awake, pissing me off. Then she'd deny she even got out of bed during the night.

'And they'd keep having a go at me. My red socks got into Tess's whites washing.

Chris blamed me when I broke his computer accidentally. I was sitting down and suddenly it was under me and I sat on it.'

Martie utters an explosive laugh.

'Not funny at the time. Within six weeks none of us was talking to either of the others. We'd communicate through notes that mysteriously vanished. Even messages left on our phones were wiped before we could hear them.'

'So to summarise' says Martie, 'you were living in a haunted house.'

'One morning we were in the kitchen, carefully avoiding each other, and suddenly the big, old, wall cupboard just pulled itself out the wall and smashed onto the floor. You could see there were six-inch rawl plugs supporting it in the wall. We looked at each other and it finally made sense. Tess swept up the glass, Chris carried the cupboard out to the back yard, and I called the owner and crapped all over him. Turned out he knew it was haunted. He thought we wouldn't notice.'

The other two are about to comment when they become aware of a steady banging sound from a room still to be explored. They exchange looks and proceed cautiously. Inside the room there is a built-in cupboard. While they watch the door of the cupboard, for no apparent reason, flaps open and shut. Don crosses to the door and blocks it from closing. For a second he feels resistance, then the door relaxes in his hand. He shuts the door.

'Yes, it's no surprise this house is possessed' says Sylvie. 'But it's nothing like Strawberry. There I thought the laws of nature were entirely suspended. So far here all we've experienced is a cupboard door that swings by itself.'

'Maybe' says Martie, 'the house is saving up for something big?'

As he says this there is a series of crashes from the corridor that echo and are magnified by the carpet-less space. They return hurriedly and see that all the doors they left casually opened have shut.

'So it's tidier than we are' says Martie lightly.

'Or is it a warning?' asks Sylvie.

'Perhaps' says Don, 'it's telling us we are under surveillance.' He speaks loudly into the air. 'It's all right. We're not trying to harm you.'

Something invisible rushes towards them along the corridor, and Martie puts out his hand. For an instant he feels a terrible coldness then it passes and they sense it moving behind them and away.

'I think it knows we're not trying to harm it. I hope it feels the same way about us.'

Attracta and Alix have chosen to explore the 19th Century Gothic Revival section. Beginning with the corridor that contains their sleeping quarters they have discovered that, as with Strawberry Manor, arriving at the end of one corridor merely presents you with the next.

'It's like I once went biking in the Greek mountains' says Alix, as he and Attracta carefully negotiate crumbling floors and gaping holes in the wall. 'Every time I thought I'd got to the top there'd be another hill to bike up. Coming down was fantastic, though, I freewheeled for miles.'

As they approach a section of the corridor with a hole in the wall, Attracta experiences a chilling sensation.

'Alix, stop' she says and he obliges.

'It's just, I've got a feeling, I mean, the hairs are standing up on the back of my neck. I've got this feeling that when we go past that hole, something in that room is going to be looking back at us.'

'So what's the problem?' asks Alix. 'We saw worse at Strawberry.'

Attracta feels herself flush with rage. 'That was before I got raped!' she snaps.

'Sorry. Not trying to be a dick' mumbles Alix.

Attracta stays rooted to the spot in the corridor while Alix moves slowly towards the broken wall. By the end of his approach he is aware he is having to consciously push his feet to take another step forward. From behind him he hears Attracta gasp. He comes level with the hole and shuts his eyes. From behind Attracta hisses with tension.

'Can you see anything?'

'No.'

'What *can* you see?'

'Nothing. I got my eyes closed.'

'Alix, please!'

Alix opens his eyes. 'Nothing. I can't see anything wrong.'

Attracta turns round and starts retracing her steps.

'Wait for me!' shouts Alix.

'I'm not waiting!' cries Attracta. She hurries down the corridor while Alix follows.

'What's your hurry?' he shouts, infected with her panic. 'I didn't see anything!'

Returning down the main stairs they meet up with the others in the kitchen.

'They do call the kitchen the heart of the home' notes Sylvie, who has already prepared tea for five.

'Food gives us energy' says Martie. 'Food equals love.'

'Sylvie gives us love' says Don, in a strange tone, and everyone looks at him.

'Sylvie, you're a fine woman' says Don as he takes his tea. The others exchange looks.

'Aren't you going to say something back?' asks Martie. 'I know I would.'

Sylvie makes sure everyone has a cup before she responds.

'Thank you, Don. I know you mean that sincerely.'

'Oh, you two, get a room' says Attracta with irritation.

'No thank you' says Sylvie. 'I did have a man I loved very much. Unlike many women today, I don't think one's emotions can just be shifted from one person to the next.'

'Swans mate for life' says Martie, as though this is relevant.

'I'm not happy' says Sylvie, lifting her cup. 'But I'm content. Most of the time. I've learned that violent emotions don't suit me well. They only lead to … disappointment.'

Attracta laughs harshly. 'Shame, Don, turned down for the first time in your life.'

'Shut up, Attracta' says Don evenly, as he takes a sip of tea.

'You lot are just like my extended family' says Alix and laughs. 'I've never been to a family gathering where there wasn't a punch up. Police attendance. Ambulance.'

'I've never been to a family gathering where any of that *did* happen' notes Martie. 'Can I hang out with you afterwards?'

'So you didn't find a door out?' asks Don of Attracta and Alix. They look guilty, then shake their heads.

'What?'

'Attracta got spooked by a hole in the wall.'

'Alix went to investigate. First he shut his eyes' says Attracta.

Don frowns. 'So there could be a door out?'

'Yes of course. We've still got whole sections we haven't explored.'

'Is anyone the slightest bit alarmed that we don't seem to be able to leave the house?' asks Sylvie, in a more than slightly alarmed tone.

'Be cool' responds Don. 'Of course there are doors out. It's a huge place and we haven't seen half of it.'

'Yeah, just a heads up, the Tudor part is definitely haunted. Slamming doors mainly' says Martie prosaically.

'I need to lie down' says Attracta. 'We can swap sections and do more exploring later.'

'Also we finally discovered Don's secret. He shared a poltergeist with two friends.'

'How did that story end?' asks Sylvie.

Don nods. 'We threatened to report the landlord to the Rent Board for non-disclosure. He cut us a deal and we left a couple of days later. Never spoke to Chris or Tess again. Something about the intimacy of what we'd experienced, and how we thought it was each other …' he shrugs. 'Some things don't last.'

'But we will?' asks Martie. 'We'll all meet up again. If I'm the last I'll definitely throw a party.'

'You sound desperate' says Alix with a grin. 'Don't you have friends of your own?'

'Of course' says Martie. 'And I'm not dissing them. But this is different.'

‘I thought we were supposed to hate each other?’ asks Attracta. ‘You don’t seem to like me much.’

Sylvie laughs. ‘You make me laugh, Attracta. Your attempts to break us up were so transparent! Family will always overcome differences in its members.’

‘But you’re not family’ says Attracta.

‘Who’s to say?’ asks Sylvie.

‘My family is me and my mum’ says Alix. ‘Plenty of room for more.’

‘Stop it! Shouts Attracta. ‘This isn’t helping!’

She storms out the room. Martie turns with a grin to Don and asks, playfully, ‘Should I go after her?’

‘Definitely’ says Don. ‘It’ll really piss her off.’

‘Anyone up for more exploration?’ asks Alix. ‘Cause I’m with Sylvie. I need to feel I can get out of this place.’

‘If the worst comes’ notes Don drily, ‘we can always throw a mock Tudor chair through a genuinely Tudor window.’

‘But in the meantime, lead on with the exploration.’

This time Sylvie and Don form a group, and Martie and Alix.

In her solitude on the first floor, Attracta listens to the feet shuffling past her door. She realises it would be a good moment to ask Don or whoever to bring her back a proper mattress, so she jumps up from the sleeping bag and opens the door. The corridor is empty. She grunts with irritation and returns to her bed. After a heartbeat she again hears noises from the corridor.

‘Just go away and leave us alone!’ she shouts from her resting place on the floor.

The noises stop and Attracta experiences a chill of fear in her heart. The only sound she can hear is her own tortured, shallow breaths. Then the noises, which now sound more like something being dragged along the floor, continue, gradually fading as whatever it is moves further down the corridor.

'I'm not scared, you bastard' she whispers to herself. She lies down in the sleeping bag, knowing she will not sleep. Except she does. Partway through her rest the door clicks open and something enters and looks down at her.

Electing to explore the Georgian section, Don and Sylvie move logically through the various corridors, up a staircase and down another. Eventually they find themselves in a glass-enclosed conservatory, perched on the end of the house like a wart on a nose. There is a glass door to the garden which Don tries, and he grunts when it does not yield.

While Sylvie is looking to see if there are any windows that aren't locked, she feels a rush of wind behind her. Don holds a metal garden chair high above his head and crashes it into one of the many full-length glass panes. The chair bounces harmlessly off the glass.

'How thick can this glass be?' asks Don angrily.

'I wonder if that's not the problem' asks Sylvie. 'I wonder if the problem is the house doesn't want us to leave?'

Waking from a deep sleep, Attracta again hears footsteps in the corridor. She determines that this time she will either confront the noise or be reassured that it's one of the other inmates. She bounces to the door and throws it open.

In the corridor is the all-too fleshy figure of a man. He has coal-black hair, large dark eyes, a sensuous mouth and a fashionable five-o-clock shadow. He is tall, with particularly large hands and a powerful chest, semi-revealed by an open shirt.

'Sorry' he says. 'Didn't know there was anyone in this wing.'

It takes Attracta a second to adjust to the vision.

'No, my bad. But who the hell are you?'

'Sorry to startle you. I'm Merlin.'

Twenty-Two Second Night

Don and Sylvie decide not to alarm the others by reporting that it may not be possible to leave the house. There's always the possibility that the glass is specially strengthened and the cause is human rather than supernatural. They join in the mood of unspoken optimism for having got through the second day basically unscathed.

Attracta, too, has decided not to share her information. Once Merlin explained that he is a PhD student, allowed by Carl to live in the house while he explores its otherworld manifestations, Attracta finds she is amused to have a secret she can keep from the others. How convenient, she thinks, that she is already in a room on her own. Merlin has promised to return once the house has settled down for the night. For some time Attracta has been thinking that keeping herself for Carl seems to be a loser's game. If he had any interest in her he would have made it known before now. Instead he's been treating her no differently than he treats the others. And those chipped cups were the last straw.

'Who wants to try the front door one last time?' asks Martie. 'It's getting towards being a full moon. Nothing lovelier than a full moon in a country garden.'

'Unless it's a ticket out of this place' says Alix 'Cause that's what I'm dreaming about right now.'

'So I guess you're pulling out of the three million pound race? asks Attracta.

Alix frowns. 'What makes you think he's gonna pay?'

'Because if he doesn't' says Don, 'I'll strangle him with my bare hands.'

'And I'll provide your airtight alibi' adds Martie.

'My report today isn't very interesting' says Attracta. 'Do you mind if I borrow your account of the closing doors?'

'I certainly do' says Martie. 'But you're welcome to your account of Alix keeping his eyes shut.'

'Piss off' says Alix, not unkindly. 'You'd have done the same.'

'I don't know why it should be' says Martie, 'I just don't find visitations that scary. Maybe that's why my gentleman caller felt welcome.'

'Unless they're under the bed' Alix reminds him with a chortle.

'That's different. Haven't you seen *Drag me to Hell?* Everyone dies.'

'You're a major slut, that's why' Attracta responds. For a moment the image of Merlin, handsome, gentle and definitely eager, swims into her mind's eye. Perhaps it was the word 'slut' because she suddenly becomes aware of a warm feeling that suffuses her body. I've never believed in love at first sight, she thinks. My mum and her many boyfriends cured me of that illusion. But if Merlin turns out to be only a percentage of what I think I see in him I'm prepared to give falling in love another go.

'I'm not such a slut' returns Martie. 'I turned down Don, didn't I?'

Sylvie and Alix laugh.

Don frowns. 'Sorry haven't you got that round the wrong way?'

Martie coyly, deliberately, bats his eyelids. 'I bet you say that to all the boys.'

Don stands and begins to make for the entrance hall. 'I don't want you to get your hopes up, Martie. But I'm going to try and open the front door. So you can enjoy the moonlight.'

Except he can't. The door, even when nudged by a series of metal prongs and a hammer found rusting under the sink, refuses to budge. Don raises the hammer to one of the full-length diamond-pane windows.

'No, don't' says Sylvie. 'Not tonight. Do it tomorrow.' What she doesn't add is that there have been more than sufficient disappointments for one day. The consequence of discovering they really are enclosed in the house, and that no way out can be found, is too great to be contemplated when they are already exhausted by the combination of country night air and the atmosphere of Borley House.

'Is that you?'

A laugh whispers its way through the chill night air. 'Of course. Who else were you expecting?'

Attracta reaches for her torch and flicks it on. Standing near the door is Merlin. Already he is beginning to unbutton his shirt. Attracta experiences a deep sigh of satisfaction as he carelessly drops his shirt on the floor. She slips off her bra and pants while he, in an erotic echo of her, adds his pants and underpants to the discards.

'Turn it off' he requests.

'But you're so beautiful' she whispers, running an appreciative hand along one muscular shoulder. 'I want to drink you in.'

'I'm shy. Please.'

Attracta turns off the torch with a smile. She likes a shy man. She likes a man who enjoys taking orders. She grunts with desire as she feels Merlin's mouth moving down her own body. She feels his breath on her warm breasts, and giggles as he tucks his tongue into her belly button. Then he moves further down and she moans as his expert tongue probes the mysteries of her feminine parts.

'I don't do anal' she says after a minute, drawn to issue a warning by Merlin's eager, wet tongue, which having thoroughly explored her front is now snaking its way round the back.

Merlin halts for a moment, then she feels his warm breath whispering in her ear. 'You sure? I've got a thirst for you which needs complete fulfilment.'

'Not tonight' she whispers. 'There will be other nights, right?'

'Of course' he replies, thrillingly. 'Thanks for asking.'

He mounts her, easily finding places to support his heavier body as she writhes helpfully. She gasps as he pushes her legs wide and slowly inserts his length.

'Oh, oh I love you' sighs Attracta. Merlin stops and Attracta feels a deep tingle of irritation.

'I mean, I love *this*' she mutters.

'I don't mind if you love me' sighs Merlin, again resuming his loving rhythm. 'I'm pretty much falling in love with you myself.'

Attracta has always needed to hold back her emotions. From her pin up days she's known her chief asset, her only asset in the world, is herself. Her physical self. She's deliberately forced herself to make love to a series of men who, to put it kindly, were not her physical match. And where has it got her? So desperate that she's willing to spend days shut up in a haunted house with a bunch of virtual strangers. Yet if she hadn't come to Borley House she wouldn't have met glamorous, handsome Merlin. She wouldn't be lying under him now. She wouldn't tell anyone in the world, because knowledge is power and she doesn't like anyone to have power over her, but Attracta has never experienced an orgasm. She has never let go enough, has never been sufficiently titillated by the sexual act to understand what it is her friends all talk about in awed and boastful descriptions.

Now, feeling Merlin's perfect understanding of the needs of her body, while he ensures he also extracts maximum enjoyment from his pelvic actions, Attracta feels entirely feminine. No longer just a good package on the outside, she finally understands something of what Don meant when he praised Sylvie for being a fine woman. After tonight, thinks Attracta, I finally get all that can pass between a man and a woman.

She gently pushes Merlin off his position on top. He grunts and slides athletically to lie next to her. She allows him to kiss her breasts, to bite her nipples gently, caressing their arousal with her finger and delighting in the savage ecstasy of sexual bliss. She feels him tuck himself between her open thighs and leaning forward so he can continue to make love to her breasts, she finds his manhood with her fingers and slides him into her. They both grunt in erotic fulfilment.

As she enjoys Merlin's powerful hands playing tenderly with her breasts, Attracta feels something wet and moving next to her thigh. She grunts. It feels like someone has slipped a wet sponge into the bed. Automatically she reaches for the torch. At the last moment Merlin realises what's coming next, and he tries to stop her.

The light clicks on. Illuminating from Attracta's viewpoint that the man who lies beneath her is … rotting. The wetness between her legs is his body in partial dissolve. Here and there bones are showing through the flesh, and when with horror she turns the light to Merlin's face she sees not only the desperate regret in his eyes, but also how the flesh is falling off and the mouth hangs to one side. The teeth, robbed of their fleshy covering, glint in the light in a rictus smile.

Attracta screams and Merlin places a hand in front of her mouth. She can see the bones in the fingers.

'Ssssh… Please…' he begs. Attracta watches in terror as he slides out from under her, collects his clothes and shuffles to the door. She is now stricken into silence, unable to even gasp in sheer horror. At the door he turns and gives her one last look of infinite regret and apology. She sees the flesh on his arm is falling off, exposing the bone. The trunk-like thighs flop over, exposing tendons and arteries. Merlin's corrupted hand reaches out and he opens the door, steps through, and closes it.

Attracta sits paralysed with shock for a few seconds before she forces herself to her feet and throws open the door. Outside there is nothing. Just the eerie glow coming from a window further down the corridor, throwing long, pale beams of light.

A minute later Don, now with a soiled mattress underneath him, sleeping contentedly in his sleeping bag, discovers he has company. Attracta and her sleeping bag have bundled up next to him.

'Attracta? What the hell?'

'I'll explain in the morning.'

Don begins to feel his way around the slender physical form that is now cuddling up next to him. He can feel her trembling. His one hand begins to rub Attracta's back, while his mouth seeks out the rest of her.

'Can we just sleep together? Please?'

Don grunts. He turns over, pulling his sleeping bag shut. After a minute Attracta hears his steady, rhythmical breathing. It takes her a lot longer to get to sleep.

Twenty-Three. Third Day

Tastelessly ingesting another desultory breakfast, the group is aware that Attracta is particularly lost in her own moody thoughts. They don't much care, they're also examining their own inner worlds and not finding much joy.

'I want the hammer' says Alix suddenly, picking it up and weighing it in his hand.

Don looks at him. 'Fancy a slice of group slaughter?'

'No way, bro' says Alix seriously. 'I'm gonna find our way out of this place.'

'I spoke about it at length in my report to Carl last night' says Sylvie. 'I've told him it's too much. That if he doesn't get us out in the next day I'm going to be pressing charges of kidnapping.'

'That's incredible' says Martie. 'It's like I'd completely forgotten there's actually a world out there, with rules and policemen and right and wrong. You're right, Sylvie. This is beyond whatever he's up to 'artistically'. This is depriving us of our freedom.'

'I bet the one who gets the three million won't bitch' notes Attracta, suddenly breaking her silence. 'It'll only be the losers who have a problem.'

'I've asked Carl to meet with us tomorrow' says Sylvie. 'I've told him if he doesn't, he'll be in a lot of trouble. He's an artist so his reputation is extremely important. I think he'll play ball.'

'What shall we do today? Press flowers? Make scrapbooks?' asks Martie.

‘I’m gonna find a way out of this house’ says Alix. ‘Oh, you’re messing with me.’

‘Not at all. Same thought. I’ll come with you. Coming, Attracta?’

She shakes her head. ‘I’ve seen enough of this place.’

Which leaves Don and Sylvie to make up the other team. Martie swirls some water around his and Alix’s breakfast things before heading up the staircase into the Georgian wing.

‘Are you planning on mixing a cake?’ asks Martie. Alix glares. Martie points to Alix’s hand, where rather than the hammer he is holding a large wooden spoon. Alix mutters an oath and begins to return to the kitchen.

‘Wait for me’ he says over his shoulder.

‘Catch up’ says Martie.

Alix strides into the kitchen and with a scowl throws down the spoon and snatches the hammer. The others look up but he doesn’t explain. He strides out, enjoying the stamp of his boots as he crosses the entrance hall and pounds up the stairs. At the end of the corridor he can see Martie just disappearing through a doorway, a door swinging closed behind him.

Alix pushes the door open and finds a further staircase going up, and one going down. He sees movement on the staircase rising to the second floor. Weird, he thinks, Martie must think there’s a way onto the roof and maybe down a metal fire escape? At some point this place must have had to comply with regulations. A fire escape makes perfect sense.

‘Wait’ calls Alix, but it seems as though Martie either doesn’t hear him, or he’s intent on finding that fire escape. Alix wants to explore the rooms behind the various half-open doors he passes but he can see Martie, always ahead, always too far to call back. So he hurries on.

Alix gets to the end of another corridor. There are two further doors in front of him. He pushes at the one but it doesn't give so Martie couldn't have gone that way. He turns the handle of the other and it also won't give. Alix steps back, puzzled. Then he sees an alcove. Inside the alcove is the access to what looks like an attic. And a ladder.

'I hate attics' mutters Alix. 'They're as bad as basements.' From his generous stock of horror movie memories he's thinking particularly of *Black Christmas* and the terrors in the attic. Literally everybody died.

Still it looks like Martie went that way, so Alix tucks the hammer into the belt of his trousers and warily climbs the shaky iron ladder. At the top Alix can see virtually nothing. There are no convenient attic windows, yet he can make out the dense shadows of beams, a sense of a restricted ceiling, a dark movement in the corner.

'Shit, man' says Alix. 'I thought you knew of a way out. This is pathetic.'

The figure in the corner moves and Alix sees that there is another dark void beyond the present room.

'What good's *that* gonna do?' he asks, sighing deeply. Some noise from the void indicates that Martie is exploring. Alix removes the hammer and clutching it in his right hand he feels his way towards the void. As his eyes get used to the gloom he can see Martie, moving around inside the void.

'Bruv' he says, 'I can't see no fire escape. Come on I'm going back.'

The figure is still for a moment, then it rushes towards him.

'Watch it, you'll knock me over!'

A second later Alix begins to feel very strange. It's as though the thick air in the wretched space is becoming heavier.

'Martie, help me. I think I'm having a seizure…'

Alix knows about seizures. His auntie used to suffer with them. Alix used to watch her, his eyes wide, seeking concealment behind his mother while his father attempted to wrestle the aunt to the ground, and force a spoon into her mouth so she didn't swallow her tongue. The heaviness in the space causes Alix to fall to his knees. He reluctantly acknowledges that he is not sharing the space with Martie.

'Please … leave me alone' he whispers, feeling the weight pressing down on him from all sides. 'What have we ever done to you?'

Don and Sylvie elect to explore more of the Tudor wing.

'This place' says Sylvie. 'You could get lost in it for a year.'

'Not so' says Don, 'I was here yesterday and already I have a pretty good mental picture of how the rooms fit with each other.'

'I read the original purpose of houses of this size is so they would act as a mini-world, a controllable universe for the head of the house. So he can look around his subjects and know he is entirely in charge. I certainly don't think any of *us* is in charge.'

They move through the Great Room, with its magnificent diamond-pane full-length windows, to where there is a further, inevitable, corridor beyond.

'Yeah, I guess if you're actually frightened of the outside world, constructing a pile like this gives you the illusion of being invincible.'

'These terrible old houses' says Sylvie, pushing open the door of another room and entering. 'I suppose it makes sense in a time where each area had its own leader, its own mini-king, with his personal army. Nowadays of course they're schools, institutions or wrecks like this.'

The room is at least thirty-foot square. The walls are bare, polished stone.

'Why on earth would you need *another* room like the Great Room?'

'Could have been a private gymnasium, I guess?'

Returning to the corridor they encounter nothing more sinister than a clutch of identical, minor rooms, gloomy with only a small slit in the wall for a window.

'Let's go back' suggests Sylvie.

'Wait, I'm looking for something …' replies Don.

Sylvie watches as he methodically searches the rest of the rooms in the present corridor. At the end of the corridor there are the inevitable staircases and a choice of going up or down.

'I'm looking for something substantial enough to make a hole in the Great Room window' Don explains as he walks up the first treads of the one staircase and then down the first few treads of the other.

'I know we have to' says Sylvie. 'It's still a shame. That window has stood against the elements for three or four hundred years.'

'Then it should come apart nicely' mutters Don grimly. He spots something possibly suitable and tries to lift it. 'I can manage this.'

The item in question is an iron fire back. At some point it's been removed from a fireplace and subsequently abandoned. Don grunts with the effort of dragging it back along the corridor and eventually into the great room.

'It looks tremendously heavy' says Sylvie. 'Do you really think you can lift it and throw it through the window?'

'I'm prodigiously strong when I'm frightened' says Don and in answer to Sylvie's wild-eyed glance he gives a tight smile. Don psyches himself up to lift the fire back. 'I can do this, I can do this' she hears him muttering. She watches him, bending over the heavy iron, her heart suddenly pounding with tension and hope, then Don lifts the fire back in one graceful, focused action and assaults the window. Sylvie is amazed at the strength of force behind the thrust, yet the window doesn't move at all. Don cries out in frustration and the fire back smashes heavily into the wooden floor.

'Nearly!' he cries. After a minute's rest he tries again. When nothing happens this time either, even though Sylvie marvels at the even greater force in Don's assault, she waits until his breathing becomes more regular before offering a suggestion.

'Don't you think it would be more effective if there were two of you? I'm thinking of Alix.'

They return to the kitchen and Sylvie boils a compensatory kettle. Alerted by the noise, Attracta appears, holding a book, the cover of which has been ripped off.

'No luck?' she asks, accepting a chipped cup of tea from Sylvie.

'Not like you to read an actual book' comments Sylvie, not unkindly.

'I don't even know what it's about' Attracta responds. 'I thought it might distract me.'

Sylvie smiles sympathetically. 'Don has a plan. Have you seen Alix?'

At that moment Martie enters, and his first question is an echo of Sylvie's.

'Have you guys seen Alix? I thought he was behind me.'

'Oh really!' cries Sylvie. 'You let him get lost!'

'No I didn't. I thought he was behind me. I mean, I kept calling him to catch up with me, but he was messing around, opening doors and stuff. I didn't want to wait for him, so as long as I could hear him behind me… I found my way to some sort of workshop area, and there's a metal emergency exit door. I couldn't get it open so I was waiting for Alix. I could hear him coming towards me, I called out for him to help me … but …'

Martie is suddenly aware how strange that moment was. That one second he could hear Alix coming up behind him, and the next it was as though the footsteps were absorbed into the walls and disappeared like vapour out of a kettle.

'So he's not here?' Martie finishes, pathetically.

'No' says Don. 'And I think we have to face another truth.' He looks at Attracta. 'I don't think Becca left here either.'

Attracta thinks before committing herself to speech. 'So what are you saying?'

Don sighs deeply. 'I think Carl knows more about this place than we do. And I think he should have filled us in.'

'It's not like Strawberry Manor. There the manifestations were… honest. The ghosts wanted us to understand them. These ones are sneaky, they're hiding in the shadows. And they're different.'

'How different?' asks Martie.

'They don't like us' says Don. 'I think they mean us harm.'

'Carl has to get us out of this place!' says Attracta. 'He can't know what we're dealing with.'

'Oh' says Don, 'I think he knows exactly. We're suckers. He dangled a huge wad of money under our noses and we went wherever he led us.'

'And' says Sylvie, 'he's been terribly smart. First he chose people who already knew of the supernatural, so we were less frightened, more ready to take a chance. Then he softened us up with Strawberry Manor. There the ghosts are … adventurous, but they're not harmful. Then he dropped us in here. And now we can't get out.'

Attracta has taken out her phone and punches letters urgently into it.

'He can't treat us like this. I've had enough and I want to go.'

'Sweetheart, none of us can go. And it looks like we're now two down' he says, glancing at Martie, who frowns and looks away.

'Don't call me Sweetheart' says Attracta. 'You don't call Sylvie 'Sweetheart', you have respect for her. I am so tired of men taking advantage of me.'

Don's mouth turns down into a frown.

'I mean it' says Attracta. 'I was born poor and hungry. Our home was a shack and it was always cold. The water was cold, my bed was cold. Even the bloody ghost in that place must have been cold. And then I grew up and my body became a beacon of interest for men. And I played the game. But I don't have to anymore. I want that three million and then I'm finally going to be free of men and their demands.'

Sylvie murmurs something encouraging and Martie nods. 'Yeah. I mean I haven't experienced it like you have, but when you look interesting people tell you all sorts of inappropriate things and it makes me uncomfortable.'

'Like' says Don ''if only you were a girl?''

'Exactly' says Martie. 'It's dumb, I know, but it really does confuse me.'

'I've something I want you to know, Attracta. I didn't plan on ever telling you.'

Don pauses for a moment, Attracta frowns and regards him steadily.

'I'm sorry. It was me who raped you. I came in through the secret panel. I don't have an excuse. You pissed me off, but I'm not putting it on you. It was all my fault.'

Attracta pushes away from the table and looks out the grimy, barred, kitchen window.

'But it could have been a ghost' says Martie. 'I mean, if my experience is anything to go by.'

Attracta turns back to Don, her eyes blazing. 'If we get out of this place, Don Shaw, I'm going to the police and these people are my witnesses.'

Don nods soberly. 'I understand. You do know I only told you because I think we're all going to die in this place?'

No one speaks. Then there is a cry.

'Stop it!' cries Sylvie. 'Just stop it. Don I'm absolutely disgusted with you. How could you!'

'I don't even know why I did it' responds Don. 'I certainly didn't enjoy it. It was as though I was propelled into it. Maybe it was the house getting to me. I don't know. I'm glad I've told you, though. Although I know you'll hate me and I obviously don't blame you.'

'Is there anything I can do?' asks Martie of Attracta.

She stares at Martie with sad eyes. 'I'm unclean' she says. 'I'd love a hot bath. I'd die for a hot bath.'

'That I can help with' responds Martie. 'I think I've worked out how to turn on the bathroom boiler.'

Nothing much is said as Martie returns to the dormitory corridor to draw Attracta's bath. Attracta continues to look out the window. When she speaks it's not clear to whom she is speaking.

'Look. Sunshine. Clouds. Far in the distance on the other side of the valley I can see a row of cars. There's a red one and a blue one and a black one. Another blue one. A silver one. Trucks, I can see trucks. I miss Becca. She's the one who'd know what to do right now. She'd hold me in her arms. Now I can see three more silver ones. Where do you think they're going? Somewhere important? Or just wasting the morning? Do you think Becca knew what was happening? Or Alix? I can see a long, long truck, I think it's one of those refrigeration trucks. People get smuggled in those trucks, they die in there. Like us. This place is a giant refrigeration truck. And there's no way out. Except the way Becca and Alix have gone.'

Don and Sylvie say nothing. After a couple of minutes Attracta turns away from the window.

'I'm going to have my bath now.'

She leaves. Sylvie begins to go after her, then turns back and instead gathers the mugs for cleaning. Don sighs heavily.

'I have never been so disappointed by anyone' says Sylvie, with her back to him.

'It won't surprise you to hear I've heard that before' says Don. 'I think every woman I've ever known has ended the relationship with some variant of that.'

Sylvie turns to Don, her eyes blazing. 'Surely you could have fought the urge? You could have told us how you were feeling before it overwhelmed you? She was your friend, for God's sake! How could you?'

Don waits for the anger in the air to subside. 'All I can say is I'm sorry. And I will take my punishment.'

'I thought you were going to protect us' Sylvie finishes, her voice breaking. Then she wipes her hand and moves out of the room, towards the entrance hall.

'You shouldn't be on your own' Don shouts after her.

'Don't follow me!' she replies.

From some hidden recess Martie has found genuine bath salts. Perhaps the last time they were used is a dozen years ago. Certainly none of the house's more recent occupants would seem to be interested in a bubble bath. Attracta strips off her clothes and places a tentative foot in the water. She sighs with pleasure as her foot is surrounded by soothingly warm water. She slides into the bath, feeling the bubbles caress her flesh, sighing again as the next wave of warmth embraces her whole body. Only her mind remains alert, bruised, grieving and as the minutes glide by and she begins to drift into an unexpected sleep, even her ravaged mind is ready to temporarily let go of her distress so she can fully enjoy the sensuous bath.

'I mustn't go to sleep' she tells herself. 'Remember poor Whitney?'

A couple of minutes later she wakes up. The water is no longer as warm and the bubbles have dispersed. Also, although a few minutes ago the sun was shining, now dark clouds appear to have exerted their will over the sky, she can barely see the perimeters of the room, with its dirty, white, glazed ceramic tiles. She half rises to turn on the hot tap. She grunts as more deliciously hot water pours into the bath and leans back to enjoy the new influx. Again a few minutes pass while Attracta drifts between consciousness and dozing and the bath relentlessly fills.

With a start Attracta realises the water has risen above the safety hole. She pulls herself together and leans forward to turn off the water. The tap won't budge.

She calls out and the door opens. But what comes into the room is not one of her friends.

She feels pulled under the water. She opens her mouth to call out and water rushes in. She opens her eyes and from under a couple of inches of smothering water she sees something watching her dispassionately. Then there is a second figure. It seems to be … Merlin! Attracta succeeds in raising a hand out of the water and Merlin grasps it. Help me! Yet he doesn't help her out of the smothering water. He only holds her hand tenderly, in sympathy. Courage, the pressure of his hand seems to be telling her. Not long now.

Sylvie has been staring out of the window in the Great Room for some time. She hears a noise behind her and turns. Don nods and shoots her a grim look.

'I'm glad to see you' says Sylvie, which surprises him. 'I mean, I heard a noise and it could have been anything.'

Don again nods. He tries to lift the fire back but this time he does not have sufficient strength.

'Sorry' he says. 'Must be having a weak moment.'

'Where's Martie? Asks Sylvie, suddenly panicked. 'From now on we really must all stay in the same room!'

They both exit and begin to call Martie's name. They see movement on the floor above and looking up are relieved to see Martie. He's rubbing his eyes.

'I fell asleep after breakfast. Didn't mean to. What's happening?'

'We have to stick together now' Sylvie explains.

'Okay. Is Attracta with you?'

'She was having a bath' says Don. 'You know that.'

Martie looks at his watch. 'That was nearly an hour ago. She'll look like a prune!'

Martie turns back to the bathroom and the others mount the stairs. As they arrive they hear Martie scream. They hurry to the bathroom.

Attracta, naked, dead, lies under the water, her beautiful hair wafting around her like golden seaweed.

'She didn't do this!' cries Martie.

'No' says Sylvie in a no-nonsense tone. 'The water's not deep enough.'

Don pulls the plug and they listen to the water cheerily drain out. Don takes towels from the radiator and covers Attracta's body.

'You're surely not going to leave her there!' howls Sylvie.

'Of course not. First I have to think.'

'What's there to think about? We have to move her to a proper place.'

Don pushes his way past the other two. They return to the corridor where they discover Don, leaning against the wall in an attitude of defeat. As they approach he lifts his head and they are alarmed to see the surrender in his eyes.

'Don't you get it? Up till now they've been content to make members of our group just disappear. So we're still thinking, maybe we've got it wrong. Maybe they have actually got out and they're going for help. Now it's changed its strategy. It's not disguising its work anymore. It doesn't care.'

Don throws his head back, banging it painfully against the wall.

'It wants us to know.'

Twenty-Four. Third Night

'I believe Carl will come and get us tomorrow. The fourth day. That's what he said. He said four days was the minimum. He must be reading our reports, he knows how terrified we are in here. I'm positive. Tomorrow he'll come and save us.'

Don looks at Martie and lets out a deep breath. For the last hour Sylvie has been quietly yet audibly intoning different variations of these sentiments. Don reaches out and covers Sylvie's hand with his own. It works in that she stops speaking on the outside.

The three are seated in the kitchen. Wordless, Martie puts a simple meal in front of each of them. He then pours coffee into cups and places these on the top right-hand side of each plate.

'I know it's only a small detail in the bigger scheme of things' he murmurs to Don, 'but have you noticed we seem to have fewer and fewer cups and plates? Just now I was able to find only three.'

'Perhaps the house has a sense of humour' grunts Don.

The three eat in silence. At a couple of junctures Sylvie puts down her fork and stares into nothingness. Then Martie stops eating, picks up Sylvie's fork and gently but firmly places it back in her hand and Sylvie, mechanically, continues eating.

'I want to say something. Again it's only a small detail, historical actually, but …'

Don smiles at Martie. The ambiguity of their relationship has dissolved into a compassionate, mainly silent, sympathy which they couldn't really analyse even if they thought to.

'It's about… the manslaughter thing.'

Sylvie's evening meal comes to a natural end and she takes her plate to the sink. Martie takes his and Don's empty plates and does likewise. Then he turns to the others.

'I don't want doing the washing up to be a distraction. I need to tell you.'

Don nods agreement, Sylvie quietly retakes her seat.

Martie sighs. 'I was younger. A friend of mine gave me a lift home from the Edinburgh Festival. I knew he fancied me and I didn't want complications on the way. As we were starting off we saw this young bloke hitch-hiking. Blond, slim, attractive in a destitute kind of way. Simon, my friend, said he didn't want to pick up any waifs and strays. I was full of the wrong kind of energy and I insisted we stop and give cutie a lift.

'Back in London Simon dropped me off and went off with the hitchhiker, whose name was Neal. A few weeks later I caught up with what had happened next. Because Neal didn't seem to have anywhere in London to stay, Simon invited him to stay at his. Turned out Neal was bi, or at least open to offers. So then Simon's really happy, finds a flat for Neal, pays the rent and food and stuff while Neal's getting established. What does Neal do? Meets a girlfriend he must have found on a rubbish dump and instantly moves her into his new flat paid for by Simon. Simon doesn't mind, he sees Neal as more of a friend, or maybe a good deed.

'Girlfriend immediately gets pregnant. After the baby's born, Neal and girlfriend break up and girlfriend takes baby back to her mother. Neal invites Simon to visit his baby daughter and Simon is horrified. The mother is an alcoholic, the home is a slum, the girlfriend is a heroin addict, the baby is neglected. Simon tells Neal how horrified he is. Neal nods in complete agreement. Goes home. Hangs himself. Simon finds out and basically has a breakdown.'

After finishing his tale Martie sits with his head bowed.

'So it's all my fault' he says. 'Because if I hadn't pushed Simon to give Neal a lift, Neal wouldn't have had a flat to move the girlfriend into. She wouldn't have got pregnant. And Neal, incapable of managing his out-of-control life, wouldn't have killed himself.'

There is a pause during which Don and Sylvie exchange a look. Sylvie coughs.

'So it's about individual responsibility. And any culpability.'

Martie doesn't look at her.

Don leans forward, stretching out a hand so Martie can see it, even though he's looking resolutely down at the rough wooden surface of the kitchen table.

'Listen to me' says Don and Martie looks up at him.

'It's also about *intention*. Okay, so you were a bit crazy making your friend stop to pick up a hitchhiker. But did you do it knowing anything of what would follow? Of course not. So you're guilty of getting your friend to do something he was reluctant to do at first. But you didn't make him pick up Neal, or pay for Neal to go into a flat. It's a terrible shame that Neal couldn't make his life work, but if there's any blame, it's Neal's. And I think that's why Neal killed himself, because he knew it was his fault.'

'Have you seriously carried this thing around with you?' asks Sylvie.

'Not all the time' says Martie, 'but when Don said Carl knew there was someone in the group … It's been on my mind since then. That's why I wanted you to know.'

'But he was only messing.'

'Accurate though.'

'It brings up an interesting point, though' Don continues. 'Is Carl culpable for what's been going on here? If he genuinely doesn't know what's going on, then he isn't. If he sent us here knowing that this house is a whole different ball game to Strawberry Manor … then he's basically and essentially a murderer.'

'I think he does know' says Sylvie. 'In my reports I've been pleading for him to come and save us. He's not answering. Yet he must be listening to our reports.'

'Unless something's happened to him' says Martie. 'Wouldn't *that* be truly ironic?'

The three sit in silence, then Sylvie goes to the sink and washes the cups, which Martie dries.

'I'm dead tired' says Don, 'Sorry, that came out wrong.'

'It's the country' says Sylvie.

'It's this house' says Martie. 'I think it likes us to sleep. It likes us to be vulnerable.'

Before dinner the three had removed Attracta's body from the bathroom and laid it to rest on the mattress in her bedroom. They locked the door although none of them felt secure that the door would remain closed.

'Come on' says Don.

The three had also decided to present a unified front by moving Don's mattress into Martie and Sylvie's room. All three begin to leave the kitchen at the same time, so they arrive at the door together. Martie chuckles.

'Group hug?'

The three come together, feeling the simple, honest warmth of each other's bodies. They are conscious only of their individual breathing. Don looks down to Sylvie and lowers his head towards hers and they kiss. Then Don turns to Martie, and the two men kiss.

Then Martie breaks away. 'Thank you, I really needed that.'

He walks out the kitchen and the other two follow.

During the night Don wakes from a restless semi-sleep. The room is pitch dark and he can hear something shuffling around. Could be an animal. He lifts his torch from where he had carefully placed it, switches it on and shines its beam in the direction of the noise. Nothing there. He becomes aware of the cold night air and the silence in the room. For a minute he lies on his back, staring up at the invisible ceiling, then he grunts, rises, dresses.

A few minutes later he is in the entrance hall. Although the massive space is silent, Don imagines, or he senses, that the house is interested. It's watching to see what he plans to do. Don tests the front door but he cannot drag it open. He walks through the chiselled stone doorway into the Tudor wing.

Once in the Great Room, he observes how the moonlight is pouring through the many diamond-paned windows. He sighs, as though imagining how many, many nights the house has been like this. How at other times the room has been filled with people, furniture, paintings, life. And how now the moon's rays pick out the ruined floor, the mess of broken bits of furniture, the graffiti scrawled on the once-splendid, now broken and wood-wormed panelling.

'Okay' he says into the hushed atmosphere of the room. 'Okay, I'm here. You don't have to hunt me down. I give myself up willingly. I volunteer. I've only got one favour to ask. Let the others go. Take me. Let me be the last victim.'

There is a particular stillness, as though the house is seriously considering his offer. Don is somewhere in the centre of the room and now he lifts his arms and turns around slowly as though wanting to maximise his presence. Or perhaps to fully convey what an exceptional specimen he is, and how the house can do no better.

There is a creaking sound. No, not creaking, it's more like something being torn from something else. Don swivels to the direction of the sound, which is coming from the full-length windows. If he's right, then what is happening is the individual pieces of glass are beginning to tear themselves out of the lead surrounds that have held them together for hundreds of years. He hears two distinct kinds of sound, one a dull thud, and the other a high-pitched squeaking. For a moment a chill of fear more terrible than any he has ever experienced runs from Don's back, though his body and out his chest. He groans in fear.

The sound from the window becomes louder, more complex, as more and more of the individual panes appear to join in the exodus. Don feels a rush of cold night air, as though someone has opened a window.

Then the individual panes of glass, still as sharp as on the day they were cut, begin to drift through the air. They assemble some feet from Don, like a swarm of bees poised to attack. Don understands what is going to happen and he moans in terror. Yet he does not move.

Suddenly, as though each separate piece is responding to a central command, the individual panes all fly at great speed towards Don. His last thought is 'My God, it's the death of a thousand cuts' yet that is not quite accurate. The oriental form of torture and death is designed to last a long time, while here all the panes strike Don at the same time. For a moment he resembles an extraordinary glass porcupine-man, then there is nothing left of Don but a last sigh as what still remains of his lifeless body falls to the mouldering floor.

Twenty-Five Last Day

Sylvie lies in her sleeping bag. She becomes aware that Martie is watching her. He sits, clothed, on his own mattress.

'Good morning' she says out of politeness.

'Hi. Don's not here.'

'Oh.'

Martie turns his back as Sylvie dresses, then he stands outside the bathroom while she sees to her morning ablutions.

'The needs of human beings' she observes, on joining him in the corridor. 'I never would have believed I would be able to wash myself in the same room where a woman drowned. But we adapt, people, don't we? If something becomes too terrible, we just make room for it.'

In the kitchen they go about organising a plain breakfast.

'I suppose we should stop pretending that Don's somewhere in the house, investigating. Or that he got out the house and help is on its way.'

'I wasn't pretending' responds Sylvie. 'I said a little silent prayer for him on our way down the stairs.'

There is a pause until Sylvie sees silent tears sliding down Martie's cheeks.

'Oh my dear! Don't give way now.'

'I don't want to … scare you. If any of us was going to get out of here, it would be him.'

There is a silence.

'If you listen carefully' says Sylvie, 'you can hear the faint hum of trucks passing by.'

'I think about the open gates' Martie responds. 'I imagine walking through them, being on the road, getting far away from here.'

Martie is about to continue, then he stops. 'Don't stop' says Sylvie, 'no point in holding back now.'

'I was thinking how my life was pretty crap before I came on this. Now all I want in the world is my life. I don't care if the three million was a con.'

Sylvie laughs quietly. 'For me it was never about the money. It was an opportunity. Which was stupid of me.'

'You're thinking of Hailey?'

'I'm always thinking of her. My hope that all parts of the supernatural world… it was a naive fantasy.'

'Do you still hope Carl will rescue us?'

Sylvie puts down her chipped mug. Her face is grim. 'No. I have no hope now.'

'Oh, sorry, I wasn't trying to upset you!'

Sylvie takes her breakfast things and washes them. Martie watches her from behind.

'I was thinking of making a banner. Nothing fancy, just S.O.S.'

Without turning, Sylvie replies 'What will you use to make the banner?'

'Sheets? And, I don't know, try and find something black, like charcoal?'

Sylvie now turns to Martie, wiping her hands on a towel.

‘That sounds like a good idea.’

‘Do you want to help?’

‘No.’

‘I thought I’d try to find a way onto the roof.’

Sylvie looks at him. ‘Good luck on that.’

‘I don’t know what else to do! I can’t sit around waiting for the house to get me!’

‘I didn’t say you should’ Sylvie rebukes. ‘I even applaud your attempts to stay positive. I don’t want to make a banner. And then not be able to open a window, get through a door. I just can’t. I don’t have the energy.’

She pauses and Martie looks at her.

‘And I’m sorry it’s me standing here and not Don.’

‘Sylvie!’

Sylvie’s expression fuses grief, anger and terror. ‘I can’t do it anymore, Martie. I want to lie down and die!’

‘Don’t say that! I don’t want to be left alone!’

Sylvie’s expression softens. ‘Oh my dear, I didn’t mean that.’

‘I know I should want to be the last one standing. Then maybe Carl will come back. But there’s been too much loss, too much fear and pain. I’m going on because I’m too frightened not to at least try. Giving up would mean that I know none of us are getting out and that’s … I can’t do it.’

Sylvie stares at Martie a long time.

'I will help you with the banner. Who knows perhaps it will be easier than I imagine.'

Despite his terror Martie finds somewhere where he can still feel excited. 'Cool beans! I'll get the sheet!'

Sylvie takes in Martie's enthusiasm and it makes her feel sad.

'But first I have to do something. You can start and I'll catch you up?'

'Sure.'

She cannot explain to Martie, but the desire to keep looking for Hailey is suddenly so powerful she can only obey the feelings in her body, dragging her away to keep searching the house.

'Good luck.'

Martie's expression drops. 'Something's happened. You're not going to help?'

Sylvie smiles absently and walks out the door. Martie continues to sit at the table. He suddenly wonders if he is in fact rooted to the chair. He discovers he can move his arms yet he still feels a strange torpor when it comes to leaving the room. He manages to make himself another cup of tea which he sets in front of him and watches grow cold. Then for a long time Martie doesn't move, as though by staying still forever he can prevent the house seeing him.

'I know you're there' says Sylvie. She has crossed the entrance hall and made her way into the Georgian wing. 'I know you watch us. How strange you must be. We really aren't very interesting. People, as individuals, usually aren't.'

Sylvie walks to the end of the corridor and hesitates. There is a staircase leading up and a second leading down. She takes the staircase going down.

‘What will you do with your days when we’re all dead?’ she asks, not expecting a reply. ‘I would have thought you’d have had more fun keeping us alive. Like mice in a laboratory. Won’t you be lonely when the last of us has gone?’

She reaches the bottom of the staircase and looks around for her next destination. She sees an entirely new wing, somehow built around the side and rear of the property. She holds up a pointing finger.

‘Should I go this way now?’

She pushes open several doors. The light down here is not good. There are indistinct shapes, probably furniture covered with cloths or blankets. She politely closes each door she opens yet when she turns round at one point most of the doors are ajar.

‘Am I the only one who knows how to shut a door?’

She is aware that the house seems to be taking her in, perhaps coming to a decision. She hears a definite sound. A child.

‘No’ she says. ‘You can’t fool me. I know Hailey isn’t here. You’re just trying to trick me.’

For a moment she considers if she can make her way back to the relative safety of the kitchen. Yet she suddenly feels overwhelmed with debilitating fatigue. She honestly doesn’t believe she can move much more than a few yards. She hears the voice again. Definitely a little girl.

‘You’re pathetic. I mean, I’m sad. I came here to try to make contact with Hailey. Now I can see that is impossible. The best I can hope for is that where I’m going, I will find her. That would be wonderful, truly wonderful.’

She remembers the man she killed. Perhaps it’s him that’s waiting for her in this house. No, that wouldn’t be justice. Justice is on her side.

She pushes open the door of a room. It is gloomy, having to contend with both small windows and half-drawn curtains. Yet it is still light enough to see that there is something in the room.

'Hailey? No, darling, I don't believe it. You're not really here. The house is trying to trick me. You're a rotten house! You're appalling!'

The little figure in the room remains where she is.

'Whatever you are, I want you to know that I don't appreciate your playing with my heart. I think you should use your time and energy better.'

Yes, she is aware that she is talking to a house. Yet reality and sanity, and boundaries and madness, are all mixed up in here, and who on the outside can understand what those inside will say? How they will step from moment to moment, propelled by their inner terror and the always imminent possibility of death?

'I'm going now. I'm going to help Martie with the banner. I was a fool to come here.'

The little figure in the room holds her arms out. Sylvie speaks, her voice cracking with emotion.

'Hailey? Oh darling, is it really you?'

What Sylvie knows is that she is willing to give her life if she can, even only for a moment, hold Hailey. She doesn't care if the house is tricking her, if she can only hold Hailey, or the essence of her, the feel, the smell, one last time, then the house has given her something she has found nowhere else. Feeling a mixture of uncertainty and hope, doubt and sudden joy, Sylvie steps into the room and away from her grief and guilt. Her arms reach out for Hailey, as the little girl's reach out for her. Between them is a dark shape which Sylvie, her attention distracted, briefly registers as a dirty rug. It is only when she steps on the 'rug' that she realises it's a hole in the floor. Sylvie is propelled through the open void, and through the space below. Time slows down so distinctly, and the fall is so great, that Sylvie has time for a number of thoughts before her body hits the concrete floor. Her head lands a micro-second after the rest of her before also slamming down onto the concrete. It would appear that after all conjecture and imagination, philosophy and betrayal, the ultimate reality is gravity.

Martie has brought a sheet from upstairs and laid it on the kitchen floor. So far he hasn't been able to find anything useful to write with. He turns from another fruitless search of a dusty cupboard and reaches for his phone.

'This is Martie. This will probably be my last report. It's been a couple of hours since I saw Sylvie. So I suppose she's also dead. That makes me the last person alive, which means, you bastard, that you owe me three million.

Oh, except I forgot. I'd be stoked if I could just walk out the door but as you know, we can't do that. So technically you don't owe me the money yet. Morally, *of course, we both know you do.*

Sylvie and Don and I have been talking about intention. Intention and culpability. Turns out I'm not culpable for my manslaughter because I didn't intend it to happen. Is that the same for you, Carl? Or have you known all along what would happen? Like all good employees we've been trying to work out what the employer is up to. It's sad that the others won't ever have a chance to fully understand what all this shit show is for.

Sylvie hoped that since today's the fourth day you'd come and get us. I think when someone finally shows, they're going to find dead bodies in most of the rooms. I hope, when you find mine, that I've got enough life left in me for me to sit up and punch you in the face.

You're a total son-of-a-bitch. You've murdered a group of decent people. I hope one day someone does something similarly vicious to you.

So now I've nothing left to say except goodbye and on behalf of all of us I curse you. I really do. I really hope you suffer.'

Martie switches off the phone. Of course, he thinks, I don't really want him to suffer. What's the point in that? All I can hope is he's as haunted by what he's done to us as we've been by him.

Martie ponders if he should do the same as the others and go looking for his destruction before it comes to find him. He is still reluctant to leave the kitchen and he slowly rinses his chipped coffee cup. As he places it in the drainer he notes that there are no other cups. For an instant he wonders if he should throw his own cup at the wall, as Don did. Instead he dries it with a cloth and puts the cup away carefully on a shelf.

His ears twitch as he hears a sound. The sound grows. It could be the sound of someone trying to open the front door from the outside. With a wild cry of hope and happiness, his eyes spontaneously filling with tears, Martie tears out of the kitchen and into the entrance hall. The sound indeed appears to be someone trying to open the door from the outside.

Martie runs to the door, pulling at the huge brass handle.

'I'm here!' Please don't leave! Push! Push!'

The door is suddenly flung wide open. The centuries of wear have worn a groove in the flagstones and the door flies open so swiftly and brutally that Martie is unable to move his foot in time. There is just enough space between the groove and the bottom of the door for Martie's foot to be agonisingly wedged in between. He cries out. At least the newcomer can help. Yet when he can see through his tears

Martie perceives that the door has opened, but there is no one on the outside.

With another cry of agony Martie rips his foot from underneath the heavy door. He no longer cares that it seems the house itself opened the door, all he can see is the driveway, sunshine, freedom. He puts a little weight on his broken foot and cries out in agony. He will have to drag his leg up the driveway. The door remains seductively open and innocent as Martie painfully drags and crawls his way, each step taking him just that little bit further from the horrors of Borley House.

As Martie hobbles the last turn of the drive he can see the wide-open main gates. He can hear the sounds of cars on the outside road. Of all the thoughts that could enter his mind, Martie is thinking that he wishes he hadn't been so condemnatory of Carl in his last report. It might make it a bit harder to prise the three million out of him. And that, of course, is his main motivation for ignoring the screaming flesh of his injured foot, as he drags it one step further from hell, towards the everyday bustle of an ordinary country road.

Martie is only about thirty feet from the gates themselves when from in front of him he hears a deep metallic groan. With a stabbing fear he realises that the great ornamental iron gates, formerly seductively chained open, are straining to close. Martie attempts to move faster.

'No. You shits! I'm so close!'

With a resounding metallic snap the chains holding the gates back give way and individual links fly into the air. Martie is only half-aware of this as he summonses every last ounce of life energy from his tortured body, his only focus to breach the gap between himself and the gates before they can entirely close.

At the last second the gravel under Martie gives way and he falls to his knees. The gates continue to close, with Martie now trapped between them. He begins to sob as the gates join, squeezing out the life of Martie, now only a temporary block in their terrible progress.

Twenty-Six. Carl

Inside I'm laughing. On the outside I've got on my most serious, most dedicated artist face. The face doesn't lie, I am indeed passionate about every aspect of my art. I'm laughing only because in front of me, in this lovely boardroom encrusted with valuable art, some of it mine, are my three agents. My British, American and Other Worldwide representatives. I have treated them all to a highly exclusive preview of my latest artwork. And they have doubts. I'm not bothered by their doubts. I know they're just giving me a preview of how the world outside is going to react to my latest masterpiece. I fucking love controversy.

'Why don't you list your objections to the piece?' I ask. I have my hand over my mouth to stop from chortling as they solemnly whisper to each other, and jot notes on a piece of paper.

As I predicted, they have three main objections:

One. The artwork takes for granted the idea that there is such a thing as the supernatural.

Two. Apparently all the people who make up the raw material of the project are real. Or they were real, but now they're dead.

Three. No one has done anything like this before and labelled it art.

The subtext in this meeting is that we all know they are commercial art whores and they will take whatever I throw at them and make it desirable to that 0.01 per cent of the world's collectors with bottomless pockets. But they also have their 'reputations' and so they have to be able to tell said potential clients that we have fully discussed all the moral and ethical dilemmas posed by the work.

So I begin. I remind them of other artworks that have used dead bodies. They argue that the corpses in this artwork are dead only because they were trapped in a house and the house killed them. I agree. This throws them. I show them the material from Strawberry Manor. I show how *I did not know* that there was something so evil in Borley House that it actually killed them. They suggest that part of the artwork should illustrate this and I have to agree with them.

In fact, it's genius. The one aspect of my art that I've been wondering about is how I'm going to avoid being prosecuted for culpable homicide, or manslaughter, or whatever. No one has mentioned murder, of course, because it's obvious that the house killed them and not me.

I then mention the august name of Gerhard Richter, the famous German visual artist. They all mutter at this point because they'd all give their right ball to represent him. I remind them that one of Richter's more controversial works was separate portraits of nine young women. The women are smiling, friendly, these are college or family portraits. It's only when you read the commentary that you discover these are the nine Chicago student nurses who were murdered by Richard Speck in the 1960s. Richter didn't have to apologise for the strength of his art statement, and neither do I intend to.

Then they say they're worried about relatives launching huge financial claims for wrongful deaths. I deliberately laugh for about fifteen seconds which I know is really pissing them off before delivering my *coup de grace:* what each of the six has in common is they have no immediate family. There *is* no one looking for them, no one galvanised by their deaths to launch a financial claim.

The three look at me strangely. One of them asks if what I've not actually done is to carry out the perfect murder. Six perfect murders. That's when my eyes look their widest and most innocent. What had I got against these people? Nothing. I was perfectly prepared to give the last one to leave three million. It's just there were no survivors. In a way, I'm the victim: the house tricked me.

It's actually seven, if you include Merlin. Merlin was my guinea pig. If he'd been able to make his way out of Borley House in one piece I'd have paid him off and gone onto another artwork. But since the house, just as I suspected it would, did for him with grace and efficiency, I knew all I needed was to enlarge my original maquette and the participants would come running.

I'm sorry and kind of sad about them as individuals, of course. Sylvie looked like a decent person, the sort of old-fashioned-values woman I thought had died out a long time ago. I don't mean died out in a pejorative sense, I'm grateful to her as I'm grateful to all my co-artists. Attracta I've been feeling really bad about, of course. Under any other circumstances I'd have been glad to take her to bed, but since I had a different intention I didn't want to fuck her and then dump her in that house. I'm not a monster, I'm a serious artist and I know what feels right.

The guys I could take or leave. They each submitted interesting reports that, in what I'm billing as my tribute to them, I've been using to illustrate various aspects of the Art.

There's a bit more general discussion. I drop in that I've had several initial responses from avant-garde galleries and hugely wealthy individuals around the world. Originally, I tell them, I was tentatively thinking of a single artwork, but with the sort of enthusiasm I'm already getting, I can see a limited edition of say six art works will bring my Art to a greater audience. Here I can't resist openly smirking as I see pound, dollar, rouble and yen signs lighting up in their greedy, grasping eyes.

'Art is a dirty business, gentlemen' I say, gathering my papers to me and thus indicating the meeting is over. 'We must approach this particular artwork with more than usual sensitivity. Six people died. My artwork is their gravestone, their inscription. We must proceed with respect, always conscious that we are only servants of Art.'

Then I get the fuck out of there. In the toilet I pause long enough to ingest the last of some highly respectable Peruvian coke I scored off my best friend. That's what best friends are for, right? Flying again, I bounce out of the building. I could take a taxi yet it's a lovely evening and my house is only a few minutes away. Which is, of course, why I insisted my agents take space in such a convenient location. Mariah famously doesn't do stairs; I don't do geography. Just going out to Strawberry Manor took me away from my studio for far too long. Thinking of Mariah gets my mind going. Images of modern icons? But doesn't everyone think Warhol when they see famous faces? Maybe famous faces in a haunted house, kind of like *I'm a Celebrity, Don't Kill Me.*' Stop with the banal thoughts, Carl. Like The Beatles, your latest Art puts you in a bracket all of your own!

Remember that 60's French artist who canned his turds and labelled them as such? Art is the art of being the first, and once you're the first it doesn't matter what it is. Warhol made images of the electric chair, and auto accidents. People put them around their dining rooms. Although he didn't have sound.

My Art does. I call it *Invitation to a Haunting*. You enter a dark room. Whispers begin from hidden speakers. These are the individual voices, the early reports of the six. Then there's visuals. Here my famous eye for graphic images comes into play. By the end of the work, the senses of the audience are screaming, and early performances have shown that some of the audience are too. Even that I'm recording so on their way out the terrified audience can listen to how other viewers have reacted.

I'm a fucking genius. And of course I'm so far on the edge, I've created a whole new edge. No one is going to be able to manipulate human beings the way I have. If anyone tries they'll be sneered at as would-be-Raeburn. Copycats. No. I've fully arrived: this is my mature work.

Up till now I've battled my inner demons, those sneaky little voices telling me I'm only recycling the work of other artists. No one has ever used people like I have. It's like that story I once read about the magician who makes birds disappear. The trick is they're crushed in the secret bottom of the cage. Birds are cheap. No one in the audience expects that every show the bird dies. That's why I'm the successful magician. I don't mind they all had to die. I didn't even have to fork out three million. The bottom line is their reports from Strawberry Manor weren't exciting enough. It's perfect I could follow it up with Borley House. There the laughing well and truly stopped.

Carl is so caught up in his inner thoughts, his ongoing internal ramblings that someone who could hear it would call his inner cacophony or insanity, that he doesn't notice the parked car with the open boot parked virtually outside his home. He is talking to himself, laughing, approving his conclusions, when someone he vaguely recognises steps from the side of the car and approaches him.

'Carl. Can I show you something?'

The newcomer – who the hell is he? – smiles and indicates that there's something of interest in the boot. Carl, for all his many, many defects, is a passionate advocate of all forms of what he's happy to call Art. He imagines that the man has a painting to display, or perhaps a model for something bigger, or a bust modelled in clay, stone or marble. Anyway, he's feeling benevolent, having planted his feet firmly in Art immortality, and he can give a sucker a break. The shadow of the boot shades the inner contents, so Carl has to lean forward. He's about to turn, puzzled and pissed off, to the strangely familiar newcomer to complain that there's nothing inside when the newcomer violently lowers the tailgate. It knocks Carl unconscious and the newcomer speedily bundles Carl into the boot and slams and locks it. Then the newcomer checks the road for witnesses but being in a part of London where most of the residents are at one or other of their other homes, there is no one around to raise the alarm.

Twenty-Seven Glen

I turn into the driveway of Borley House. I note that the iron gates are again securely chained. I debate whether I should leave the car wedged so the gates can't close again but I don't want to carry Carl all the way up the drive. So I park near to the front door. Which is still conveniently open. I know something about how tricksy and deadly this house is so I don't yet go inside. Instead I haul Carl out the boot and slap him around till he wakes up. As he does I see his eyes widen. He can't do much in the way of movement, of course, because of the nylon cord around his hands and feet.

'What – who the fuck are you?'

'You remember me. I'm Glen Davis. I was there that night you invited the six you'd selected for your experiment. Only the whole thing made me sick and I left.'

I watch as Carl tests his bonds and see a look of cunning enter his dazed eyes.

'Glen, yeah I remember. It's not an experiment anymore, you know, now it's a fully-formed work of Art.'

I have to laugh. 'I don't know much about art. I'm a rugby man.'

'Art involves sacrifice' grunts Carl. 'You can say what you like about me, but I am a serious artist.'

'You're a conman. And a murderer.'

Carl considers this.

'How much do you know?'

I smile. 'Interesting question. Let's start with who I am. I'm Merlin's brother.'

The look on Carl's face changes. Now he looks seriously panicked.

'So, Merlin's brother, what are you looking for? Revenge?'

'Why would I need revenge? Unless you've done something to Merlin?'

Carl shakes his head slowly. 'I knew I made a mistake with the first one. He had an ex-wife. And, now I remember him saying, a brother…'

'I know *everything*.'

'That's crap' says Carl. 'Only way you could know is if you had all the tapes, all the reports. And I've been scrupulous. None of my assistants have heard everything on the tapes. I've hand picked a couple of early audiences so none of them were you. This morning, only my three agents. I doubt you were hiding under the table.'

I draw close enough to Carl to feel his breath on my skin. I hiss '*Merlin told me everything*.'

Carl pulls away from me. He looks up at the house. The Great Room on the left has lost its glass. Yet there are no faces staring out, no threat I can't talk my way out of, he so obviously thinks.

'So you must know how much I promised I would give the last person to leave the house. I'm gonna be totally honest with you, I'm that sort of person, I'm a very honest artist. I can give you the three million pounds. Technically I guess we could say you *are* the last person to leave.'

'Three million. Yeah, I thought that was a very interesting sum. More than a million, not so unbelievable as five. Well calculated, Carl. Perhaps that's your real strength as an artist. You know exactly how much the market can bear. You know exactly how much money sways a person. Makes them do very stupid things to themselves.'

'Look, I'll give it to you right now. Untie me and I'll transfer the three million from my account into yours.'

'And then what?'

'You let me go. You've got your share.'

'But what would stop me taking the money and then killing you?'

'Not everyone is a killer. Most people aren't. You're no killer. You're angry and right now you're probably a bit insane but you're not going to kill me.'

I pretend to think.

'Of course. You win. I'm angry but I'm not a killer.' I cut the plastic tie around Carl's hands. He flexes them and looks at me reproachfully. Then he withdraws his phone from his pocket.

'Now my legs' he says.

'After I get my money' I reply.

Carl scowls and presses a number of buttons.

'It says I'm trying to exceed my daily maximum' he says. 'My maximum is five hundred thousand. Even that was a bitch to arrange.'

I think. 'Tell me all the numbers I will need. I'll use them exactly six times. One time for each of your victims.'

I keep making him go over the numbers until I wear Carl down and I believe him when he gives me them one more time.

'What's to stop you changing the numbers when you walk out of here?' I ask.

'You can trust me.'

I can't help laughing at that, and Carl frowns.

'Now untie me.'

Instead I fireman lift him over my shoulder. Of course he realises what I'm about to do and he struggles, but I feel filled with the rage of righteousness and his fear makes him weak, while my anger makes me temporarily invincible.

I dump him on the floor of the entrance hall and glance around.

'Nice room. Too bad you didn't put some cash into doing it up. This is a shit hole.'

Carl looks wildly around him. He can't walk but he can crawl and he tries to crawl back out the front door. I laugh.

'Am I going to have to tie you to the bannister?' I ask. Carl stops. There is a sound and a hidden door on the side of the staircase creaks open. Carl cries out, a sound drowned by my even louder shout.

'Of course! Perfect!'

Carl struggles mightily, his body writhing and flapping, like a beached seal. That's the disadvantage of being an artist, perhaps: all that sensitivity and insufficient muscle.

I set him down next to the entrance to the basement.

'Please' he moans. 'I'll give you everything I've got.'

'Thanks. I've already got it.'

I step back and turn towards the still open front door.

'I'm not doing this for me. I'm doing it for Merlin, Martie, Sylvie, Don, Alix, Attracta and Becca. So whatever I do with your money, it's got to be better than what you did with it.'

Then I turn and walk back towards the front door. From behind me I hear a flood of obscenities that suddenly fade away. I don't look back, I'm not a sadist.

Ahead of me the door, fortunately, continues to remain open.

I blink as I come out into the daylight. I can even hear birds and when the wind blows, the far-off sounds of the road beyond the gates. I get into my car and hold my breath but the ignition takes first time. I begin to drive slowly down the drive. I'm gambling that whatever's in the house is now fully occupied and nothing will stop me leaving. Just before the house would be lost in the bend of trees I stop and look back. The front door has shut again.

I inhale mightily. 'I win, Merlin' I whisper.

Then I guide my car around the last bend, and head for the open gates and the life beyond Borley House.

POSTSCRIPT

The disappearance of noted Brit Artist Carl Raeburn caused its own sensation. Although several houses along the street where he lived carried CCTV, for the time when Carl was believed to have been travelling home all the CCTVs were mysteriously turned off.

His greatest Art, *Invitation to a Haunting*, drew a celebrity crowd for its highly publicised opening. Unfortunately first there was a power cut and then when the electricity returned several of the objects had become electrified. Several successful lawsuits on behalf of those electrocuted took the shine off the Art, and the exhibit was closed to the public.

Distant relatives of Carl Raeburn inherited his estate. They sold off everything they could, including Strawberry Manor, which was bought by Glen Davis, and turned into a home for indigent artists in memory of his brother Merlin. A specially commissioned painting in the magnificent hall also pays tribute to the six volunteers who disappeared: Martie, Sylvie, Don, Alix, Becca and Attracta are painted sitting together, smiling happily, forever a kind of family.

No one was willing to take over Borley House and a number of fires so undermined the already fragile buildings that eventually the council flattened the enormous structure. Money from the Carl Raeburn estate went to establish a magnificent public park. It has become a local legend, however, that no one can be persuaded to visit the park after dark.

Printed in Great Britain
by Amazon

64836697R10154